Gables of Legacy

VOLUME FIVE

The
MIRACLE

Gables of Legacy

VOLUME FIVE

The
MIRACLE

a novel

ANITA
STANSFIELD

Covenant Communications, Inc.

Cover images: map © Photodisc, Inc./Getty Images; linen photography by Leon Woodward.

Cover design copyrighted 2003 by Covenant Communications, Inc.

Published by Covenant Communications, Inc.
American Fork, Utah

Printed in Canada
First Printing: October 2003

10 09 08 07 06 05 04 03   10 9 8 7 6 5 4 3 2 1

ISBN 1-59156-321-6

In loving memory of my dear friend, Jacqui

Chapter One

South Queensland, Australia

Emma Hamilton sat on her bedroom floor, surrounded by three pieces of luggage and multiple piles of clothing, books, and personal items that would need to fit into them. She pushed a hand through her shoulder-length brown hair and sighed loudly.

"Don't they have a web site to teach you how to pack this stuff?" Emma said to her mother, Emily, who was going through the closet in search of empty wire hangers.

"If they do, I don't know about it," Emily said. "Don't worry. I've helped missionaries pack before. I'm certain we'll manage."

Emma's mind wandered as she considered the missionaries that her mother had helped prepare for their missions. There had been her two brothers, James and Jess. James had gone out before Jess, even though he was younger, since Jess had made some bad choices in his life and needed time to get on track. And there had been Emma's half-sister, Allison. There had also been Sean, who was a sort-of foster brother that Emma's parents had taken in when his family disowned him after he joined the Church. These four missionaries who had gone before her had one thing in common that Emma couldn't help feeling disheartened about. Prior to their leaving for the Missionary Training Center, Michael Hamilton had given them a father's blessing. Emma had actually not been born yet when it happened with Sean, but she knew it had because the family had talked about it. She'd been too young to recall it happening with Allison, but she recalled clearly the blessings that had been given to Jess and James.

For some reason she had clung to these beautiful moments in her family experience. James was now gone from this earth, since he'd been killed in a car accident a few years ago, along with his wife, Krista. Jess had survived that accident, but he had suffered greatly because of it, since he'd not only lost his brother and sister-in-law, but he'd also lost his best friend. The loss had been horrible for the entire family, but Emma knew beyond any doubt that it had been their time to go. She had found peace with losing her brother, James, and having Jess in her life still gave her a big brother to look up to and lean on. They were as close as siblings could be, in spite of living on separate continents.

Emma had been able to find the same kind of peace after losing her father to cancer. She knew it had been his time to go, and she had felt the Comforter close to her as she watched her father pass away. But in the time since his death, a tangible emptiness had continued to grow inside of her. She had been close to Michael Hamilton in a way that no one but he or she fully understood. There was no one in her life that helped fill that hole. She could count many blessings in her life and she had much to be grateful for, but she missed her father beyond description. And now, within days of leaving for the MTC in Utah, she ached for the father's blessing that she knew he would have given her, had he been alive to do it.

"What are you thinking about?" Emily asked, startling Emma and returning her thoughts to the present.

"Nothing really," Emma said.

"Are you nervous?"

"A little, perhaps, but not really. It's not like I'm going to some third-world country or something."

Emily chuckled as she carefully folded the pajamas Emma would take. "No, you're certainly not. Ironic, isn't it."

"Yes, it is," Emma said, briefly pondering the ironies for the hundredth time. She had been called to serve a mission on Temple Square in Salt Lake City. While the gospel was being spread to the far corners of the world, Emma would be sharing it smack-dab in the middle of the Mormon capital, where the world came to see the landmarks of the Church. Another irony was the fact that Jess had served in the same area; not specifically on Temple Square, since only sister missionaries served there, but he had done most of his proselyting in the Salt Lake valley. Emma didn't believe in coincidences, especially when it came to matters that were obviously in the Lord's hands. And she felt a secret thrill in wondering if some specific purpose might be met by her serving where her brother had. Or perhaps it was something they might never understand.

"You know," Emily said, "we'll never be ready if you just sit there and daydream."

"Sorry," Emma said and began dividing her belongings into three categories. The smallest of her bags she would carry on the plane and it would contain her most needed belongings. If her luggage was temporarily waylaid, at least she'd have what she needed. The second piece of luggage would contain things she would need for her brief stay at the MTC, and the third piece would not be opened until she actually reached her apartment in Salt Lake City.

"It sure is a lot of stuff," Emma commented.

"Surprisingly enough," Emily said, "it's supposed to be everything you'll need to live for eighteen months." She chuckled. "But I know better. As I said, I've done this before. You'll be writing to say you need this or that, and I'll be sending packages, and then you'll send home boxes of stuff you don't need any more."

"If I need something, I'll write to Allison. I think the shipping will be a lot less."

"True," Emily chuckled again.

That was another irony of Emma's mission call. While technically her home was Australia, she had been going to BYU and living with her sister's family in Provo—an hour's drive from where she would be serving her mission. Of course, Jess had gone to BYU as well, and he had dealt with the same irony. But Emma already knew it would be an added challenge to know that members of her family were so close, while it was strictly against the rules to see them.

Later that evening Emma found Jess in the nursery, playing with his children. She appreciated the way he lived here with his wife and children in the huge family home where they had all grown up. Jess had fully taken over the family businesses following their father's death, and Emma knew it was a great blessing for their mother to have Jess's family here with her. In return, Emily had been a great help and support for Jess and his wife, Tamra, especially during Tamra's recent pregnancy with twins, and subsequently as she helped care for the two babies and their brother who wasn't even a year older. Jess was now surrounded by the three little boys. The twins, Tyson and Joshua, were crawling around him and giggling, while their brother, little Michael, sat close by, playing with an assortment of plastic animals. Emma sat in the rocking chair and Evelyn immediately climbed on her lap. Evelyn was James and Krista's daughter; she had been an infant when her parents were killed. Jess and Tamra had officially adopted her soon after their marriage, and she was now learning to read. She was continually bringing storybooks to Emma and they would sit together and sound out the words.

After two stories, Evelyn went to find Grandma and see what she was doing, which left Emma alone in the nursery with Jess and the babies.

"How you doing?" he asked.

"I'm okay. How are you?"

"Beyond the fact that I dread having you leave, I'm fine."

"You should be plenty used to my being gone," Emma said.

"And I always miss you. It just never seems right here without you. And this will be different. You won't be home for holidays and vacations. We won't even be able to talk on the phone."

Emma forced a smile then looked toward the window. "Yes, but . . . it will be worth it."

"Yes, I know it will," Jess said. "My mission is one of the greatest experiences of my life, in spite of certain . . . disappointments."

Emma turned back to him in surprise. "Disappointments? Why?"

"Well, it was hard. But then, a mission is. You know that."

"Yes, I know. I'm not expecting it to be easy. You're not going to scare me out of going by telling me it will be hard."

"I didn't figure I would."

"But why was it disappointing?"

"Well," Jess was thoughtful for a long minute, "I think sometimes that, overall, my mission was more for my own growth. I mean . . . I went prepared, and I went for the right reasons, but . . . it's just that I had no obvious success stories. I never baptized anyone. Of course, that's really irrelevant because with transfers and the often slow progression of the conversion process, performing a baptism is not necessarily a measure of success as a missionary, and I know that. Still . . . I simply have no success stories in my missionary journals. I taught more discussions than I can count, and I had some great experiences and met some great people, but I never actually saw anyone come into the Church because of my influence."

"Murphy did," she said, and he chuckled.

"Yes, well, Murphy lives across the lawn. We grew up together. He works for us. The fact that he finally got smart and came around has little to do with my mission, and I think our father's influence had a lot more to do with it than anything I said or did. I was just there to answer his questions at the right time."

"Obviously you had the right answers," Emma said, then she found her mind wandering from the mention of her father. Oh, how she missed him!

"Where are you?" he asked, startling her.

"Just thinking," she said, then took the conversation back to the topic at hand. "You never know what seeds you planted on your mission, Jess."

"That's just it. I will probably never know. At least not in this life."

"The important thing is that you went, and as you said, it was one of the best experiences of your life. I'm counting on it being the same for me."

"I'm sure it will be," Jess said. "And I dare say that you are far more mature—emotionally and spiritually—than I was when I went out."

She laughed softly. "I don't know about that. I feel like a little girl leaving home for the first time."

"You nervous?"

"Sort of, I guess," she said, looking at her hands folded in her lap.

"Hey," he said, moving a little closer, "I was thinking and . . . well, it's completely up to you, and if you don't want me to, I would understand, but . . . could I give you a blessing before you go? The way Dad gave one to me?"

Emma met her brother's eyes, absorbing the love and sincerity there. He couldn't have possibly known how troubled she'd been over that very thing, because she'd said nothing to anyone. She felt a perceptible warmth fill her as she reached for his hand and said, "I would like that very much. Thank you."

The night before Emma was leaving, Jess, Tamra, and Emily all went into town to meet with a member of the stake presidency who set Emma apart as a missionary. Tamra's Aunt Rhea, who also lived with them, stayed with the children. When they returned home, the children had all been put to bed and Rhea joined them as they gathered to listen to Jess give Emma a blessing. Rhea was not a member of the Church, but she had gained a deep respect for the gospel, and she enjoyed participating in family home evening and other events that affected the family. They were all hopeful that eventually the Spirit would touch her enough that she would take the plunge and be baptized.

Emma hadn't been thinking of her father when Jess laid his hands on her head, but as he spoke her full name and proceeded with the blessing, she was amazed at how his voice sounded so very much like their father's. Listening to the words flow eloquently, Emma tried to tell herself it was only her imagination, but as the blessing went on, her emotions deepened and she knew beyond any doubt that her father was present, with his hands upon her head as well as Jess's.

In the blessing Emma was told that the location of her mission had not been happenstance, that the Lord was mindful of her and her afflictions, and she would be led to great blessings and opportunities as a direct result of *where* she would be serving. She was also told that in the same respect, her family would reap great blessings as well. She was given specific guidance, great promises of spiritual strength, and an outpouring of love from her Father in Heaven.

After the "amen" had been spoken, Emma opened her eyes to see that she wasn't the only one with tears streaking her face. The others were all crying as well—even Rhea. After sharing lengthy embraces, Emma went to bed, knowing she now needed to keep the mission rules, which included an early bedtime.

The following morning Emma shared final good-byes with everyone but her mother and Jess before they drove the ten minutes to the hangar on their land where the family's private planes were kept. Being isolated as they were, the planes were a great blessing, and Jess himself was often at the controls. He flew Emma and their mother to Sydney, where the two of them would be going on to the States. Emily would see Emma to the MTC, then spend some time with Allison and her family before returning home.

Emma found it more difficult than she'd expected to say good-bye to Jess at the airport. He hugged her tightly and she felt extremely hesitant, almost afraid, to let go. With tears in his eyes he stepped back, saying, "I'm going to leave now, before I really lose it. I'll write." He took her shoulders into his hands and pressed a kiss to her brow, then he turned to hug their mother and walked away. Emma watched him go, leaning her head against her mother's shoulder. She prayed that the next eighteen months would not be too difficult for any of them.

* * *

Emma settled easily into her mission. She loved the MTC and was thrilled when she was finally able to be in the heart of Salt Lake City with the purpose of sharing the gospel. Letters came regularly from family members, so many that it took her hours on her preparation days to write letters in response. But the love and support of her family was not something she took for granted. Her companion, Sister Symonette, from France, only got an occasional letter from her father, and that was all. Emma enjoyed sharing her letters from home with this sweet sister, and after Emma told her family in letters about her companion's situation, Sister Symonette's mail increased. She not only got letters from members of Emma's family, but she got them from youth and primary children in a couple of different wards. Answering them gave Sister Symonette something to do on P-days while Emma wrote letters to her family.

Emma found she loved working on Temple Square, especially after the Christmas lights were put up for the holiday season. She loved the magical feel of the Square, and the way so many people came there to feel the strong Spirit that was present amidst the beauty. But as Christmas quickly approached, Emma became unexpectedly homesick. In spite of having spent a great deal of time away from home in the past, she had never been gone for Christmas. Her thoughts strayed far too often to what her family was doing, and she harbored a secret longing to be with them. Combined with her longing for home, she felt anew the grief of her father's death. She missed him deeply and had to remind herself that even if she were home, he would not be there.

Emma also found it ironic to recall the many times she had come to Temple Square as a visitor with family and friends, just to see the lights and peruse the displays in the visitors' centers. She thought of her sister's family, living an hour away, and it was difficult to stick to the rules and not make contact with Allison. She prayed and studied her scriptures more vigorously, attempting to focus more fully on her purpose for being there. She fasted more than once that she could be comforted and strengthened. She found that she did feel better and more able to stay focused, but still, she missed her home and family and decided that she would be glad when Christmas was over.

* * *

Scott Ivie sunk onto his leather couch with a harsh sigh. He lost track of the time as he stared at the unopened box of Christmas decorations, and another containing the artificial tree, waiting to be assembled. But he just couldn't bring himself to do it. What point was there in having a Christmas tree? He had no one to celebrate with. No family, no friends close enough to share such moments with. Of course, at one time, he'd been quite accustomed to such a situation. But that was before Callie had come into his life. They had shared pleasant Christmases together, and then he had embraced the gospel of Jesus Christ, and his love and gratitude for the holiday and all it represented had deepened. But Callie had resented his joining the Church, and the changes he had made in his lifestyle did not suit her at all. Scott had prayerfully pursued every avenue he could think of to compromise and communicate and overcome the problem. He respected the marriage vows they shared and fought with everything inside of him to keep their union together. But a day had come when she'd walked out on him and filed for a divorce. The loss was devastating, but he'd had to wonder if it was for the best. He wasn't certain he could have spent the rest of his life with a woman who simply didn't share the same goals and values that he had. He knew in his heart that he could never achieve his spiritual potential or be truly happy if he'd remained married to Callie. And in all honesty, he knew that he was the one who had changed. When they had met and married, he had been living the life she still enjoyed. Much of their free time had been spent in bars, surrounded by people who were crude and base. At home they had often watched questionable television programs and movies, and it wasn't uncommon for them to both get drunk on Saturday nights and sleep it off all day Sunday.

Scott had put such habits behind him before he'd stepped into the waters of baptism, but Callie had not been able to grasp, to any degree, the reasons for his convictions. Neither could she understand that some changes in *her* life could make her happier, even if she wanted nothing to do with the Church. In spite of believing their separation was for the best, there was a place in Scott's heart that loved Callie. And her absence in his life had been difficult to face. He reminded himself hourly as he went to work and church and kept his life together, that his choices would bring greater blessings into his life. But there were moments when he just felt so completely lonely that he truly wondered what he'd been thinking.

Knowing there was only one source to find any peace over the matter, Scott pressed his head into his hands and poured his soul out in prayer. Long before he'd become exposed to the gospel, he had held strongly the belief of God's existence, and he credited prayer with getting him through a youth that was far from ideal. Orphaned at an early age, he'd been passed through many foster homes and had finally ended up living on a boys' ranch in Montana, where he had stayed until he was old enough to be on his own. He had worked his way through school, attaining first a bachelor's degree and then an MBA at the University of Utah. Upon graduation, he'd acquired a good position with a good company in the same city, working hard to move up the corporate ladder. The main element that he credited for getting him this far was the power of prayer. He certainly wasn't going to discredit that power now.

"Please, dear Father," he prayed aloud, "I know there must be more to life than this. Guide me, Father; show me the way. Help me find purpose and meaning; help me make a difference in this world. Help me lift someone else's spirits that my own might be comforted."

Scott paused his prayer to contemplate the possible opportunities for service that might get his mind off of his own misery. But nothing came to him, so he prayed on, repeating the same phrases over and over until an idea came clearly to his mind. He had the distinct impression that he should visit Temple Square, but he balked at the idea, certain it would do nothing but dredge up more difficult memories. In spite of Callie's aversion to the Church and its teachings, she had loved Temple Square at Christmastime, and they had gone there together many times, since it was less than a ten-minute drive from the home they had shared—the home where he now sat alone, staring at the boxes of Christmas decor.

When the idea persisted, Scott put on his coat and made the short drive. He parked at the mall and walked across the street through the brisk winter evening into the Square. The memories assaulted him with such power that he could only force himself to put one foot in front of the other until he was standing before the Christus statue in the north visitors' center. He gazed at it for endless minutes, silently praying for answers while the physical image of Christ before him somehow made it easier to imagine his pleas being heard.

He didn't get any obvious answers, but he found that he did feel better as he wandered back outside, ambling slowly with his gloved hands clasped behind his back, taking in the beauty of every tree filled with tiny lights. Every once in a while he took a picture with the camera hanging on a strap around his neck. The camera had been an expensive investment many years ago, and now it had become an extension of himself, kept in good repair and frequently close by in order to capture the moments of his life.

Scott paused on the west side of the temple and gazed upward, marveling as always at its majesty and beauty. It occurred to him that it had been a few weeks since he'd attended the temple, and perhaps that was part of the problem. He silently examined his schedule to determine a time when he could go, until his thoughts were interrupted by a feminine voice with a thick French accent.

"Excuse me," she said. "Do you have any questions that we might answer?"

Scott turned to see two sister missionaries. A quick glance at their name tags told him they were Sisters Symonette and Hamilton. The name *Hamilton* tugged at something familiar in his mind, but he couldn't place it. They were both attractive young women, wearing stylish black boots, long black wool coats, and gloves. Sister Hamilton was wearing a wool hat over her dark, sleek hair that curled under at the bottom.

Scott smiled warmly at them and answered, "No, but thank you. I was actually trying to figure when I could get to the temple, since it's been a while. So, I think I've had the important questions already answered."

"That is good then," Sister Symonette said, then she informed him which days the temple would be closed for the holidays, and Scott thanked her.

"So," Scott said, enjoying the distraction, "you're French, I take it. Where exactly do you come from?"

Sister Symonette told him about the village in southern France where she had been born and raised, and they talked for several minutes before he turned to the silent Sister Hamilton and said, "You haven't got much to say."

Emma felt startled to realize this man was addressing her. She was almost ashamed to realize how preoccupied she'd become with looking at him. He was tall and broad-shouldered, with thick, almost black hair and brows. His features had a refined quality that was distinctly masculine—rugged but very distinguished. He wore a long, brown leather coat, with leather gloves on his hands. She couldn't deny that she found him attractive, but she reminded herself that she was serving a mission and had no business appraising a man this way. Her thoughts were in no way inappropriate, but simply not where her head was supposed to be.

When she realized he was expecting her to speak, she cleared her throat and said, "I'm just listening. I like Sister Symonette's descriptions of home."

Scott's heart quickened unexpectedly at the sound of this woman's distinct Australian accent. The accent combined with the name triggered a distant memory and forced it to the front of his mind. At her expectant expression he cleared his throat and said, "Yes, I can understand that. She speaks beautifully."

A long moment later, she asked, "Is something wrong?"

"No, uh . . . yes . . . I mean . . . nothing's wrong. I just have to ask . . . forgive me, but I once knew an elder who served in this area . . . his name was Hamilton; he was Australian. I can't help wondering if . . ."

Scott's heart went from quickened to racing when there was no mistaking the light that filled Sister Hamilton's eyes. "My brother served in this area not so many years ago," she said. "Perhaps it could be him."

Scott laughed aloud then felt compelled to explain. "I don't remember his companion's name, but I met them at some fast food place where we were both eating lunch. We talked and I gave them my phone number and address. They persisted with me even though I was difficult, until one day I just told them I didn't want to see them again. I was pretty rude about it. But there was something Elder Hamilton had said to me that haunted me. It stuck in my brain like glue and I couldn't shake it. Some months later I came here to Temple Square and got the ball rolling again. I took the discussions from some elders, but Elder Hamilton had gone home. I've always wished that I could just talk to that man for five minutes, just to thank him, and to apologize. I don't think he has any idea how he changed my life."

Emma listened to this man's story with a growing hope in her heart. She thought of her brother's feelings about his mission, his belief that he had not really made a difference for anyone. Could it be possible that this meeting was not coincidence at all? Her hand was nearly trembling as she reached into her deep coat pocket to pull out her wallet. Without saying anything, she flipped it open to where pictures of her family members were kept. She held up a copy of Jess and Tamra's engagement picture and watched this man's eyes fill with tears.

"That's him," he said breathlessly. Then he laughed. "I can't believe it." He took the wallet and held it close to his face, as if he thought his eyes were deceiving him. "It really is him." He looked directly at Emma. "My prayers have been answered."

Emma wanted to say that this could likely be a great blessing to Jess as well, but she didn't get a chance before he asked, "Is there some way I could get in touch with him? I don't want to impose or be inappropriate, but . . . I would so love to just send him a letter, or . . ."

"I could give you his email address," she said. "I'm certain he wouldn't mind."

"Oh, that would be wonderful!" he said with so much enthusiasm that Emma couldn't help laughing. For the first time in many days she felt true joy in her heart, and she realized that her prayers had been answered as well. This man's appearance, for some reason, had left her feeling comforted and strengthened, and she felt better. His excitement and the "coincidence" of their coming together let her know that God was indeed mindful of her—and of him, whatever his name was. And Jess, as well.

"Might I ask your name?" Emma asked as he reached into his pocket for something to write with.

"Scott Ivie," he said, handing her two business cards. "Keep one, if you like. And on the other, would you mind writing his address?"

He handed her a pen and she wrote it down. Giving him back the pen and card, he stared at the address incredulously.

"Thank you," he said. "Thank you so much." He shook each of their hands vigorously, wished them a merry Christmas, and walked away.

Emma watched him leave, but the passing days did not erase him from her memory. Christmas came and went, being less difficult than she'd expected, and she began the new year with a fresh zeal for serving with all her heart and soul. But always in the back of her mind hovered the image of Scott Ivie. She wondered if she might ever see him again, but reminded herself to keep her thoughts trained on the work she had been set apart to do. Still, she couldn't help hoping that she hadn't seen the last of Scott Ivie.

* * *

Scott returned from his little jaunt to Temple Square and nearly went straight to the computer to send Sister Hamilton's brother an email. Then he realized that he needed to think about what to say exactly. Since he'd never believed such an opportunity would ever actually present itself, he'd never considered how he might handle it. Instead Scott put on a Christmas CD, then he put together his Christmas tree and put the lights on it. By the time it was finished he was exhausted and went to bed, and the following day he was especially busy at work. That evening he finished decorating the tree and cleaned up the mess before he sat at the computer to compose a rough draft of a letter to Brother Hamilton. He felt pretty good about it, but he wanted to let it sit for a day or two and be sure that he was saying exactly what he wanted to say. He might not have had so much difficulty putting his words together if he didn't find his thoughts continually drawn to *Sister* Hamilton. He didn't understand it and he couldn't explain it, but memories of her clung to his thoughts like snow to a cold earth.

On Christmas Eve he finally sent the letter, along with a prayer that it would be well received. He went to bed with no gifts beneath the tree, but his heart felt full, and the next morning he got up early and went to a local soup kitchen where he spent the day working to serve some decent meals to those in need. He even took a couple of trips to purchase more food from his own pocket to contribute to this great Christmas dinner. He went home late and felt exhausted but gratified with a day well spent, going straight to bed without even thinking to check his email. Scott wasn't in the habit of getting anything personal there, but he woke up in the middle of the night and was startled by the thought that he should check it. He couldn't help hoping that he might actually get a reply to his careful letter. And he prayed that he wouldn't be disappointed.

Connecting to the Internet, Scott reminded himself that this man was likely very busy with the holiday, and could even be out of town with relatives and wouldn't be checking his email for days. But when the in-box screen came up, there it was: a message from j&t-downunder@BD&H.com.

Scott took a deep breath and attempted to quell his pounding heart as he clicked the mouse and waited for the message to come up. He let out a one-syllable laugh when he realized the message was at least as long as the one he had sent. It began, *Dear Scott, What a wonderful Christmas gift you have given me.* Jess went on to explain his feelings about his mission, and how he'd always wondered if he'd made a difference. He spoke of the irony of his sister now serving in the same area, and his speculations on what purpose there might be in that. Deep inside he'd hoped that some connection might be made, but he'd never dreamed that something so incredible would come up so soon, when she'd only been out a couple of months. He also wrote how good it was to hear from someone who had seen his sister, since he missed her terribly. He finished by saying, *Thank you again, Scott, for taking the time to share your experience with me, and for brightening my holiday. I hope that you'll keep in touch and share more about yourself with me. I would love to get to know you better. God bless always, Jess Hamilton.*

Scott sat back in his chair after he'd read the letter twice. He silently thanked God for sending him a miracle, then he quickly composed another letter to send back, hoping deep inside that he might have actually found a true friend—even if he was halfway around the world.

* * *

Emma and her companion were just sitting down to write their weekly letters when a knock came at the door. Emma went to answer it, and for a long moment the world seemed to stop as she found herself facing Scott Ivie, and neither of them could seem to come up with anything to say. Looking into his eyes she felt as if she were facing a childhood friend, one she had known and loved for many years, and she had now come face-to-face with him in a time and place that felt foreign and strange. Emma looked away and cleared her head, reminding herself of who she was and what she was doing here. Indulging in some silly infatuation with a man she had barely met once was ridiculous at best, even if she weren't serving a mission.

"Hello," he finally said and she bravely looked at him again to see him smiling. She could almost believe that his feelings for her were similar and he was pleased with the evidence that she was less than indifferent toward him.

"Hello," she replied, forcing a straight face. "What may we do for you?"

"Well," he glanced at the box in his hands that she just now noticed—a nondescript bakery box. "It is Valentine's Day, is it not?"

Emma had to think about it. "Now that you mention it, I suppose it is."

She gathered the words to reprimand him for coming here with some offering of romance on a romantic holiday when he knew she was a missionary. But his smile broadened as he said, "I am here on behalf of your brother." He pushed the box toward her. "Apparently you have a deep love for pastries from a particular German bakery here in the city. He sent me very specific instructions on when and what I was supposed to deliver. So, Happy Valentine's Day from your family, and your mother said to remind you to share with your companion; there's plenty."

Emma became so flustered that all she could do was take the box and say, "Thank you, Brother Ivie." She looked at the box in her hands and felt the love of her family on the other side of the world. She couldn't keep her voice from cracking as she added, "Your efforts are very much appreciated."

"Glad to do it," he said, smiling again. "Now, is there anything else you need? Anything I can do to help you sisters? Do you have enough to eat? Anything I can pick up for you?"

Emma smiled back. "We're fine, really. But thank you."

"You have my number if you need anything," he said. Again she wanted to accuse him of trying to flirt with her, when he clearly knew how unacceptable that was. But he added very genuinely, "I'd be privileged to do anything I can to help build the kingdom."

"Just keep gathering those referrals," she said, attempting to maintain an emotional distance.

"I do my best," he said and the knot in Emma's throat thickened until she could only manage to say, "Thank you," as she closed the door.

"Who was that?" Sister Symonette asked, coming out of the bathroom.

"A delivery from home," Emma said, finding it easier to force back her emotion now that Scott Ivie wasn't staring her in the face. She took the box eagerly to their little table and opened it carefully, laughing out loud as the familiar delicacies came into view. "Take your pick," Emma said. "They're all wonderful."

"Oh my," Sister Symonette said. "It has been so long since I've had such a treat. I do miss European pastries."

"These are from a German bakery that I always loved, and their methods are very authentic."

Emma picked up a little white frosted cake and closed her eyes as she sunk her teeth into the velvety frosting. She made a noise of pleasure as the fluffy white cake and raspberry filling found its way into her mouth. Then she laughed, somehow feeling less lonely for home than she had in many weeks.

Chapter Two

Scott clicked on "Send" with the mouse and leaned back in his chair, marveling that his letter would be arriving in Australia in seconds. He contemplated his gratitude for living in the computer age as he considered the friendship he had developed with Jess Hamilton. Most of their written conversations had focused on spiritual and doctrinal matters. Their relationship had naturally begun there, since Jess's serving a mission had been the initial seed that had sprouted into the desire that had led Scott to making the gospel a part of his life. Scott knew very little about Jess personally beyond the fact that he had some great spiritual insight, and he knew the doctrine of the gospel in a way that Scott envied. Jess had grown up in the Church and had been raised with gospel principles, while Scott still felt like an infant in spiritual matters at times. Through the weeks they had been regularly emailing back and forth, Scott had learned more than he'd learned in the time since he'd joined the Church. He found their communications stimulating and thought-provoking. And given the poor state of his social life, he was especially grateful to have a connection to someone—even if he was halfway around the world. He looked forward to the messages he received almost daily, and found he was going about his days with more motivation.

Scott's work kept him very busy, as did his calling in the elders quorum presidency. His ward members were kind and well-meaning, but he had never felt really connected with any one person since he'd joined the Church. The missionaries had been wonderful, the bishopric the same. People had welcomed him into the fold and treated him well. But when he'd changed his values, he'd lost his friends, and eventually his wife. He'd gained much through embracing the gospel that far outweighed what he had lost, and he had no regrets. But the long-distance friendship he'd gained with Jess Hamilton had filled something in him, and he was truly grateful.

The downside of the situation was the hovering obsession he had with Jess Hamilton's baby sister. She was serving a mission and he had no business entertaining romantic thoughts about her, but keeping her from his mind was an impossible feat. He'd almost been dismayed when Jess had requested that he make the Valentine's Day delivery, knowing that if he saw her again his thoughts would surely get the better of him. Seeing her had made him realize that he'd not imagined what he felt for her, and he could only pray that his feelings were not deceiving him, and that one day in the future their paths might cross again. His friendship with her brother gave him the hope that such a thing might be possible. Still, when Sister Hamilton completed her mission, she would return home to a different continent, and he had difficulty imagining how they might ever meet again.

Knowing that this, as with every matter in his life, simply had to be put into the Lord's hands, Scott did his best to put it there and not think about her. He felt certain that either his feelings would dwindle as some pointless infatuation, or he *would* meet her again one day, when the time and circumstances were appropriate. In the meantime, he completely resisted any temptation to go to Temple Square or in the vicinity where the missionaries labored. It was simply better for him to stay away.

On a bright spring morning Scott went into the high-rise where he worked and instantly felt something different the moment he stepped into his office. He couldn't help feeling nervous when his assistant said, "Mr. Barton wants to see you immediately."

While there were always speculations flying about possible cutbacks in the company, Scott went into Mr. Barton's lavish office with a prayer in his heart that his employment would not be in jeopardy. He knew that he was considered a hard worker, honest and competent, and he hoped those qualities would be noted if cutbacks were, indeed, being mandated.

"Ivie," Mr. Barton said, motioning to one of the big leather chairs opposite the desk where he was sitting. "Have a seat. Would you like a cup of coffee?"

"No, thank you, sir."

"Oh, that's right. You don't drink coffee, do you."

"Not anymore. But thank you."

"Smart move," he said. "You'll probably live a lot longer than I will."

"It's never too late to quit," Scott said, but Mr. Barton just laughed.

"So, what can I do for you?" Scott asked, not wanting to endure the suspense any longer. "I was told you wanted to see me."

"Yes, indeed," Mr. Barton said. "We've got some big changes underway, young man. We're branching out and the merger has necessitated that we take some action and quickly."

"Merger?" Scott asked. There had been rumors of that as well, but nothing he'd been willing to pay any attention to.

"Yes, sir." Mr. Barton laughed, which left Scott to assume that the changes were favorable. "It's a done deal and we've got some serious work to do."

Scott breathed an audible sigh as the mood of the meeting indicated he was not looking at a possible layoff or demotion. "So, here's the deal, young man. I've never held back on letting you know that you're one of the best on my team. So, I'm giving you first choice. Of course, you can stay here if you want, but a transfer could mean a significant raise."

Scott's heart quickened. A transfer? It was true that he had no family connections or friends here. Still, he liked his ward and neighborhood. He liked his home. Did he really want to leave this city where he'd gotten his education and worked for many years? Then again, not being in the same city as a sister missionary that he had fallen for could be a good thing. He reminded himself that he wouldn't be asked to make a decision right there on the spot, and tried to focus on what Mr. Barton had to say.

"With the merger we will be moving our people into offices already established by our sister companies around the world. There are three locations where we need good people willing to keep the ball rolling and keep an eye on our interests. I'm giving you first choice, or as I said, you can stay here if you like, but . . ."

Scott cleared his throat and asked, "Where exactly are these locations?"

"Well, one is Seoul," he said. "I know you don't speak Korean, but actually we have someone who does. Went on a church mission there, or something. So I really think he's the best choice there. If you really *want* to go to Korea, we could—"

"No, that's all right," Scott said. "I don't know that I'd necessarily enjoy that. What are the other choices?"

"London and Brisbane," Mr. Barton said.

Scott had no trouble knowing where London was, but he felt a little stupid as he asked, "Pardon my ignorance, but where exactly is Brisbane?"

"Pronounced 'Bris-bun' by the locals, I understand," he said. "It's in Australia."

Scott's heart did a somersault. He literally bit his lip to keep from shouting, "I'll take it!" He considered some fasting and prayer to be in order, rather than impulsively jumping on something simply because it suited what he wanted. But three days later, after much fasting and prayer, Scott knew beyond any doubt that his Heavenly Father wanted him to move to Australia. Within a few days the deal was official, he'd applied for his visa, and the house was on the market. The company would provide him with an apartment for the first three months to allow some time for the house to sell so that he could purchase something new. They would also cover all of his moving expenses, although he figured there was really very little worth taking to Australia beyond his clothing and personal belongings. He figured such things as furniture and dishes and linens could all be purchased in Australia, and there was little that had any sentimental value to him. So he cleared out the house, had a great yard sale and had the rest picked up by Deseret Industries for charity. He became so busy with his preparations to move that his emails to Jess became brief and less frequent. He wanted to let him know about the move, but he wanted to take some time composing his email, and he'd hardly had a moment to think.

Scott was amazed at how smoothly his preparations went. He was even able to sell his car with the agreement that the buyers could take it over the night before he would fly out. He shipped most of his belongings as soon as the visa came through, then he sat in a nearly empty house, contemplating the memories and the future before him.

Finding some real time on his hands, now that everything was as ready as it could be, he connected to the Internet with the intention of letting Jess know that he was moving to the same continent. He reminded himself that just because Jess's frequent emails had filled a void in Scott's life did not necessarily mean that Scott might have had the same effect on Jess. And then it occurred to him that he actually had no idea where Jess Hamilton lived. Australia. That was all he knew. And it was a big continent. He knew that the majority of the population was in the east, but that was still a big area. He began his email by asking where the Hamiltons resided, then he reached a mental block and couldn't put a coherent sentence together. Then he recalled that in one of his first messages, Jess had sent a phone number, and he felt suddenly compelled to call him. He didn't even think about what he might say as he punched the number into the phone, then he marveled at how quickly it began to ring.

"Hello," a woman's voice said.

"I'm looking for Jess Hamilton," he said, then it occurred to him that there was likely a huge time difference. He was grateful that the sound of her voice had not indicated being awakened in the middle of the night.

"Just a minute," the woman said, and he realized she was American, although there was a subtle hint of an accent in her voice, as if she'd been down under for many years. He'd expected to hear a thicker accent, like unto Sister Hamilton. In the background he could hear her saying, "Do you know where Jess is?"

He distinctly heard another woman with a similar accent say, "In the nursery with the boys, I believe."

Then the woman who had answered the phone said, "Jess, pick up the phone," and he realized she had likely spoken into an intercom. A click sounded only a second later.

"Got it," a male voice said, and the expected Australian accent came through clearly, even in those two simple words. Following another click as the extension was hung up, he said, "Hello."

"Am I speaking to Jess Hamilton?" Scott asked, suddenly feeling nervous.

"It's me."

"Well, this is Scott Ivie," he said and heard immediate laughter.

"It's about time you called me. I wondered if I'd ever get to hear your voice."

"You could have called me, you know," Scott said.

"I know, but I didn't want to be too pushy." There was humor in the way he said it, and he laughed again. "It's really you. I can't believe it. How are you, my friend?"

Scott felt warmed by his reference to friendship, and said brightly, "I'm doing well. And you?"

"Quite well, thank you. I really have been thinking that I'd like to call you. I'm glad you got past the procrastinating better than I did."

"Well, I actually called to ask how far you live from Brisbane."

Jess chuckled. "You actually pronounced it right; I'm impressed."

"I practiced," Scott said and Jess laughed again, as if he just couldn't contain his joy over this conversation, which deepened Scott's gratitude for the friendship they had gained. With any luck, it would now have the opportunity to move beyond the Internet.

"Brisbane," Jess said. "Well, that would be about a half-day's drive—on a good day."

"You're kidding," Scott said and let out a one-syllable laugh. He had considered being told that a half-day's flight would make it possible for them to actually see each other again.

"So, what's the deal?" Jess asked. "Please tell me you're coming to Brisbane on a business trip and you have an extra day. That would be so amazing!"

Scott chuckled again. "I'm afraid it's better than that. Well, better from my perspective, at least. I don't know if *you'll* think it's better, but . . ."

"Try me," Jess said expectantly.

"I'm moving to Brisbane. I leave the day after tomorrow."

"You're kidding," Jess said in the same tone Scott had used a moment earlier.

"Quite serious. My company gave me the choice between London and Brisbane. And they were anxious to get me there in a hurry."

Jess was quiet for a long minute and Scott's nervousness returned. Would this man have some aversion to actually having him permanently on the same continent? Did he fear that he would become continually aggravated by some guy who was practically a stranger?

Scott was searching for the words to appropriately clarify himself when Jess spoke again, and his voice had a distinct tinge of emotion. "Forgive me," he said. "I'm not sure if I can explain why your coming means so much to me, but I'm going to try."

"I was hoping you would."

"It's like . . . well, from that first email you sent, I've just felt something . . . significant. It's as if the Spirit was telling me to sit up and take notice, only it was . . . subtle. Still, undeniable."

Scott sighed and shook his head in disbelief. He felt something wonderful evolving as he admitted, "Yeah, I know exactly what you mean."

"You do?" Jess asked, excitement in his voice.

"Yes, I do," Scott said assuredly.

"Well, then," Jess said with the same tone, "it would seem we have an adventure ahead of us."

"It would seem so," Scott said.

They talked for only a few more minutes and Scott promised to call again as soon as he was settled in Brisbane. For nearly an hour after he got off the phone, Scott stared at the wall and pondered what he was feeling. His thoughts naturally strayed to Jess's missionary sister, and he couldn't deny his attraction to her. But what he felt now had nothing to do with her. He felt a deep kinship with Jess Hamilton, but when it came to personal matters, he knew absolutely nothing about the man beyond the fact that he was married and had children, and his mother was living in the same home. They shared the same religion, and through their communication on deep spiritual and doctrinal matters, Scott knew that Jess had a strong testimony and great deal of knowledge. And that was all. But the prospect of meeting him and spending some time together gave him a feeling of assurance that he recognized. The same Spirit that had let him know the Church was true, and had given him the conviction to embrace the gospel and live it, was letting him know now that his life was on the right track—and a very important one. He felt as if his leaving the States now was putting his feet on the path that would lead to his destiny. And he felt a secret thrill to discover what that destiny might be.

* * *

Scott thoroughly enjoyed most aspects of his move and settling into a new job and a new apartment. He felt confident and competent in the work that was expected of him, and he enjoyed exploring this new city during the little snatches of time that he found. Attending church made him feel at home among the Saints there, and he felt peace at the evidence of a universal gospel.

A few days after his arrival, he'd emailed Jess to let him know he'd arrived on the continent, and that he would call when he had some time. Three weeks later, on a Wednesday afternoon, he called from his office. The same woman who had answered before told him that Jess was at work, and she gave him an office number.

"Are you sure it's all right for me to call him at work?" Scott asked.

The woman laughed. "Absolutely; it's not a problem."

Scott carefully dialed the number and was momentarily startled when he heard a woman answer by saying, "Byrnehouse-Davies Home for Boys. May I help you?"

Instantly Scott felt a thousand little memories parade through his mind and back again. Having spent many years of his youth living at a boys' ranch, it felt oddly comforting to have the phone in his hand connected to what he assumed was a similar institution. Then he wondered momentarily if he really had the right number. Could it be possible that this man he'd felt such kinship for worked in such a place?

"Hello?" the voice said, startling him to an answer.

"Hello," Scott said. "I'm looking for Jess Hamilton. I was told that he—"

"He's on another call. Would you like his voice mail?"

"That would be great. Thank you."

A moment later he heard Jess's recorded voice saying, "You've reached Jess Hamilton at the Byrnehouse-Davies Home for Boys. Your call is important to us. Please leave a detailed message after the beep, and I will get back to you as soon as humanly possible. Thank you, and have a great day."

Following the beep, Scott said, "Hi. It's Scott Ivie. I believe I can actually take some time off this weekend. I was thinking of doing a little exploring and wondered if it might be a good time to see you. I can do whatever is most convenient for you." He then repeated his home and office numbers and hung up the phone. Less than ten minutes later, Jess called back.

"How much exploring did you want to do?" Jess asked.

"I'm pretty open," Scott said. "With the hours I've put in since I got here, I'm taking Friday off."

"Well, I'll give you some options, if you're interested."

"I am," Scott said. "You're the resident expert here."

Jess chuckled and went on. "I could probably get away for a couple of days and come to Brisbane. I've been there enough that I could likely give you a favorable tour. I could meet you part way somewhere and do whatever we find to do. Or, if you're up to it, you could come here."

"I want to do what's easiest for you," Scott said. "I don't want to take time out of your schedule and pull you away from home. But neither do I want to invade you and—"

"Let me rephrase that. If you're up to the drive, we would love to have you come and be our guest."

Scott absorbed the invitation, unable to deny his excitement at the prospect. "Well, that sounds great. Is there a place you could recommend close by that I might get a room?"

"No," Jess chuckled. "The closest place to get a room is an hour away. But I can assure you we have room for you. Isolated as we are, we're quite accustomed to overnight guests. If you can leave early Friday morning, you should be able to get here that afternoon. I can take off early if I'm a good boy and get my work under control, and we can just . . . hang out and get to know each other better. I'll do my best to keep the kids under control." He chuckled. "However, if that's not the kind of weekend you had in mind, I'm certainly not going to be offended."

"No, it sounds wonderful," Scott said, "if you're certain I wouldn't be imposing."

"Imposing?" He laughed. "My dear friend, I have been looking forward to this for weeks. So, if you can get yourself here, I'll make sure you're well cared for. And we'd love to have you go to church with us on Sunday, if you'd like."

"It sounds perfect," Scott said.

"Great. If you've got something to write with, I'll give you directions."

Scott listened and wrote down the landmarks, realizing there wasn't actually an address. Jess finished by saying, "And soon after the road becomes paved again, you'll go beneath an iron archway that says, 'Byrnehouse-Davies.'"

"Oh, so this is where you work."

"This is where we do everything. The house is attached to the boys' home. I guess you could say it goes with the job."

Scott had another of those moments of disbelief. "Amazing. I'd like to talk to you about that sometime."

"About what?"

"Well, lots of things, actually. We'll save it for the weekend."

"I'll be waiting. Why don't you come to the boys' home, and I'll just work until you get here. You can't miss it. The sign over the door is pretty easy to read, and there are three gables on the upper story."

"Great," Scott said, jotting the word 'gables' on his notes and circling it. "I'll see you Friday afternoon, then. And I do have a mobile phone, in case I get lost."

"You won't," Jess said, but he took the number in case there was any reason he might need to talk to him while he was en route.

Scott got off the phone and laughed out loud. He had a feeling this could end up being a really great weekend. And unless his feelings were completely deceiving him, he had to believe that his little trip to Byrnehouse-Davies could hold great significance for his life.

* * *

Scott set out Friday morning with the sun barely peeking over the eastern horizon. He enjoyed the drive and the scenery he encountered, and stopped often to get out and take pictures. He'd always heard Australia was a beautiful country, but he was experiencing the evidence firsthand. Beyond enjoying his surroundings, he had to admit that he felt comfortable in this setting. He felt as if he'd come home.

Scott began to get a jittery sensation as he turned off the main highway onto neatly groomed dirt roads, just as Jess's directions had indicated. He noticed what looked like a small airplane hangar near a long stretch of land that looked as if it had been used for a runway.

On the side of the hangar was a boldly painted logo: BD&H. He recalled the letters from Jess's email address. He suspected the "BD" was Byrnehouse-Davies, and he realized this company Jess worked for must be quite well off.

Scott was actually surprised when the road became paved again and he knew he was getting close. The iron archway appeared, just as Jess had described it, and that jittery sensation increased as he drove beneath it. As he drove a little farther, his view of the trees receded into the background, and a large building appeared in front of him. It had a look that was a combination of a hotel and a school, with a high roof and three gables jutting outward from the upper story.

"The gables," he said aloud and was seized by an inner trembling that made him feel hot and cold at the same time. He pulled the car into a parking place between two others and turned off the engine. The sign above the door clearly read: Byrnehouse-Davies Home for Boys. And once again a mass of memories lunged at him from his youth. Could that be the reason he felt as if he were coming home as he stepped out of the car and stood before the beautiful structure?

Scott took a deep breath and tugged on his leather jacket before he started toward the door. A quick glance at his watch told him it was 2:42. Considering his stops for meals and to use three rolls of film, he'd made pretty good time. He felt as nervous and excited as a child on Christmas Eve as he pushed open one of the large double doors. He was struck by the beauty of the building that was even more evident inside. He suspected it had been built in the Victorian era, and it had been well preserved. He turned his attention to the office just off the main hall and stepped through the open door. The woman at the first desk looked up and smiled. "I'd bet you're Mr. Ivie," she said.

"You must be psychic," he said, extending a hand to take hers.

"Psychic, heck," she said. "He's talked of little else all day."

Scott chuckled. "And you are?"

"Just call me Madge," she said. "Everybody else does."

"Well, it's a pleasure to meet you, Madge."

"And you. Have a seat. As usual, he's on the phone. But I'll let him know you're here."

Scott expected her to push some button on her phone, but she stood and moved to an open doorway, looking into a room that was beyond Scott's view. She made some comical hand signals and returned to her desk.

"He'll be out soon," she said, and Scott took a seat in one of three sturdy wooden chairs that he suspected were as old as the building.

Barely a minute later, he caught movement and looked up to see Jess Hamilton coming out of that open doorway. He hadn't changed much beyond his hair being longer than the standard missionary haircut. But then, Scott had seen the more recent photo from his sister's wallet. Jess laughed as Scott came to his feet and extended a hand that Jess shook heartily.

"Scott Ivie," he said as if he couldn't believe it. "It's really you."

"It's me," he said, and Jess hugged him as if they were long lost brothers. Scott felt something nearly electric occur from the embrace.

Jess drew back and looked into his eyes. They were of equal height and met each other eye to eye. Jess sighed and said, "You've changed. Same features, but a different man."

Scott smiled. "I don't have to tell you why."

"No, you don't have to tell me why." Jess laughed again as if his happiness could not be contained. "You met Madge?"

"I did," Scott said.

"Well, Madge," Jess said. "I'm out of here. If something comes up, Beulah will take care of it. I already talked to her."

"Have a nice weekend," Madge said and waved comically as they left the office.

Moving into the huge hall, Scott said, "This is a beautiful place. Where I was raised didn't have such a . . . beauty to it."

Jess stopped walking toward the door and looked at Scott as if he'd become polka-dotted. "You were raised in a boys' home?"

"Well, they called it a ranch, actually. But, yes, I was. They couldn't find a foster home that would keep me for long, so I ended up there when I was eleven, and stayed until I was old enough to be on my own."

"That's incredible," Jess said.

Scott looked around again. "Quite a coincidence, don't you think?"

"I don't believe in coincidences," Jess said.

Scott met his eyes. "Neither do I."

Jess motioned toward the stairs. "Would you like a tour before we go to the house?"

"Oh, I would," Scott said, unable to hide his enthusiasm.

Jess led the way through many halls and up a beautiful staircase, showing him the cafeteria, the library, the dorms, and the game room. They peeked into one-way windows in the classroom doors to see the boys being taught. As they toured the facility, Scott felt a growing combination of deep sorrow and inexplicable joy. Memories of his youth churned into the present, leaving him feeling strangely disconcerted. And then Jess ushered him into a room that took his breath away even before any explanation was given. It was vacant of any furnishings, and three large gabled windows lured him to move across the room.

"This is the gabled attic," Jess said. "The home was specifically built around this room as a symbol of something that held great meaning for my great-great-grandparents. This room is used for a number of different activities, and is rumored to have a certain magic about it."

"That's not difficult to imagine," Scott said, amazed at the spirit of the room that seemed to tangibly surround him, like a warm blanket. The sensation reminded him of currying horses as a boy, and the abstract sense of security he'd felt at the time.

"You must read the plaque," Jess said. "My wife found the words recorded in my great-great-grandmother's journal. It was her idea to put them on a plaque."

Scott moved closer and shifted his head until he could clearly read the words.

This morning I walked through the completed Byrnehouse-Davies Home for Boys, and while every part of it is beautiful and pragmatic there is no question that the gabled attic is the heart of the Home, as we had hoped it would be. When we embarked on building this home as a refuge for boys whose situations have left them at great disadvantage, we wanted the structure itself to be a tangible symbol of all we have endured to bring us to a point where such an endeavor was possible. Through much pondering and discussion, we made the decision to call upon the poetry written by Jess's mother, the key to uncovering the reasons for the heart of our trials and hardships. Through the gable facing east, I see my source of pain. By looking east through the gabled window, we found the answers that eventually made it possible to merge the Byrnehouse and Davies names, and to have the means to fulfill Jess's dream of helping boys with no control over the circumstances that have marred their precious spirits. For us, the source of pain is deep and personal, as it is with all human beings who fight to rise above the difficulties of this world to make something meaningful and rich of their lives. My deepest prayer is that every boy who has the opportunity to stand at these gabled windows and watch the sun rise will leave here changed for the better and more capable of finding a life of happiness and peace.

It took Scott a ridiculously long time to read it, since his eyes kept misting over and he had to fight the tears back rather than start crying in front of this man whom he barely knew. No one could ever fully understand how this woman's words, written more than a century ago, spoke to his soul.

"That's extraordinary," Scott said, hearing evidence of the emotion he was feeling in his voice.

Jess just put a hand to his shoulder and said quietly, "Yes, it is."

Scott was reluctant to leave the attic, and Jess must have sensed it when he said, "You can come back and spend as much time here as you like."

"Thank you," Scott said. "I might do that."

They walked back downstairs and toward the front doors near the office. Jess said, "It would probably be easier for you to move your car around to the house, so I'll ride along and you won't get lost."

"Wise plan," Scott said and they stepped outside. He noticed a large van that hadn't been there when he'd come in. On the side was that same logo: BD&H. "So, what's the H for?" he asked.

Jess looked surprised but simply said, "Uh . . . that would be Hamilton."

Scott was momentarily taken aback and realized his shock wasn't missed by Jess. Only then did the idea connect in his mind that the plaque in the gabled attic had been written by Jess's great-great-grand-mother. As they both got into the car, Jess said, "You didn't know."

"I'm still not sure I know. In truth, I know nothing about you beyond your spiritual convictions."

"Which is all that matters, really," Jess said as Scott backed the car up and headed the direction Jess was pointing. "Just follow the drive through the trees and park at the end near the house."

"So what is it that I should know?" Scott asked just as his view of the trees receded and the drive turned, and an incredible vista opened up in front of him. He became immediately breathless and unconsciously stopped the car, just feeling the need to absorb the view.

"Incredible, isn't it?" Jess said. "No matter how many times I see it, I'm just amazed at what a beautiful place this is."

"It certainly is," Scott said, almost afraid of the growing sensation inside of him that he had come home.

Chapter Three

The first thing Scott noticed was the beautiful, large buildings that could be nothing but horse stables. There were several corrals, a gallops, and even a track. Stating the obvious, he said, "You have horses."

"Yeah," Jess chuckled. "We certainly have horses."

Once Scott assimilated one more ironic piece of information, his eyes took in the full breadth of the scene. To his left was a large, beautiful Victorian home. And he could see from here that it connected into the boys' home, as he'd been told. Another much smaller home was across the huge rolling lawn, and in the distance, beyond the stables and track, an endless stretch of land merged into the mountain range in the distance.

"It's beautiful," Scott said, oblivious to his odd behavior until Jess chuckled and cleared his throat loudly.

"If you want to park the car up there at the end of the drive," Jess said, "I'll tell you the story."

"The story?" Scott asked, bringing himself back to the moment as he drove forward.

They got out of the car while Scott could hardly tear his eyes from the horses that were being trained in different corrals, and the extraordinary landscape beyond them.

"Is something wrong?" Jess asked, reminding him that he wasn't alone.

"It's just . . . like an image out of my dreams," he said. Scott found himself wishing for his camera, but it would have distracted him from absorbing the reality of his surroundings. He would be sure to take lots of pictures before he went home.

"Really?" Jess sounded intrigued.

"On the ranch where I grew up there were a couple of horses, and the opportunity to ride was a privilege that had to be earned. Many of the boys were indifferent toward the horses. But I worked very hard to do everything just right so I could ride each week. The other boys would complain when their turn came to feed or curry the horses, but I would trade just about anything I had to be able to just . . . touch them and be close to them." He gave a humorless chuckle and shook his head. "They were my best friends. It seemed they understood me, when no one else did. And riding was like . . . being set free from everything else in my life that was . . . well, certainly less than favorable."

Scott heard himself baring his soul, saying words aloud that he had only told one other person, and Callie had listened with a certain indifference. He turned to Jess to study his reaction and was surprised—though perhaps he shouldn't have been—to see complete understanding in his eyes. To test it a little further, he asked, "Does that sound crazy?"

"No," Jess said, his gaze moving to the fine animal being ridden around the gallops, "it doesn't sound crazy. You're talking to a man whose earliest memory is being in the saddle with my father. I don't share the intense love for horses that others in my family have, but they are a source of comfort to me. They're amazing animals."

"And what exactly is done with them here?"

"We breed and train for many different purposes. The most prominent is the racing stock."

"Really?" Scott said and chuckled.

"Is that funny?"

"Well, for a number of years my greatest pastime was the races. When I joined the Church I had to put my attention elsewhere since the temptation to gamble was a little too strong."

Jess chuckled. "Well, we like a good race around here, but we keep the bets in pocket change."

Scott laughed, then inhaled deeply, as if he could pull his surroundings more fully into himself before he said, "You were going to tell me a story."

"Ah yes." Jess ambled slowly across the huge lawn toward the corrals, and Scott matched his gait. "Well, I'll give you the nutshell version. As I understand it, the story began with a man named

Benjamin Davies. He was the son of Welsh coal miners, and he came to Australia to make his fortune. He homesteaded this land and made enough money mining gold to build a beautiful home and buy some good horses, good racing stock. Ben married a woman named Emma, and their son, Jess Davies, inherited everything. But soon after his father's death, the house was burned to the ground by an arsonist."

"Really?" Scott asked, astonished.

"Really. So Jess sunk everything he had to rebuild the house, then he struggled to stay afloat. A young woman named Alexa Byrnehouse came to Jess for a job when she was disowned by her father. He hired her to train his prize horse for a race, with everything he owned staked on her success. She won the race and they fell in love. They married and eventually inherited her father's fortune, and the Byrnehouse-Davies name was established. With that fortune Jess and Alexa founded the boys' home. Their daughter, Emma, eventually married a man who had been raised in the home and then stayed on to work. That's a rather colorful story which I will save for another time. His name was Michael Hamilton. Michael and Emma had several daughters and one son, Jesse, who is my grandfather."

"And your father?" Scott asked as they approached the rail around the track and leaned against it.

"Jess Michael Hamilton, the third." He spoke the name with a certain reverence and added gently, "He died of cancer last year."

"Oh, I'm sorry," Scott said.

"Yes, well . . . it's been one of the most difficult things we've ever faced, but . . . life has a way of going on."

Scott found his mind briefly wandering to Sister Hamilton, who was serving a mission in Salt Lake City. He thought of her facing the loss of her father, and his heart ached for her in a way that made no logical sense considering how he'd spent a total of fifteen minutes in her presence, if that. He attempted to ease his curiosity on several counts as he said, "So I assume your work entails overseeing the boys' home."

"Mostly that. Actually I oversee everything in one way or another, but my interests keep me more in the boys' home while I leave the horse business mostly to the stable master; he's a good man. He lives in the smaller house there, which is actually older than the main house."

"Still, the responsibility must be quite a burden for you."

"At times it's seemed that way, but I have many good people working for me. We manage. It's very gratifying work, for the most part."

"Forgive me if I'm prying, but . . ."

"No, ask anything you like." Jess grinned. "I'll likely get even."

Scott smiled and asked, "What of your siblings? Or are there just the two of you?"

"Technically there are seven of us."

"Seven?" Scott asked. Being an only child and orphaned at that, it was difficult to comprehend such a family.

"My mother was married previously and had three daughters, which she brought to Australia when she married my father."

"Your mother is American, then."

"She is, and so are my half-sisters, technically."

Scott wondered about the sister serving a mission, but she was obviously younger than Jess. He listened as Jess went on to explain, "I am the oldest of my father's children, and then there is my brother James. And many years later came the twins."

"Twins?"

"Tyson and Emma are twins, although Tyson died soon after birth. That left Emma to be the baby of the family."

Emma, Scott repeated in his mind while his heart quickened. He forced a straight voice as he asked, "And Emma would be your sister serving a mission on Temple Square?"

"That's right," Jess said brightly, as if just hearing her mentioned added to his happiness.

"So there would be you and James, and four sisters."

Jess sighed loudly and Scott turned to look at him, sensing something difficult even before he said, "James and his wife were killed in a car accident not so many years ago."

Scott's heart ached as he heard of this tragedy. Three deaths in the family in only a few years. Scott had never lost a loved one to death, which was most likely due to the fact that he'd never had any loved ones. Of course, he'd lost his parents at an early age, but he wasn't even certain he remembered them, so it was difficult to feel any sorrow for the loss. "I'm so sorry," Scott said again, thinking it sounded trite.

"Yes, well . . . that was one of the *other* most difficult things I've lived through. But as I said, life goes on, and we have been very blessed."

"And you have taken over a great legacy here."

"Yes, I have. And I have struggled much with wondering if I could ever be worthy or adequate to do all that is required of me. Eventually I realized that my best is good enough, so I just take it one day at a time and do the best I can." Again he said, "We have been very blessed."

Jess turned to lean his back against the rail and Scott did the same, taking in the view of the house and yard, surrounded by magnificent trees and spacious lawns. The serenity in the air was a stark contrast to the busy city life he'd become accustomed to. But he liked it. He liked it a lot.

Following several minutes of comfortable silence, while Scott attempted to digest all that had been said, he commented, "So, your . . . who was it? Your great-grandfather was raised in the boys' home?"

"That's right."

"And he turned out all right, huh?"

Jess chuckled. "He was amazing. There are stories recorded in a number of different family journals."

"So there's hope for me, you think?"

Jess looked at Scott and chuckled. "You don't seem to be doing too badly."

"You don't even know me."

"Just give me a few more minutes," Jess said, slapping his shoulder playfully as they moved back toward the house. "What I know seems pretty amazing."

"Well, the feeling is mutual," Scott said humbly, so in awe of all he was seeing and feeling that he could hardly keep his thoughts straight.

"You should come in and meet the family. They'll wonder where we ran off to."

"I'd like that very much," Scott said.

"And perhaps in the morning we could go riding."

"Really?" Scott laughed. "I can't even remember the last time I was on a horse."

"Well then, it's about time you get on one again."

Jess quickened his pace as they walked across the lawn toward the house. "It must be getting close to supper time now," Jess said.

They stopped for a moment at the car where Scott got his overnight bag and his camera bag and slung them over his shoulder before he locked up the car and stuffed the keys into the pocket of his jeans. They were a only a few steps from the side door of the house when it flew open and a little girl with reddish-blonde hair came running.

"Daddy!" she said and flung herself into Jess's arms.

Jess laughed and twirled around with her. "How's my favorite girl?"

Scott watched the reunion with interest while something incongruous struck him.

"This is Evelyn," Jess said to Scott. Then to Evelyn, "This is my friend, Scott. He's going to stay with us for a few days."

"We're having Aunt Rhea's homemade chicken soup with fat noodles for supper," Evelyn said. "And chocolate mousse that Daddy made last night."

"It sounds wonderful," Scott said to the child before she got down and went into the house ahead of them.

"Forgive me if I'm prying again, but . . . if I calculate the time since you were serving a mission, isn't she just a little too old to be yours?"

Jess laughed. "I like the way you just cut to the chase, Scott. You and I are going to get along great; I can tell. Yes, Evelyn is too old to be mine. Tamra and I adopted her. She's my brother's daughter."

Scott recalled the brother and his wife who were killed in an accident. "Oh, I see," he said. "Well, I can stop worrying over that one."

"Indeed," Jess said, and they stepped into the house.

From where Scott stood in a long hall, with stairs going up close by, the house looked cozy and had a homey feel. A pleasant aroma filtered from the kitchen and he realized he was hungry.

"I'll show you the room you'll be using," Jess said. "And you can freshen up a bit if you like." He glanced at his watch. "We'll eat in about ten or fifteen minutes."

"Sounds great," Scott said and followed Jess up the stairs.

The room he was given almost reminded him of something out of a bed and breakfast. The furnishings were likely original to the house, and it was decorated with an inviting, cozy charm—right down to the homemade quilt on the bed, and another folded on a quilt stand near the foot of the bed. A private bathroom branched off the room in one direction, and in the other direction it connected into what Jess called a sitting room. Scott examined the view out the window and almost felt as if he were dreaming.

"Extraordinary," he whispered to himself and went down the stairs to the kitchen. He entered quietly to see Evelyn putting napkins beneath the forks beside each place setting. Three women were hovering near the stove taking tastes from a pot of soup and laughing. The most unusual feature of the room was the three highchairs lined up along one side of the table. Jess had two bibs tucked beneath his arm while he put a third on one of the little boys seated there.

Jess glanced over his shoulder and saw Scott in the doorway. "Oh, there you are," he said and the women all turned at once. "Come in. Come in," Jess said. "Make yourself at home."

"Thank you," Scott said.

"I'll make the introductions," Jess said, continuing his bib duty. "Scott, this lovely lady is my mother, Emily Hamilton."

Scott took the outstretched hand of an attractive middle-aged woman, startled by the thought that appeared in his mind: *Emma's mother.* He took her hand, saying, "It is such a pleasure, Sister Hamilton."

"The pleasure is purely ours, Scott. And please . . . call me Emily."

"This lovely lady is my sweet wife, Tamra," Jess said, motioning toward the youngest of the three women, who was significantly taller than the other two, with long red hair.

"Hello, Scott," she said, shaking his hand as well. "It's so good to finally meet you. You will never know the happiness you've given my husband."

Scott glanced toward Jess who was smiling sheepishly. "And this lovely lady," he motioned toward the third woman who was thin and dressed garishly, "is Tamra's Aunt Rhea. She stays here to keep us all in line."

"And she does a fine job of it," Emily said.

"So good to meet you," Rhea said.

"And you," Scott replied.

"Well, shall we eat?" Emily said. "We can't agree on whether the soup needs more salt or not, so you'll all just have to adjust it in your own bowls."

"I dare say we can do that," Jess said as he helped his wife dish up some drained noodles into three little bowls.

"I haven't met these handsome boys," Scott said, taking the chair that Emily motioned him into.

"How silly of me," Jess said. "I can't forget the royalty of the household. This is Michael," he said, pointing to the oldest of the three, who offered a silly grin that made Scott chuckle.

"Jess Michael Hamilton, the fifth, to be exact," Rhea said proudly.

"Of course," Scott said.

"And these are the twins," Jess added and Scott was surprised. He was thinking they looked too close in age to be from different pregnancies, but they looked nothing the same, so he had assumed that perhaps they were tending someone else's child. "Joshua and Tyson," he said, putting little cups with spillproof lids in front of them.

"Wow," Scott said, "that must keep you busy."

Tamra snorted a laugh that made everyone else laugh. "Three boys with the oldest barely two," she said, "and they're all as rambunctious and obnoxious as their father."

"How would you know?" Jess asked, pretending to be insulted.

"I told her," Emily said. "Believe me when I tell you that I know exactly how rambunctious and obnoxious you were at that age."

"I think you're going senile, Mother," Jess said. "I was a perfect angel, and you know it."

"Of course," Emily said with a trace of sarcasm.

They were all seated and Jess offered a blessing on the food, in which he expressed gratitude at having Scott present with them. The meal proceeded with much conversation and laughter as hot rolls and fresh vegetables were passed around to go with the soup—the best soup Scott had ever eaten. He complimented Rhea who humbly declared that Tamra had helped her, then he found he was quite content to observe his surroundings. He'd certainly been invited to dinner before with families in his ward, or families of people he worked with. But it had never felt like this.

Scott tried to determine what it was exactly that made him feel as if he were somehow in a dream; the kind of dream that stuck in your memory, as if you were supposed to ponder it and learn something significant. He'd spent time with real families before, and it wasn't new for him to wonder what it might have been like to grow up in such a family. Instead he'd been passed from one family to another, and not one of them stood out as having given him any measure of love or security worth holding onto. Yet, in this room right now he felt as if a lifetime of love and security were being poured out to him, simply as an overflowing of the love they all shared for each other. He felt deeply comforted, and at the same time comfortable; perhaps more comfortable than he had ever felt in his life. And he wondered why. *Why?* In pondering the question, it occurred to him that perhaps he was simply fantasizing because of his attraction to Emma Hamilton. Perhaps his infatuation for her had prompted him to imagine what it might be like to marry into such a family. But he had to admit in all honesty that he'd not been thinking of her at all when the feelings of security had overtaken him.

When they'd all had their fill of soup, and the babies had made a glorious mess, Evelyn helped her mother serve the chocolate mousse that Jess had made. "His father taught him how to make it," Tamra said to Scott. "I insisted that Michael could not leave us until he taught Jess the really important things."

"I still can't make it the way he did," Jess said.

"But you make animal pancakes every bit as well as he did," Emily said proudly, then they all laughed.

Scott's feelings of peace deepened as he observed the way they discussed their deceased husband and father, and the love for him was still so readily evident in his absence. But for the evidence of their love, they were not upset in talking about him, but rather comforted.

When the meal was finished, Jess and Emily took the children upstairs to bathe them and get them ready for bed. Rhea dug in cleaning up the high chairs and the mess beneath them on the floor. Tamra cleared the table. Scott felt helpless for only a moment before he took the empty pan from the stove to the sink and began to wash it.

"Oh, you don't need to do that," Tamra insisted.

"I'm happy to," he said. "It's nice to feel useful, believe me. And I always preferred to have the pans washed first, which makes the rest of the dishes not seem quite so ominous."

"I think I like that idea," Rhea said. She commented a moment later, "You seem to be pretty good at that."

"Oh, unfortunately I'm a little too good at cleaning things," he said.

"Why do you say that?" Tamra asked with a chuckle.

"Well, I must confess that I struggle some with OCD."

"What is that?" Rhea asked.

"Obsessive Compulsive Disorder," he said. "In English, I just have an obsession with keeping things clean and tidy."

"Oh, I think I would like that kind of obsession in a man," Tamra said.

"What kind of obsession?" Jess asked, coming into the kitchen to get one of the boy's little blankets that he'd forgotten.

"Scott has an obsession with keeping things clean and tidy," Tamra said as if it were a unique gift.

"Really?" Jess said. "Yes, I do believe my wife would like that." He winked at Tamra.

"I'm afraid it's rather annoying," Scott admitted. "I'm aware of it and I can laugh about it, but my ex-wife didn't necessarily appreciate it. She got used to it after a while, however. She just learned to let me pick up after her."

Tamra chuckled. Jess waved comically and left the room.

"So," Tamra said, standing beside Scott to rinse dishes that would go into the dishwasher, "tell us about yourself, Scott. I asked Jess to tell me about you, and he knew absolutely nothing."

"Well, that made us fairly equal, I'm afraid. We were so busy discussing the gospel in those emails that we never thought to ask any personal questions."

"Must be a man thing," Rhea said.

"Must be," Tamra agreed. "But you will tell us about yourself now, won't you?"

"There really isn't much to tell," Scott said, "beyond my having an ex-wife and a problem with OCD."

Tamra probed him with questions and he told her the bare minimum of his background. When the kitchen was cleaned up and the children all in bed, the adults gathered in what Jess called the lounge room. And Scott was coerced into repeating what he'd told Tamra and Rhea in the kitchen.

"And he spent several years of his youth in a boys' home," Jess said as if he'd declared that Scott had royal blood.

"Really?" Tamra and Emily both said as if they agreed with Jess.

"It was called a ranch, actually. And yes, I really did."

He went on to tell them what that was like, and of the love for horses that he'd gained through those years.

"It's just too weird," Jess interjected. "There are too many coincidences here." He hummed the theme song to *The Twilight Zone* and they all laughed.

Emily asked him more questions about his upbringing before the conversation finally began to include the others in the room. Scott learned that Tamra was a convert to the Church who had suffered a great deal of abuse while growing up in a dysfunctional family; she had obviously risen above her background marvelously. Her Aunt Rhea was her mother's sister who had always been more of a mother to her than her own mother. She wasn't a member of the Church, but her living in the Hamilton household had obviously taught her much of its principles. She was obviously a good woman who fit well into the family.

As the evening deepened Scott learned about Emily's first marriage, which had been difficult. And he heard the love story behind her marriage to Michael Hamilton. He marveled at the way her eyes glowed as she spoke of her deceased husband, and he determined that he wanted to feel that way about a woman. He was taken off guard when Emma popped into his mind in the same moment. He forced his mind back to the conversation and learned that Jess had actually been rather rebellious in his youth, but he'd finally turned his life around and served a mission. When that point came up, Scott felt compelled to express his gratitude for the sacrifices made in this family, by Jess and those who had loved and supported him while he had served. The seeds he had planted in Scott's heart had changed his life irrevocably. The room became hushed, even reverent as Scott heard himself sharing his testimony and what the gospel meant in his life. And then he expressed his gratitude to the family for supporting Emma on her mission, making it possible for him to find Jess again, and to be here now. He told them the story of how he'd felt so alone following his divorce, and he'd felt prompted to go to Temple Square and the connection had been made.

"It's truly a miracle," Emily said.

"I think we've heard of many miracles tonight," Tamra said.

"Indeed we have," Rhea agreed.

"It's good to have you with us, Scott," Emily said with a tenderness that threatened to make him cry.

"It certainly is," Jess added with equal sincerity.

"Well, for me," Scott admitted, "I can't even say how good it is to be here. Forgive me if I get a little mushy, but—"

"Oh, we like mushy," Tamra interjected.

"Anyway," Scott chuckled, grateful for some relief of the tension, "I've known many people who have been kind and compassionate about the lack of family in my life, but I have never been around such a fine family, and I've never felt quite so comfortable in someone else's home as I have today."

"You don't even know us yet," Jess said. "Just give us time."

"I'd like to do that," Scott said and glanced at his watch. "But seeing that it's nearly one o'clock, I'm sure I've kept all of you up plenty late."

"Oh, my goodness," Tamra said. "It's really true what they say: time flies when you're having fun."

"Indeed," Scott said and came to his feet. "Thank you again, for everything."

"Our pleasure," Emily said and hugged him tightly. He absorbed her motherly embrace as if it could somehow make up for the lack of a mother figure in his life. "Sleep as late as you like in the morning, and make yourself at home. If you need something you can't find, just ask."

"I will, thank you," he said and turned to shake Jess's hand, but he ended up getting an embrace from him as well. Then Tamra and Rhea followed his example, with Rhea pinching his cheek like the proverbial aunt and saying, "Such a sweet boy."

Jess walked into the hall beside Scott, saying, "Don't forget that we're going riding in the morning, if you're up to it."

"Oh, I'll be up to it," Scott said.

An hour later Scott was still wide awake, so thoroughly caught up in the miraculous events of this day, and all that had led up to it. Long after he'd finished with his usual prayer, he found himself spontaneously thanking God for orchestrating such an incredible chain of events. He contemplated the bits and pieces of these people's lives that he'd heard through the conversations they'd shared, and he marveled that he felt so at home among them. He finally slept with the anticipation of another marvelous day, and he woke to find his room filled with the light of dawn. The room itself was lovely, and he wondered what the walls might tell of the history they had seen in this great house, and the generations of fine people who had lived here.

Not wanting to waste another minute of this day in bed, he got up and took a quick shower. He dressed in jeans and a white polo shirt and running shoes. If he had known he was going riding, he might have come better prepared. Although, it had been so many years since he'd ridden that he concluded he really didn't have anything in his wardrobe that was any more suitable than what he had on. With his bed made and his room tidy, he went quietly down to the kitchen, not wanting to stir anyone else if they were sleeping late. He entered to find Emily sitting at the table with a steaming cup of cocoa beside her, reading a magazine.

"Oh, hello," she said.

"Good morning," he replied, setting his camera on the table. "I didn't know if anyone would be up and about, but I figured I could manage to find myself some hot water."

"It's already heated in that teapot on the stove. I enjoy my hot cocoa every morning."

Scott poured himself a cup of hot water and eased a chair out. "May I?" he asked.

"Oh, of course." She slid the can of cocoa mix toward him.

"No, thank you," he said, producing an herbal tea bag from his shirt pocket. "I brought my own. Silly habit," he added as he stuck it into the water and stirred it with a spoon. "But it's helped me break the morning coffee habit. I'm afraid that cocoa is usually a little too sweet for me."

"Well, whatever that is, it smells very good," Emily said, inhaling the steam that rose from his cup.

"I'm not sure, actually," he said. "I have quite a variety and I just grabbed a few for the trip."

He chuckled and she asked, "Is something funny?"

"I just realized I'm discussing herbal tea with a lovely lady. It's something I might have dreamed of doing in my youth."

"Well," Emily smiled, "dreams do come true, you know."

"Coming from you, I believe that."

"Something occurred to me last night after you went to bed. After you shared some of your experiences with us, I realized that you have some amazing things in common with someone else I know."

"Really? Who?" he asked.

"Well, let me tell you this much first. He wasn't orphaned, but he grew up in a horrible situation with unspeakable abuse. He ended up living on the streets at a very young age until he was picked up by the law at the age of eleven and put into our boys' home." Scott lifted his brows as he listened. "He stayed here until he was old enough to be on his own, and then he actually worked in the stables after that. He did leave eventually but ended up making some bad choices and went to prison for a while. However, through a series of miracles that are rather incredible, he eventually became the administrator of the boys' home and married into the family. He was an amazing man." She smiled. "And he loved the horses. I believe he declared more than once that his love for horses had taught him how to love."

"Extraordinary," Scott said breathlessly. "Who is this man? I should like to meet him."

"Well, that might be possible one day. But I hope it won't be too soon. He died when my husband was a child. It was his grandfather, Michael Hamilton."

Scott was momentarily flabbergasted. "Really. Wow. And how do you know all of this? Did your husband remember or—"

"He was an avid journal keeper, as many of our ancestors have been. It's something we are truly grateful for. Their stories have left us with a great legacy."

"I should like to read that story, or is it exclusively for family?"

"Heavens no," she said. "You'd be welcome to read it. I'll dig it up for you."

"Thank you," he said. "I'll look forward to it."

They chatted comfortably while his tea steeped and became cool enough for him to drink. Soon afterward Jess and Tamra arrived with the children and the kitchen became noisy with delightful activity. Scott's offers to help with breakfast were vehemently refused, but he rather enjoyed watching Jess make animal pancakes for his children. He was pleasantly surprised to have a nearly perfect Mickey Mouse pancake put onto his own plate.

"I bet you've never had breakfast look quite like that before," Jess said to him.

"No, I can't say that I have."

"Well, eat hearty. If you can get that one down, I'll make you a bunny."

"And I thought I had seen it all," Scott said as he spread butter over Mickey's ears.

When breakfast was finished, Emily shooed Jess and Scott out the door, insisting that she would take care of the dishes. "Have a wonderful time and don't hurry," she said.

"I need a few minutes," Jess said, glancing down at his bare feet. "I'll meet you on the veranda." Scott felt confused. "The long porch on the side of the house."

"Ah," Scott said. "I'll be there."

He had no trouble finding the veranda, and he quickly made himself comfortable with his feet propped up on the rail. The view was as magnificent as it had been yesterday, and he resisted the urge to literally pinch himself. He snapped some pictures, wishing they would do justice to what his eyes could see. But they would stir his memories, if nothing else.

He'd not sat there for long before Jess appeared wearing a white shirt with leather suspenders over it, attached to dark riding breeches and classic, black riding boots. On his head was a flat-brimmed, well-worn hat.

"Very nice," Scott said. "Do you have a copyright on the ensemble?"

"Hardly," Jess snorted. "It's rather common attire around here."

"Then you must tell me where I can acquire such . . . Australian attire."

Jess laughed, as if the very idea would be a pleasure. "After lunch, we can do just that, and if you can't afford it, we'll work out a deal."

"Oh, I can afford it," Scott said, and they laughed together as they headed toward the stable.

Jess took notice of the camera hanging around Scott's neck. "You look like a tourist."

"Aren't I?" he asked, then snapped a picture of Jess walking beside him. Jess just laughed again.

Chapter Four

During the next few hours Scott found his senses overwhelmed and his spirit completely exhilarated. It only took him a couple of minutes to feel completely comfortable on the well-trained stallion, and he absorbed the experience as one that he'd missed far more than he'd admitted. The beauty of the scenery they encountered was breathtaking. The conversation he shared with Jess was stimulating and nearly eerie at times as they almost seemed to anticipate each other's thoughts and ideas.

While Scott was replacing the roll of film in his camera, Jess said, "That's the third roll this morning. You *are* like a tourist."

"It's a hobby of mine actually. I take it rather seriously."

"Do tell," Jess said.

"Well, I just . . . seem to see everything around me through a camera lens, whether I have a camera or not. I'm always noticing what would make a good picture. For every roll I shoot I usually end up with three or four that are really worth saving; pictures that just have an artistic feel to them."

"Incredible," Jess said. "I'd love to see your work."

"Well, I'll bring some with me next time, if you like me enough to invite me back."

"No question there," Jess said with a grin.

They returned to find the women sitting on the veranda eating sandwiches and drinking lemonade while the children played close by on the lawn. After caring for the horses, Jess and Scott walked toward the house with the sound of feminine laughter floating to their ears.

"Now, there's a lovely sight," Jess said, and Scott heartily agreed. He snapped a couple of pictures. He couldn't help thinking that the sight would be made lovelier if Emma Hamilton were among the group. He wondered how she was doing, and he couldn't deny that he felt lonely for her, even though he wondered how that could be when she had never been a part of his life. Still, he missed her, and he prayed that when her mission was complete, their paths might cross again. Given the situation developing with her family, he considered it a likely prospect, even though his being here now had absolutely nothing to do with her—beyond the fact that she had been the liaison that had made this possible.

As he and Jess stepped onto the veranda, Emily motioned to a plate of sandwiches covered with plastic wrap, and some clean plates and glasses sitting near the pitcher of lemonade.

"You look like a tourist," Tamra said, pointing at Scott's camera.

Jess laughed heartily. "That's what I said. But actually, he's a real photographer."

"That depends on your definition of 'real,'" Scott said. "I keep a camera with me most of the time, and I enjoy the results."

"That's marvelous," Emily said and motioned him toward a chair.

They visited while they ate and Scott felt more at home every moment he was with these people. He took a chance by snapping some pictures of them, wondering if they had any idea how quickly he was growing to love them. In response to their surprise he said, "Just collecting memories. Don't pay any attention."

When they had finished eating, Jess said, "I hope you ladies don't mind, but I must take Scott shopping. He is apparently concerned that he doesn't have the right attire to fit in around here, and we certainly want him to fit in."

"Oh, of course," Tamra said facetiously. Then to Scott, "He bought me a pair of those boots before he'd hardly said, 'how do you do' to me. I think it *is* a requirement."

"Hardly," Emily laughed. "But it doesn't hurt."

"So, if I get a pair of those boots, does that make me officially fit in?"

"Oh, that was clinched the minute you got out of the car," Jess said. "The boots are just a necessary evil."

"Evil?" Scott echoed.

Tamra laughed and said, "You must understand, Scott, that this is a man who only wears shoes when he absolutely has to." Scott glanced at Jess to see that he had pulled off his boots and stockings, probably before they had eaten.

"That's right," Jess said. "And if I have to wear shoes, they'd better be pretty darn comfortable. Hey," he said as if he'd just had a great enlightenment, "maybe I have some OCD behavior about shoes." They all laughed before he added, "But those boots," he motioned toward them, "are simply something you need if you're going to ride horses more than once a year."

"Well, on the chance that I get invited back," Scott said, "I must have some of those boots."

While Jess was pulling his boots back on so they could leave, Emily said, "Well, you boys have a good time. Since Jess watched the children while Tamra and I went into town last Saturday, I'd say he's earned a day out."

After Jess had hugged all of his children, his wife, his mother, and Rhea, they walked together to a structure that had to be at least as old as the house.

"The carriage house," Jess said, as if he'd sensed Scott's curiosity. He opened one of the huge doors to reveal two Toyota Land Cruisers, a sedan, and a variety of historical wheeled vehicles sitting further back, in the shadows.

"Extraordinary," Scott said and they climbed into one of the Cruisers and headed away from the house. Their comfortable conversation of earlier picked up again easily through the hour's drive to the nearest town. Scott had a glorious time picking out some new clothes, admitting to Jess that he'd only brought to Australia a minimal selection of the things he'd really liked and needed. When he tried on a pair of those classic boots, he had to admit they were comfortable and he liked the way they felt. Jess picked up Scott's camera and took a couple of pictures of him as he comically modeled his new apparel. Their last stop was to buy a suitable hat to wear riding in sun or rain. "With a perfect Australian flair," Scott said when he tried it on.

"Do I look Australian?" Scott asked and Jess snapped a picture of him.

"Did you want to?"

"Oh, I think I could get used to it."

"In that case, you look Australian."

When they returned to the house, talking and laughing, the women fussed and swooned over Scott's new look. "Here, give me that," Tamra said, taking Scott's camera, then she made him and Jess do several different poses together.

"The only problem," Scott said, "is that Jess's hat and boots look well worn, and I still look like a tourist."

"The only way to make them look worn is to wear them a lot," Jess said. "We'll have to work on that."

Over supper with the family and while visiting again into the night, Scott wondered if he'd ever laughed so much in his life. At moments he felt completely a part of this family, and at others he felt like a child outside the window of a candy store, desperately wanting to fully partake of experiences that he'd coveted all his life. Discreetly snapping pictures, he felt like a reporter, quietly observing and mentally taking notes as if he might write a feature article entitled, "What makes the ideal family tick."

When they finally dispersed to go to bed, since church was early and the drive long, Scott said, "I think I'll go out to the veranda for a few minutes before I turn in." As he sat and enjoyed the peaceful night air, he dreaded having to return to Brisbane tomorrow. He wondered if the Hamiltons would ever invite him back, or if this would be a once-in-a-life-time experience. His thoughts were interrupted when Emily appeared beside him.

"May I?" she asked, motioning to a chair.

"Of course. It's your home."

"But I didn't want to invade your privacy if you were wanting some time alone."

"I've had way too much time alone to ever turn down an offer for company," he said.

"I wonder if we could talk," she said in a tone that made it evident she had something specific on her mind.

"Of course," he said again, hoping that he'd not done something inappropriate, something to offend her or one of her family members.

"First of all, I was just wondering if you've had a good time."

"Oh," he laughed and shook his head, "this weekend has been one of the highlights of my life."

"I hope you'll come and visit us often," she said sincerely and he wanted to jump out of his chair and hug her.

"I can't think of anywhere I would rather spend my time off, but I don't want to intrude or—"

"You're not intruding, Scott, I can assure you. You've been a delight to have in our home, and a perfect gentleman. If the boys in our home could be raised with such fine manners, we would consider ourselves very successful."

Scott chuckled. "You're very sweet, but I'm not sure it had much to do with my upbringing. It was more a fetish of mine. I recall being constantly annoyed with the other boys I grew up with when they would be impolite and inappropriate."

"Then it's a gift you brought with you to this world," she said and he could only smile. He'd never looked at it that way. He'd wondered if it was just another form of his OCD behaviors.

Following a long minute of silence, Emily said, "There's something else I want to say. I'm just not sure where to begin."

"I'm not in trouble, am I?" he asked, hoping to eliminate the tension he was feeling, wondering if he'd overstepped his bounds somewhere. He was so unaccustomed to interacting with a family to this extent, that he felt as if he had been at sea for endless years and he was suddenly trying to walk on dry ground while his sea legs threatened to buckle beneath him.

"Certainly not," Emily chuckled. "In fact, I want to thank you."

"Thank me? Whatever for?"

Emily looked directly at him, and he was grateful for the outdoor lighting that made her expression clearly visible. "You've filled a void in his life, Scott," she said, and he knew she was talking about Jess. "There was a marked change in him from the day he received that first email from you, and that change has blossomed in your presence. He has been more like his real self today than I have seen since his father was diagnosed with cancer." Emily leaned closer and put her hand over his where it rested on the arm of the chair. "But it's more than that. I've been watching him interact with you, seeing a side of him that I've not seen for years; a purely delightful, completely happy side. And it just occurred to me, that . . ." She sighed loudly. "You see, Jess lost his brother and his best friend in an accident. Gradually as he healed, his father became his best friend, and then he lost his father to cancer."

Scott felt his heart tighten and a knot gather in his throat. He'd been so preoccupied with the miracle of this experience for him, that it hadn't even occurred to him that his being here might have made a positive difference to somebody else. He could feel where this was going, but he was still unprepared for how the tears filled his eyes when she went on to say, "I didn't fully realize until I saw the way he was with you, that . . . well, you've filled a hole, Scott. I have seen a miracle manifest itself here today." She met his eyes directly, apparently unsurprised by the tears she saw on his face. "You have become his brother, his best friend." She sighed and said more brightly, "And for that you must know that you will always have a place in our home. To see the way Jess lights up in your presence, I'd say the more you are here, the better."

"It's a nice thought," Scott said, "but I don't want to be here too much and wear out my welcome. I don't want to distract him from his work and his family."

"Oh, he's not going to neglect either of those. He knows he doesn't need to babysit you. I'll tell you what I've told every other person who has spent a great deal of time in our home. If I have cause for concern, if something needs to be said, I'll not be holding back."

Scott smiled. "A true mother, in every respect. And I'm glad of it. I feel rather unsure of myself in such situations, and I certainly wouldn't want to do anything inappropriate. If I know you'll keep me straight, then I can stop worrying."

"Oh, there's no need to worry, Scott. Just promise you'll come back every possible chance you get, and I promise to let you know if I sense even the tiniest bit of a problem."

"It's a deal," he said and squeezed her hand.

Scott had trouble sleeping again that night as the depth of this miracle settled in deeper. The conversation he'd had with Emily was like icing on a glorious and beautiful cake, and he was truly grateful.

Going to church with the Hamiltons the following morning just added to his contentment. His only regret was that it would have been inappropriate to take his camera into the church building. He just had to hold those memories in his heart. People were warm and friendly and he quickly realized that being with the Hamiltons had a certain prestige attached to it; not because they were affluent, but because they were known as such kind and giving people.

As the meetings drew to an end, Scott felt decidedly depressed. He had driven his own car to the meeting, since he really needed to be on his way home, and it was silly to drive an hour to the house and then back again. When the meetings finally ended, it took him more than twenty minutes to say his good-byes in the parking lot. He was even going to miss the children, even though they had hardly paid him any mind. He was surprised when Emily handed him a small cooler and a thermos.

"What is this?" he asked.

"Some food to get you home," she said, "so you won't have to buy food on Sunday."

"You're terribly sweet," he said, wondering if anyone had ever packed a lunch for him in his entire life. "I'm certain that whatever it is will be far better than anything I could buy."

"Well, it comes with more love, if nothing else."

It was that word *love* that finally choked him up. While he was attempting to control his emotion, Emily touched his face and said, "You remember what I said. We'll be hoping to see you again soon."

He nodded and swallowed hard. "I'll bring these back," he lifted the cooler and thermos, "when I see you again."

"And when will that be?" Jess asked, looking almost as depressed as he felt. "Next weekend?"

"Would that be possible?" Tamra asked as if she too would sincerely miss him.

"I don't know," he said. "I'll see how the week goes and call you."

He thanked them all once more and reluctantly got in his car and drove away. Once alone, tears spilled down his cheeks. He realized then that one of the disadvantages of having close family relationships was the loneliness you had to deal with when you couldn't be with them.

Scott's apartment felt empty and cold when he arrived, and it had nothing to do with the temperature. He called Emily to let her know he had arrived safely, as she'd made him promise to do. And once again she repeated her invitation for him to return, as if she sensed the underlying doubt he had that his eagerness to be with them might not match with their desire to have him there.

It wasn't difficult to get up the next morning and get to work. All over again he felt like the lonely teenage boy with the incentive of riding a horse if he did all of his work and kept his grades up. He knew now that if he could stay on top of his responsibilities, he might be able to take an extra day off again and make it back to the place he considered heaven on earth. By Thursday it was looking good, but just to be sure he phoned his superior, Mr. Barton, in Utah and explained the situation.

"Listen," he said, "I was wondering how you'd feel about my working longer hours four days a week as a standard, and taking three-day weekends." He briefly explained the situation and Mr. Barton responded eagerly, "If you can keep those people in line down there, and stay on top of everything—and I know you will—I don't care how or when you do it."

Scott got off the phone and laughed out loud. He hurried to email Jess and tell him what his boss had said. He finished by writing, "Unless you have any protests, I will be on my way back in the morning." He got a response less then ten minutes later that clearly expressed Jess's enthusiasm. He ended his email with the words, "Why don't we just make a habit out of this? It might keep me out of the doghouse. The women have all taken the opportunity to tell me that I'm grumpier when you're not around, so you'd better hurry."

The following morning the drive seemed longer than last week as he eagerly anticipated his destination. When he pulled the car up beside the house and stepped out, the peace and comfort he'd found there rushed back into him. And then Emily Hamilton came running out the side door and flung her arms around him. He impulsively lifted her off the ground to hug her tightly, and he couldn't resist saying, "Hello, Mother."

She laughed and hugged him again. He thought momentarily of her private conversation with him about the hole he'd filled in Jess's life, after the loss of a brother and a best friend. It occurred to him now that in the same respect, Emily had lost a son and a son's friend. Perhaps he had filled something in her as well; the obvious joy in her expression made the idea fairly clear. She was a mother who had lost her son, and he was a man who had never known a mother. And it seemed they were a perfect match. His little remaining doubt about overstepping his bounds completely dissipated when she said with a glisten of moisture in her eyes, "Welcome home, Scott. We missed you."

Inside the house he received similar greetings from Rhea and Tamra, and little Evelyn even ran to hug him. Five weekends later she was calling him "Uncle Scotty" and he had started leaving some of his belongings there in "his room." He'd settled comfortably into a pattern where he didn't feel like he intruded on whatever the family needed to be doing, but he felt comfortable being a part of their meals and activities. At least once each weekend he went riding with Jess, and occasionally Tamra joined them. Once in a while Scott went out on his own, enjoying the opportunity to explore this beautiful country on horseback, always with his camera in tow.

He enjoyed going to church with the Hamiltons, and wondered if his ward in Brisbane believed he was inactive. Tamra suggested that he have his records transferred to their ward, and Jess agreed to see the ward clerk and make it happen. Scott quickly came to dread church, however, when he inevitably started home afterward. Deciding he'd like to spread his weekend out a little more, he worked Friday morning and arrived late evening, then he didn't have to start home until Monday morning. He found that with his laptop and a mobile phone, he was able to keep up on whatever might happen in his absence. Less than two months since his arrival in Australia, he had to admit that his life was good—better than it ever had been. And every once in a while he allowed himself to wonder what it might be like when Emma Hamilton came home.

On a Friday afternoon with heavy rains, Scott was relieved to finally arrive *home.* As he often did, he parked in front of the boys' home and went inside to see Jess first. He teased Madge and Shirley in the front office, then knocked at Jess's office door before he pushed it open to see Jess looking as if he might melt into the chair. Stress and concern seeped from his expression.

"Oh, good, you're here," Jess said. "I can stop worrying." He glanced toward the window where rain was still pouring. "I have an aversion to driving in the rain."

"Why is that?" Scott asked, sitting in one of the chairs across from Jess and putting his feet on the edge of the desk.

"Well, that would have something to do with the time I rolled the Cruiser and ended up hanging upside down in my seatbelt, wondering why I wasn't dead."

"You're joking," he said, astonished.

"No, I'm quite serious." His frown deepened. "I have an aversion to driving in the rain."

"Is that why you look like you want to hurt somebody?"

Jess sighed loudly. "No, I just . . . it's one of those days when everything hits."

"Like what? Tell me. Maybe I can help."

"I don't think so, but—"

"Tell me anyway. What are friends for?"

"Okay. Well, Murphy is gone for a week because his wife's sister is getting married, and heaven knows the man deserves a vacation. But one of the stable hands quit yesterday; just up and left, and I had to fire one the day before that. The guy was actually stoned, and that's not the first time it's happened. The drug and alcohol abuse we get with the hands is ridiculous. And since another one is out with the flu, we're extremely shorthanded. On top of the extra work that has to be managed there, I have to hire two more men. And I don't see how I have time to do that when one of my assistants here is out with a sinus infection and I am barely treading water as it is."

"So let me help."

"With what?" Jess almost sounded insulted.

Scott chuckled. "Do you think I'm that incompetent?"

"No, of course not, but . . ."

"Okay, well consider this, my friend, I have an MBA and a great deal of hands-on experience in business administration, and I know a fair amount about horses. I really think I could manage hiring some stable hands and helping keep the animals cared for in the meantime."

"But . . . it's the weekend. You can't do hiring when—"

"So I'll stay into next week until I can take care of it. Everything's under control at work. As long as I can plug my laptop into the Internet—which I usually do when I'm here anyway—I can handle everything from here for a few days."

"I really don't want to put you out like that," Jess said.

"Put me out?" Scott tried not to feel insulted. "Jess, you have given me a weekend retreat for weeks now. You've fed me and taken me in and made me a part of your home and family. And you're worried about putting me out? Good heavens, man, let me earn my keep. Your mother won't even let me pay for groceries. And I was pretty insistent, but she got down right mean about it."

Jess chuckled. "She can be that way."

"Let me do this, Jess. It would be a pleasure." Jess hesitated still and Scott added, "Is there a reason you don't want me to do it? If you think I can't handle it, or you'd prefer that I keep out of the businesses, then—"

"No, it's not that at all. I just . . . well, are you sure?"

"Of course I'm sure."

"Well then, I accept your offer." Jess smiled, obviously feeling better. "Thank you."

That evening at supper, Scott said, "I have a gift for you. I'll show it to you when we're finished here."

"For who?" Jess asked.

"All of you," Scott said. "You'll have to share."

"I can't wait," Tamra said.

Much later, after the children were in bed, the adults were gathered in the lounge room with the nursery monitor close by, as always. Scott set a wrapped package on the coffee table and said, "Emily, why don't you do the honors?"

"Okay, I will," she said and carefully unwrapped the box, then opened the lid. She glanced at Scott, looking slightly confused, then she lifted a photo album out and opened it, and her face filled with enlightenment.

"Oh, pictures!" Tamra exclaimed and moved quickly to sit beside Emily. Rhea pushed onto the couch beside Tamra and Jess sat on the other side of Emily. For the next hour Scott leaned back and watched them turn slowly through the pages filled with photos he had taken of their home, the stables, the land, the boys' home, and all of the people who lived and worked here. They laughed and commented on the beauty and artistic perspective of many of the photos. They talked through the memories that the pictures represented, some funny, some tender. And Scott felt as if he'd been a part of their lives forever.

When they finally finished going through the thick album, Emily said, "Oh, Scott, that's beautiful. We have a lot of photo albums, but there are so many things in there that I don't think anyone has ever thought to take pictures of. You've captured so much of the beauty that I think we take for granted here." She rose and crossed the room and he stood to accept her embrace. "Thank you," she said again. "You are such a blessing to us."

Scott felt startled by her statement, and even more so when she asked, "Is something wrong?" He wasn't sure if he liked the way she had come to read him so easily.

Scott debated brushing the question off, but the intensity in her eyes compelled him to admit, "I sometimes worry that I'm wearing out my welcome. It amazes me that you would feel that way about my being here."

"I assure you that's not the case. You are far from the first lost soul we have taken into this family."

"And some become permanent," Tamra said. "Like me."

Scott didn't want to admit how his thoughts had actually strayed to such a possibility, but he felt a little better when Emily added, "But you don't have to marry into the family to become a permanent part of it. Sean's living proof of that."

"That's true," Jess said, then he went on to explain to Scott about Sean O'Hara, who had been disowned by his family when he'd joined the Church, and the Hamiltons had taken him in. That had been many years ago, and he was still actively a part of the family, even though he lived in the States.

"I would love to meet him," Scott said.

"Oh, I'm sure you will," Emily said, as if his being around in the future was something she simply took for granted. A moment later, she asked, "Forgive me if I'm being nosy, Scott, but I've sensed that you really are concerned about wearing out your welcome. Yet, from my perspective, you're polite and gracious and always appropriate. And I've come to know you well enough to believe that you would be sensitive to any difficulties related to your presence . . . if there were any, which there are not. May I ask why?"

Scott glanced down and swallowed carefully. He knew the answer to the question, but it was difficult to say. He reminded himself that these people had always been completely open and honest with him, even about many of the sensitive issues that had occurred in their lives. He looked back up at Emily and met her eyes firmly. "I believe it goes back to the foster home thing when I was a kid. Nobody wanted me, you see." He forced a smile in an attempt to cover the underlying pain that still rose in him when he thought about his youth. "Looking back, I know I was difficult and obnoxious, but I also know that my behavior was just a desperate measure for attention and security." He paused and added, "I went through more than two dozen foster homes between my father's death and my going into the boys' ranch at the age of eleven."

"Good heavens," Emily said, her compassion evident.

"And through all of that, I hardly have a single positive memory. It wasn't until I was about fifteen when it clicked for me that I had to be nice if I wanted to get anywhere in this world, and I had to admit that my bad behavior had kept me from having a family. I determined then that I would always do my best to be good."

"It must have worked," Tamra said in a voice that made him realize she was crying. "You have a family now." She actually reached for his hand and squeezed it.

"Yes," Scott laughed softly, "and it only took me until I was thirty years old to get it." He then noticed that Emily and Rhea both had tears as well. "Hey, what is this? There's no need to cry for me. I have been very blessed—especially since I came to Australia. I'm just about the happiest man alive."

"Just about?" Rhea asked. "What's missing?"

"I suspect he could use a good wife," Jess said. "And he doesn't realize that the only reason I'm nice to him is my secret hope that he'll marry Emma when she comes home."

Scott's heart thudded in his ears. The comment had completely caught him off guard, and he wondered if Jess had somehow sensed the feelings he'd never spoken of to anyone.

"Oh, wouldn't that be perfect," Tamra said.

"Perfect for who?" Jess asked in mock astonishment. "My sister's a shrew."

"Oh, she is not!" Emily defended with a smile. "She has an occasional short fuse, but I've rarely seen her get angry."

"Short fuse?" Jess laughed. "Mother, what she has is a very long memory. When she gets angry she holds onto it for weeks. She's stubborn and willful, and I love her. But she's going to need an awfully patient man."

"Well then," Scott said, trying to keep his voice light, "that settles it. My ex-wife declared that I was anything but patient, so I couldn't possibly be the one for Emma."

"Maybe your ex-wife was an idiot," Tamra said and Jess laughed.

"Otherwise," Jess said, "she would still have the good sense to be your wife."

"In that case," Scott said, "I'm glad she's an idiot. Sadly, my life has improved immensely in her absence."

"Well, I for one am glad she dumped you," Jess said, "if only so you could come and live with us." He added more to the women, "And now he's going to be our temporary help in the stables."

"Really?" Tamra said. "Do tell."

Jess went on to explain what he would be doing, and Scott had to admit that he was looking forward to making a tangible contribution to the family.

The following few days he spent a great deal of time working in the stables and seeing that everything was kept under control. He contacted an employment agency first thing Monday morning and before he left to go back to Brisbane on Thursday, he had hired two stable hands, and with Jess's approval he had made arrangements with a local agency that did random drug and alcohol testing of employees while they were on the job. And all employees had been informed that they would be fired on the spot if the tiniest increment of such substances showed up in their blood while they were working. He reported to Jess what he'd done, finishing with the statement, "If they want to drink they can do it with discretion on their time off and make sure it wears off before they come back to work. After all, I did."

"You've been drinking?" Jess pretended to be astonished.

"Not recently," Scott chuckled. "But I used to drink pretty heavily on Friday and Saturday nights, and I'd sleep it off on Sunday. It was a nasty habit, but I never let it affect my work week. I knew I'd lose a good job if I did."

Scott hated the drive back to Brisbane, and he had barely been there a few hours before he was longing to go back home. *Home,* he thought as he looked around his apartment. He forced his discomfort at being there out of his head and concentrated on his work. But the next day he came down with a bad head-cold combined with the body aches and fever of the flu. He ended up in bed, handling his business over the information highway. He wanted desperately to be on the road to Byrnehouse-Davies and Hamilton Station, but he knew he didn't feel well enough to make the drive, and he didn't want to give the family his germs. So he called to let them know he wasn't coming.

"What's wrong?" Emily demanded after he told her. "Are you sick? You sound terrible."

"I'm afraid I am," he said.

"Well, you should be here where we can take care of you. I would even make you chicken soup."

"Wow," he said. "I've never had a mother make me chicken soup when I was sick."

"Never?"

"Nope."

"Well, it's about time you did. Next time you get sick, see if you can arrange to do it here."

"I'll see what I can do," he chuckled. "But I really don't want to share my germs with you."

"Oh," she scoffed, "we're very good at germ management. It's a big house. We'd just quarantine you to your room and deliver everything you needed."

"Sounds heavenly," he admitted.

"So will you end up terribly behind on your work?" she asked.

"Not really," he said. "I can do most of it from home, actually. Occasionally I have to show my face for a meeting, but there are none of those until the end of next week."

"Well, that's good then," she said. "You take good care of yourself."

"I'll do my best," he said. They visited a few more minutes before he hung up, feeling downright depressed. But all he could was endure this illness and pray that it wouldn't be long before he could be with his family again.

Chapter Five

Three days into Scott's illness, he still felt horrible. He slept when he could, even taking powerful cold medicine to help him do that. Then he improved just enough that he felt restless, without feeling good enough to do anything about it. His work was as under control as it could be. He was flipping through a string of useless television channels when the phone rang. A quick glance at the caller ID quickened his heart and he answered eagerly.

"How are you?" Emily's voice asked.

"Improving slowly," he said.

"Well, I hope you get feeling better enough to get here this weekend. We miss you."

"Well, I've been hoping the same, but actually, I have to go apartment hunting this weekend. The one I'm in is temporary, provided by the company. I've got to be out in a few weeks, but at least my house in Utah has sold."

"Oh," Emily said, her disappointment evident in a way that warmed his heart. At least she missed him as much as he missed her. "Well, one of the reasons I called is to tell you that I'm emailing you something, but since I'm fairly computer illiterate, I want you to call me in an hour if you don't get it and I'll have Jess help me try it again."

"Oooh, I can't wait," he said.

"Well, I hope you'll enjoy it. Perhaps it will help pass the time."

"Thank you," he said. "I'll call if I don't get it."

Scott hung up the phone and quickly connected to the Internet, and there it was, a message from Emily Hamilton that read, 'Thought you might enjoy this. Get better. Love, Mom.' He smiled as he felt her love penetrate him, then he noticed that the attachment was rather large. His phone rang and he hurried to press the print button, knowing his eyes hurt too badly to read on the computer screen for long.

Scott finished his phone call and returned to the computer. It had finished printing, and a significant stack of pages, typed manuscript style, were stacked in one side of the printer. He picked up the stack and read at the top of the first one: *Personal History. Michael William Hamilton.* And the date of the first entry was late in the nineteenth century.

"Extraordinary," Scott said and immediately settled into a comfortable chair to begin reading. Over the next couple of days he pretty much read and slept and saw to the minimum communications with the office. He marveled at the life of this great man, and even more so at how much he related to him. Emily had mentioned that they had some things in common, and they certainly did. But more amazing was how Scott related so strongly to the feelings this man had recorded. And there was one line in particular that Scott went back and read so many times that he finally had to copy it down. He wrote it on a little piece of paper and stuck it into the pages of Moroni, chapter seven, which was one of his favorites. He took it out often and read, "My love for Emma defies all logic, but it is such an integral part of me that I cannot deny it, any more than I can deny the existence of God. Michael W. Hamilton, 1912." The fact that the first Michael Hamilton had secretly loved a woman named Emma was a tender coincidence. The fact that the Emma who Scott harbored secret feelings for was the great-granddaughter of the man he was reading about was nothing less than astonishing.

Scott completely read the history twice before he got feeling well enough to go into the office. Everything was running so smoothly that he didn't stay long, but when he returned to his apartment he nearly turned around and went back to the office. He hated it there. Deciding that he needed to do something about that, Scott started checking the newspaper ads, thinking perhaps that he should bypass apartment hunting and just find himself a nice home, a place where he could feel comfortable and at peace. Perhaps that was the problem. Once he got a home of his own, he could settle in better and enjoy the time he spent here in the city. He simply wouldn't allow himself to think of how he'd far rather be elsewhere this weekend. He wondered if it had been a mistake to have his membership records transferred to the Hamiltons' ward. Perhaps he should have made more effort to settle in here, and he considered that maybe he should cut his visits back to once or twice a month. He didn't like the idea, but feeling so torn between two places, he couldn't see any other solution.

That evening Scott called to thank Emily for the history, and when she asked how soon they might see him again, he cautiously said that he would just have to see. He ignored the disappointment in her voice and steered his mind to prayer. That was the only way he knew he could find peace and the right answers for his future.

The following afternoon, Scott was looking over a fax he'd just gotten from the office when the phone rang.

"Hello, my friend," Jess's voice said eagerly when Scott answered.

"Well, hello," Scott said brightly.

"How are you feeling?"

"Much better, thank you. And how are you?"

"We're all fine, barring that we miss seeing your happy, smiling face."

Scott wondered why he felt so uneasy hearing such a comment while he was contemplating buying a home here in Brisbane and making a commitment to spend some significant time in it. He felt confused and he wasn't sure what to do about it.

"Well, I miss you too," he admitted honestly. "All of you."

"On that note," Jess said, "I confess there is a purpose to my call."

"Okay."

"We had a little family council yesterday morning and discussed something, then we all gave it some time for pondering and prayer, and we reconvened this morning to discuss it again." Scott felt his heart sink. Would Jess tell him that they had to make some cutbacks on the time Scott spent in their home? He could certainly understand, but it made him heartsick, nevertheless.

"The thing is," Jess said, "the vote was unanimous and eager."

"Okay," Scott said, managing to keep his voice steady.

"Well . . . my biggest concern is that I just don't want to be too pushy. I mean . . . what I'm asking is pretty presumptuous, but we feel like we should ask, and they tell me I'm the patriarch of the family so I'm the one who has to talk to you."

"Get on with it," Scott said, wishing it hadn't sounded so brusque.

"Well, it was Mom's idea—and a good one at that, I think. She said you mentioned some things that wouldn't leave her head, and well . . . the thing is, we think you should just blow the apartment hunting and come and live with us." Scott sucked in his breath, then clamped a hand over his mouth to keep from audibly making a fool of himself.

"Are you still with me?" Jess asked.

"I'm here," Scott said and put that hand back in place for noise control.

"Well, this is the way we see it, but we may not have all the facts. You can do the majority of your work from home as long as you have a computer, a phone, and a fax machine. That's covered. And your house in the States sold, right? So you can probably afford to stay in a hotel when you have to go to Brisbane for meetings. And that would be, what? Once a month? Twice at most?"

"That's right," Scott managed to say.

"You can turn your sitting room into an office; bring in whatever you want or need to be comfortable." He paused. "What do you think, Scott? Am I being too pushy? Is this terribly presumptuous of us, or—"

"No, not presumptuous or pushy, Jess." He finally allowed an audible laugh to come out. "I just . . . can't believe it. I mean . . . are you sure? It just seems too good to be true."

"Really?" Jess asked and laughed. "Well, of course I'm sure; we're sure. We had a family council over it, for heaven's sake."

"I should like to see what that is like."

"Well, next time something comes up, we'll be sure to include you. That shouldn't be too difficult if you're living under the same roof. Please tell me you'll come. I think my mother will cry if you say no. And yes, I said that to try and make you feel guilty and manipulate you into coming."

"It worked," Scott said and Jess laughed. "Although, I think you had me back at 'blow the apartment hunting.'" He laughed. "I don't know what to say."

"Don't say anything. Just rent a truck and get here. Do you need me to come and help you move?"

"Nah," Scott said, "I don't have much. This apartment is furnished. I got rid of most everything I had before I came here. I just have some boxes, mostly. It shouldn't be too complicated."

"And you really think it will work with your job?"

"I do," Scott said. "My boss has told me more than once that as long as I keep everything under control, he doesn't care when or how I do it."

"Okay, well . . . when may we expect you?"

Scott thought about it. "I'll leave in ten minutes." They both laughed. "No, seriously, if I don't have to find an apartment, I could pack up tomorrow and be on my way Saturday morning."

"Great," Jess said. "We'll see you Saturday afternoon."

Scott got off the phone and let out a whoop of pure joy before he went straight to his knees and thanked God for sending this miracle into his life. He figured he was just about the happiest man alive. And he was well on the path to eliminating the "just about" part.

* * *

When Scott arrived at the station with the rented truck, towing his car behind it, he was met by a happy and eager welcoming committee. With their help it took little time to unload the small truck and carry his belongings up to the rooms that would now be his permanently. Then Jess followed him into town so that he could turn the truck in. While they were in town Scott purchased some office furniture and equipment that was scheduled to be delivered the following Tuesday. As they returned home for supper, Scott loved the feel of knowing that he didn't have to dread going back to Brisbane. When he needed to go back, it would only be for a brief business trip here and there.

On Monday Scott thoroughly enjoyed unpacking the boxes that had remained packed through his brief stay in the apartment in Brisbane. It truly felt like home as he saw things that were precious to him becoming a part of the bedroom, then he unloaded his books in the sitting room that would become his office. As he pulled them out and put them onto the empty shelves, he pondered over many of them with fond memories of the great things he'd learned, and the stories he'd enjoyed. His books were considered some of his most precious possessions, mostly because he only kept the ones that had left deep impressions on him. If he read a book that didn't touch him, he would take it to the used book store and trade it for something else. He had many fond memories of exploring the shelves in search of a new treasure he might find in some out-of-print book.

As Scott pulled a particular book out of the box, he only had to glance at the cover to recall how much he'd enjoyed that particular novel. In fact, it was part of a set and he'd read the entire collection twice through. But as the cover came fully into view, he heard himself laugh as the name of the author struck him. He found it humorous to think that a successful author would have a name that had become so familiar to him personally. Surely Michael Hamilton was not such an uncommon name. He was contemplating showing the book to Jess when he realized that the author's name was actually printed as J. Michael Hamilton. That narrowed the coincidence down a little. He opened to read on the inside of the dust cover, just curious over what the "J" might stand for. And then he practically hyperventilated as he read, *J. Michael Hamilton, born in Queensland, Australia.* And further down, . . . *Beyond his lifetime experience with the breeding and racing of horses . . .* That was simply three too many coincidences.

"I can't believe it," Scott said to the empty room. He laughed. "I can't believe it," he said again. But more startling than the realization that this book was one more connection to this family he had become a part of, was what he felt when he'd read it—and the others in the six-book set. He'd rarely had fiction affect him so deeply, and in fact, on his most recent reading of the set, after his divorce, he had at times almost felt that . . .

A knock at the door startled him.

"Yes," he called, moving toward the door.

Tamra stuck her head in, "Evelyn didn't sneak in here, did she?"

"No, I haven't seen her," he said.

"Okay. She's probably with Rhea. Just checking."

When Tamra was gone, Scott didn't wait another minute before he went to Jess's office in the boys' home.

"Hello," Jess said, looking up from the paperwork on his desk. "What's up?"

"Okay, you can sing that *Twilight Zone* music now."

"Why?" Jess laughed.

"Because I was just unpacking some of my stuff, and I discovered something really weird."

"Okay," Jess said and hummed the music while he wore an exaggerated expression of expectancy.

Scott set the book down on the desk. Jess's eyes answered every question. Scott sat down, saying, "The name, combined with being born in Queensland and having vast experiences with horses leads me to believe that you know the author of that book."

"Quite well, actually."

"Your father," Scott said, simply needing clarification.

"That's right," Jess said, picking up the book to thumb through it. "First edition," he said.

"Yes, I have a complete set—unless he wrote more than six."

"No, six is all."

"I bought them in a used book store several years ago. I read them all right after I got them, and then I reread them after my divorce. I can honestly say I felt drawn to them, and . . ." Scott hesitated, wondering if he should really share what he was thinking. It seemed so strange, so illogical, and yet . . . he knew. In his heart he knew that what he'd felt was real. And given what he knew now, it could not be a coincidence.

"Is something wrong?" Jess asked, his voice warm and concerned.

"Not wrong, but . . . Can I tell you something?"

"Of course," Jess said easily.

Scott stood up to close the door, then he sat back down. While he was searching for the right words, he realized that he couldn't come up with any.

"Yes?" Jess said.

Scott recalled something that might help and said, "You know what? I want to share something with you, but . . . I believe the experience is recorded in my journal, and I think it might be better if you just read it . . . whenever it's convenient."

He was surprised when Jess said, "How about now? I could use a break."

"Okay," Scott said, and they walked together back into the house and to Scott's rooms. "I think I can find it fairly fast, because I know it was after my divorce, and not many weeks before the holidays. I remember it was autumn and it was cold."

He thumbed through the appropriate journal while Jess said, "So you keep a journal. That's pretty big stuff in this family."

"Yes, I've noticed," Scott said. He walked to the little sofa and sat down while he turned pages and scanned them, then his heart leapt when he caught it. He motioned for Jess to sit down beside him. "Read this." He pointed to the spot on the page.

"Out loud?"

"Sure."

"Okay," Jess said and cleared his throat. "'I am very much enjoying the novels I'm reading. They keep me distracted from Callie's absence, and in a way I could never describe, the stories actually give me an abstract kind of comfort. At times I almost feel as if the author himself were sitting beside me . . .'" Jess gasped and stopped reading. He looked up at Scott and an unspoken understanding passed between their eyes. He looked back at the journal and took a deep breath before he continued reading, "'. . . Beside me, keeping me from being alone, giving me hope that the future might still hold good things for me. In my reading of the Book of Mormon today I was . . .' That's something else," Jess added.

"No, keep reading," Scott said. "There's a connection."

Jess continued, his expression betraying that he was having difficulty absorbing the implications. "'. . . today I was struck deeply by verse twenty-nine in my favorite chapter, Moroni, seven.'"

Jess looked up again, looking almost ashen.

"What?" Scott asked.

"I know that verse; I know it by heart. 'And because he hath done this, my beloved brethren, have miracles ceased?'" Scott joined him and they finished the verse audibly, together. "'Behold I say unto you, Nay; neither have angels ceased to minister unto the children of men.'"

Following a long minute of incredulous silence, Scott asked quietly, "Am I crazy, Jess, to be thinking what I'm thinking?"

"I don't know. Tell me what you're thinking, and I'll tell you if you're crazy."

In a hushed voice he said intently, "I felt your father with me, Jess. I don't recall at the time consciously thinking that the author of that book had been specifically sent to minister to me through a difficult time, but looking at what I wrote, it's like I knew that was the case, even if I didn't fully recognize it. And when I looked at the book a while ago, the memory came back to me with such perfect clarity, and I *knew* it had been him." He gave an incredulous laugh. "Do you know what this means?"

"I think so," Jess said with a reverent awe in his countenance, "but tell me anyway."

"Why would I have an experience like that, if my being here right now had not been somehow foreordained?"

As soon as he said it, Scott felt warm tears burn into his eyes just before the warmth spread throughout him. He knew the feeling well. He'd not encountered it frequently, but he knew it was the Spirit confirming the truth of what he'd just said. He was searching for the words to tell Jess what he was feeling when he realized from the tears in Jess's eyes and the expression on his face that he had felt it too. There was no need for him to explain.

They sat together in silence for several minutes before Jess said, "I think you need to have a conversation with my mother."

Jess and Scott talked for a while longer, analyzing certain elements of a miracle that simply felt incomprehensible to either one of them. But they both had a testimony of the ministering of angels, and they could not deny what they had felt. They finally parted with a firm embrace before Jess said, "I could never tell you how grateful I am for your friendship, and the brotherhood we've come to share. And now it seems that my father somehow knew you could fill some part of the void he left in our lives. It's incredible."

"Yes, it is."

"And I'm grateful."

"Amen," Scott said and they embraced again.

Jess returned to his office to see to some necessary work. Scott picked up the novel and his journal and went to find Emily. He checked all the usual rooms on the main floor where he often found her, and wondered if she'd gone for a walk or something. He went back upstairs and found Tamra and Rhea in the nursery with the children, but they hadn't seen Emily. He couldn't recall it ever being this difficult to find her.

"Try her rooms," Tamra said and Scott went there, knocking on the partially open door to her bedroom.

"Come in," she called and he felt a deep relief. "Oh, hello," she said with a smile when she saw him. "What a pleasant surprise." She set aside the book she'd been reading.

"I don't want to interrupt anything, but . . . I was wondering if I could tell you something."

"Of course," she said. "I can read anytime. Let's go in here and sit down."

She led him through a side door into a sitting room, and he realized that practically every bedroom in this house had a sitting room attached.

"What have you got there?" she asked once they were seated side by side.

Scott handed her the novel and saw her smile. "Ah, you've found his books. You're welcome to read them if you—"

"No, this belongs to me," he said. "I bought the entire set at a used book store years ago."

Emily looked pleasantly astonished. "That's incredible," she said.

"Yes, it is," he said, "but that's not the half of it." She gazed at him expectantly and he searched for the words to begin. "I should start at the beginning. You know my story, but let me share a few details with you. When Callie and I separated, I knew beyond any doubt that it was the right thing. But in spite of her lack of values and her negative influence on me, she was the only family I had ever known. My friends were her friends, and once we were no longer together, I felt cut off from every social connection that had ever meant anything to me. I had the gospel, and I had a good ward. But I felt no close personal connections there."

"You were understandably very lonely," she said with compassion.

"Yes, I was," he said. "And that's when all the doubts started creeping in. Had I done the right thing? Maybe joining the Church and changing had been stupid. Maybe I would have been better off with Callie. Perhaps she'd been right when she'd called me a fool." Scott took a deep breath, appreciating the way Emily put a gentle hand over his. Her compassion and insight never stopped surprising him. "I prayed," he went on. "I prayed a great deal, but shaking those negative feelings was extremely difficult, and they hovered with me a long time. I finally felt that what I needed was a distraction, and I went to the book case looking for something reliable that I could count on to lift my spirits. I came across these books and felt excited about digging in, because I'd read them years earlier and the experience had been positive and powerful. For that very reason I had kept them rather than trading them in."

"And the books lifted your spirits," Emily guessed with a smile.

"They certainly did," he said with enthusiasm. "But there's more than that." He sighed and his voice sobered. "Emily, I know that you're a woman who understands the spiritual workings of this world we live in, and I know I can share this with you and not have you think I'm crazy." Her brow furrowed but she said nothing. "Let me back up a bit first and tell you that I always instinctively believed that this world was made up of more than we could see. But being surrounded by the world on every side, with no opportunity for spiritual explanation, I began to believe there was simply something strange about me. When I met Jess as a missionary, I was in a particularly defiant point in my life. It was only months later that something he'd said struck me, and I sought out the Church. Of course, you knew that part, but the point is that . . . well, I've always had a deep respect and perhaps a . . . sensitivity to spiritual happenings that defy all logic. Am I making any sense?"

"Absolutely," she said, and her smile was full of understanding. He considered it a miracle in and of itself that he could be sharing such thoughts and feelings with someone and not be considered insane. Conversations with Callie came to mind, times when he'd wished that he'd just kept his mouth shut, and kept his most sacred feelings to himself.

"Okay, well . . . with that in mind, I—"

"Wait," Emily said, "before you go on, would you mind telling me what it was that Jess said that ended up having so much meaning for you?"

Scott smiled, still recalling the words clearly. "He told me that there was much more to this world than we could see or hear, and that God was very mindful of me."

Emily smiled and squeezed his hand. "Okay, go on."

"This is my journal," he said as he opened it to the appropriate page. "And I would like you to read what I wrote . . . during that time I just told you about."

"When you were reading Michael's books."

"That's right."

He handed her the book and pointed to the right spot. He watched her carefully as she read, and was not surprised when she looked up at him, astonished. She turned her eyes back to the book and read on while tears rose in her eyes then spilled down her face. She was silent for a long minute while he wondered if her tears came simply from a tender reminder of her deceased husband. He wondered if perhaps he was making more out of this than it really was, or perhaps she would, in spite of her apparent spiritual sensitivity, believe he had too vivid an imagination. But she finally looked into his eyes and said easily, "I always knew that he liked you, but I had no idea that he'd actually spent time with you. Apparently he was looking out for you, making sure you became a part of our family." She touched his face and smiled. "Apparently your being here was meant to be." She laughed softly. "Of course, I already knew that, but a little validation never hurts."

"Wait a minute," he said. "You knew that he liked me? But . . ."

"I just . . . felt it. I'm sure you understand."

Impulsively Scott threw his arms around her and just held her tightly, relishing in the long, firm response of her embrace. When he drew back she put both her hands to his face, saying with emotion, "I love you, Scott, as much as I ever loved my own sons."

Scott suddenly found it impossible to speak. He tried to force the tears back, but they refused and he found his face pressed to Emily's shoulder while he cried like a baby. In the motherly comfort of her arms, he cried for the motherless life he had lived, and the contrasting joy he knew now that he had finally found a home.

* * *

Scott had no trouble settling into the Hamilton household. He did his best to find ways to help and do his part, since Jess blatantly refused any offer to pay rent. So Scott washed dishes whenever the women would let him, and he was always searching for household tasks that needed doing. He preferred keeping his work a secret and made a game out of seeing if he could accomplish the cleaning of a bathroom or some serious vacuuming when no one was around.

He was thrilled when Jess invited him to go on a brief trip in the plane to see to some business. Scott enjoyed the experience so much that he signed up for flight lessons as soon as they returned home. Jess said it would be nice to have someone else who could fly the planes, since he and Murphy were the only ones, and there were times when it would be nice to send someone else on those faraway errands.

Scott made a habit of frequent visits to the boys' home, usually timing it so that he could share library time with the boys. He got to know each of them by name, and enjoyed sharing story time with the younger ones and helping them pick out books to borrow. One day when one of the staff members was ill, Scott was invited to read a story to the boys and he thoroughly enjoyed it. He stayed for lunch in the cafeteria, which he enjoyed so much that he began doing that frequently as well.

Scott also made a habit of checking in regularly with Murphy and seeing what he could do to help around the stables. Or sometimes he'd just clean out some stalls or wash down some horses without waiting for an assignment. He got to know Murphy well, and they enjoyed some good conversations, especially given that the stable master and his wife were recent converts to the Church.

Scott gained a deep contentment with his new life that was deepened further when he was called into the bishop's office and asked to teach Sunday School to the fourteen-year-old youth. The class tended to be a little noisy, but they were good kids and he thoroughly enjoyed the calling.

Scott was just beginning to believe that life could get no better when Jess knocked at his office door.

"Can I talk to you?" Jess asked, peering around the door.

"Sure. Have a seat."

Jess sauntered in and sat down. "This is business," he said, crossing his ankle over his knee.

"Really?" Scott's voice betrayed his interest.

"Murphy tells me you've given him a number of suggestions that are making things run much more efficiently. He tells me you're rather amazing."

Scott made a dubious noise. "I just know and love horses, Jess."

"I think there's more to it than that. You obviously have a good head for business and, combined with your other talents, you've made a difference. You're taking a business that's more than a century old and turning it on its ear."

"I'm sorry," Scott said, not certain what Jess meant exactly.

"Don't apologize. It's wonderful. If you didn't have such a good job, I'd offer you one."

"Doing what?"

"Well, don't sound so defensive. It was Murphy's idea. You could oversee the entire horse operation, handle all of the business end of it, and leave Murphy to oversee the hands and keep them in line."

Scott felt so excited he could hardly remain in his seat. He was reminded of how he'd felt when Jess had invited him to come and live in this home. But he kept his voice as steady as his expression, reminding himself that this was business. He tested Jess by saying, "You couldn't match my salary."

"Well, I could if I wanted to, but if I want to keep my profit margins where they're at, you're right, I couldn't match your salary. But the job includes room and board."

With that the conversation went from business to personal in a hurry. "Oh, that's rich coming from you. The job includes room and board? Would that be the room and board I'm already getting for nothing because you blatantly refuse a single dollar of rent?"

Jess just smirked. "If I started charging you rent, could I manipulate you into quitting your job and taking this one? Or . . . maybe you could do both. You've told me that with things going smoothly in Brisbane, you're not having to put in so many hours. You don't appear to have much of a social life. I'll take you on part time."

"Done," Scott said.

Jess laughed. "Don't you want to think about it? Don't you want to know what it pays or—"

"Not really," Scott said. "It's the job of my dreams. I'm not going to quibble over details. Eventually I might be willing to quit my other job, but I don't know if I'm ready for that yet. So, we'll give it some time."

Jess grinned and they shook on it, and within days Scott became fully involved as an employee of Byrnehouse-Davies & Hamilton,

Incorporated. He felt comfortable with the work he'd been asked to do, and gratified to see how well he and Murphy worked together. Murphy seemed to greatly appreciate having certain responsibilities lifted from his shoulders and admitted that this was especially good since he had a baby on the way.

As the months passed, Scott's contentment deepened further. He even did some dating and enjoyed an occasional outing with some fine women, most of whom he'd met through singles functions related to the Church. But he couldn't help comparing each woman to Emma. And even though he hardly knew her, he could not deny the intensity of his feelings for her, feelings that not another human being alive was aware of. He was amazed at how his attraction to her clung to his memory, even though he'd not communicated with her directly since he'd delivered German pastries to her door in Salt Lake City. He could only hope that when the time came for her to return from her mission, the circumstances might be conducive to getting to know her better. And with any luck, she would feel some measure of attraction to him, as well. He wondered occasionally if he should let her family know how he felt, but he figured it was better left unsaid. His being here had nothing to do with his feelings for Emma, and he didn't want anybody to think that it did.

Another miracle in Scott's life came through a growing friendship with Jess's wife, Tamra. He found that they had much in common, having both come from a difficult upbringing and being converts to the Church. But he found their common bonds went much deeper as she shared with him her experiences in initially coming to this place. In fact, Tamra admitted that she felt undoubtedly lured there by one of Jess's ancestors from the other side of the veil.

"Which one?" Scott asked eagerly, recalling his keen interest in Michael Hamilton the first.

"Alexandra Byrnehouse-Davies," she said with aplomb. "And her story is remarkable."

"Where does she fit into the family line?" he asked.

"She is *the* matriarch of the family."

"She is Emma's mother, then," Scott said and Tamra smiled.

"That's right. And it was her husband, Jess, who began the tradition of taking in lost souls."

"Lost souls?" Scott echoed, recalling that he'd heard that phrase come up before, but he'd never heard any explanation.

"That's right. His journals tell of how he hired people who were lost and in need, and then he opened the boys' home and the rest is history. The tradition continues today. And I'm living proof."

Scott thought about that a minute and said, "I guess that means I am too."

"I think you would definitely qualify as a lost soul."

"But not anymore," he said proudly.

"No," Tamra said, "we are among the lucky few who actually get taken into the family."

"Yes, but *you* married into the family."

"Yes, but you might be interested to know that I felt very much a part of the family before Jess ever came to his senses. My being at home here had nothing to do with him, initially."

Scott liked hearing her say that, and it spurred much more conversation between them, although he said nothing about his feelings for Emma. She directed him to the typed copies of all the other family journals that he'd not read, and he began using every minute of spare time discovering the ancestors of this incredible family. When he had read everything there was to read, he found that he was especially drawn to the two Michaels: Jess's great-grandfather, and his father. He had studied the former's history extensively, and he'd heard much talk of the latter. But one Sunday afternoon he felt compelled to go to Emily and say, "Would you mind telling me more about your husband? I would like to know him better."

"I can think of little more enjoyable than that," she said and took him to her bedroom where she knelt next to a large cedar chest at the foot of her bed. "Slightly rugged, but fine and sturdy," she said, pressing her hands over the chest. "Just like Michael."

She opened the chest and began bringing out one keepsake after another, explaining the meaning and sentiment attached to each. She showed him pictures and letters and mementos, and gradually the life she had shared with Michael Hamilton became clear and vivid in his mind. He marveled at the light in her eyes as she spoke of him, and in spite of the way she obviously missed him, he could feel her peace and the strength of her love that had transcended the veil of death that had temporarily separated her from her husband.

When she reached into the chest to pull out the final item from the bottom, she became suddenly emotional.

"What is it?" he asked as she lifted out a well-worn pair of classic black riding boots—much like the ones that Scott had bought for himself when he'd first come here. He knew from a glance that they were too small to be Michael's.

"Oh, the memories just . . . took me off guard."

"Michael bought them for you?"

"Yes, he did," she said, "when I came here during college. They were my reward for having learned to ride. And then I went home and put them away in my cedar chest and married another man. Many years later I dug them out to wear to see Michael again; that's when he came back into my life. I felt it was appropriate that they be kept here."

She looked around herself at the contents of the chest that were spread out all over the floor, and looked suddenly distant and sad.

"What is it?" Scott asked.

"There are moments when I just . . . miss him terribly." She started to cry. "I don't have any trouble knowing that we'll be together again. I just miss him."

"That's certainly understandable," he said and put his arms around her. She cried for a few minutes, then dried her tears and began putting the contents back into the chest, continuing her reminiscing as she did, and her sorrow turned to laughter.

When it was all put away she closed the chest and once again pressed her hands over it, saying, "Slightly rugged, fine and sturdy."

"He's an amazing man," Scott said.

Emily smiled at him and came to her feet. "He's not the only one. Come along, son. Let's get something to eat. I'm suddenly starving." She took his hand as they went down the stairs, while Scott silently thanked God for this mother he had been given.

Chapter Six

Scott experienced a new level of excitement when he had the opportunity to share Thanksgiving with his new family. Even though it was an American holiday, it was a strong Hamilton tradition, since Emily was American. She made a point of mentioning that he and Tamra were as well.

Following the best Thanksgiving of his life, the weeks moved quickly toward Christmas. Packages had been sent to Emma, as well as other family members. Apparently this would be a quiet Christmas, since Jess's sisters had all made the decision to remain at home or be with other relatives. Emily actually admitted to feeling some relief. She loved to have her family together, but she confessed that when they all came at once it was exhausting. For Scott, he wanted to get to know the other family members that he'd only heard about, but he was already surrounded with far more people than he was accustomed to. Having the entire family together would probably be pretty overwhelming. Still, it was an adventure he looked forward to in the future.

As the house took on a distinct Christmas atmosphere, Scott felt like a giddy child inside. He had a marvelous time purchasing gifts for everyone in the family, including the children who had all warmed up to him. Less than a week before Christmas he drove to Brisbane for two days of meetings, with the plan of returning home the day before Christmas Eve. He rarely had to go to Brisbane these days, since he'd facilitated his management by consolidating the necessary meetings, thus keeping his trips to a minimum. He didn't want to leave home in the midst of the excitement of Christmas preparations, but it had to be done so that other employees could finish up important business and be with their own families for the holidays.

The meetings went well and he enjoyed giving each of the employees he worked with a token Christmas gift. He drove toward home feeling deeply comforted with the anticipation of celebrating Christmas with his family. He contemplated the meaning of the holiday, and the many miracles that had come into his life through his commitment to striving to live a Christ-like life. He prayed silently over many miles, expressing his deep gratitude, and his renewal of that commitment.

* * *

Emily watched Scott drive away in the early morning light for his trip to Brisbane and she said a silent prayer that he would travel safely. She looked forward to his return and the Christmas they would share together. She sat down to look through her recipes, contemplating what other Christmas goodies she might make today once breakfast was over. She wished she had asked Scott what he might like. She so wanted to make this Christmas memorable for him. But then, she anticipated that he would be with them for many years to come. She knew that eventually he would marry and have a family of his own. But secretly she hoped that his work here at the station would become full-time and permanent, and then he might raise his family right here. She could never explain how he had filled the hole that had existed since the death of her son. She'd always anticipated that James would live here and raise his family, and the thought of Scott filling that place was appealing indeed.

When the phone rang Emily reached for it absently, hoping as always that it might be one of her children. Those were her favorite phone calls.

"Sister Hamilton?" a serious male voice said.

"Yes," she said.

She heard a stifled chuckle. "I guess I should clarify, since there are two Sister Hamiltons in your home. Is this Emily?"

"Yes, it is," she said, wondering if this was a new executive secretary calling her for an appointment with the bishop; perhaps she was in for a new Church calling.

But the voice on the other end of the phone introduced himself as the mission president and she sat down, feeling a dread come into her chest as he said, "It would be better to have this conversation face-to-face, but given my schedule and the distance between us, it's simply not feasible. I'm calling about your daughter, Emma, who is serving a mission in Utah."

"Is she all right?" Emily asked as memories of losing loved ones in the past catapulted into her mind.

"She's having some health problems, but relatively speaking, she's fine."

Emily blew out a long breath as her panic subsided to a more reasonable level.

"However, it is serious enough that she will no longer be able to serve."

Emily kicked herself inwardly for relaxing too soon. What could be so serious? Emma had said nothing in her letters; there had been no indication whatsoever of a problem.

"Okay," Emily said, "so . . ."

"She's on her way home now, Sister Hamilton. I have no specific information on the problem itself. All I can tell you for certain is that her flight will be arriving in Sydney in about eight hours. I realize the notice is terribly short. So I need to know what we can do to help get her home. We can arrange for a connecting flight to Brisbane or—"

"No, that's all right," Emily said. "My son flies a private plane. He can go and get her."

She wrote down the flight information, thanked the mission president and hung up the phone. Then she cried. She cried harder than she had since she'd lost Michael, grateful that the family was still upstairs just getting the morning routine underway. Knowing they would be coming down soon, she got her emotions under control, took a glance at herself in the mirror, and stoically went to find Jess and Tamra. They were in the nursery, each dressing one of the wiggly twins.

"Hello, Mother," Jess said, seeing her in the open doorway. Then he did a double take. "What's wrong?" he demanded and Tamra shot her gaze toward Emily as well.

When Emily hesitated, Jess left the child half dressed and jumped to his feet, repeating firmly, "What's wrong, Mother?"

Not wanting to draw out her explanation and cause them any further panic, she quickly said, "Emma's on her way home. She'll be arriving in Sydney in about eight hours."

"Good heavens," Tamra said, standing up as well. "What's happened?"

"Health problems; that's all they told me."

Jess put a hand over the center of his chest. "I don't like the sound of that. Forgive me, for saying it; I know it sounds crass, but I can't help thinking I'd almost prefer hearing that she just couldn't handle being missionary any longer. I mean . . . not really, but . . . health problems serious enough to have her sent home; that scares me."

Emily felt momentarily startled but had to admit, "I know what you mean, but we all know we're grateful that's not the problem. I would prefer that she be able to finish her mission without *any* problems. But I learned a long time ago that we often don't get what we want or expect in this life." Her tears surfaced again and Jess drew her into his arms. How grateful she was to be sharing her home with family that loved and supported her.

Once the shock wore off a bit for all of them, they set to work rearranging plans so that Jess could pick up Emma, and Emily could hurry and finish up the absolutely necessary preparations left for Christmas and get Emma's room ready. Rhea would help Tamra with the children while they both did what they could to help Emily. Emily very much wanted to go with Jess and be with him when Emma got off the plane, but she knew it wasn't practical. Whatever the problem was, she would be much better prepared to handle the situation when Emma arrived if she kept working now. Until they returned home, all she could do was pray that all would be well, whatever the problem may be.

* * *

Emma was one of the last to leave the plane. She simply didn't have the strength to stand in the aisle and wait, or fight her way out. So she sat until the plane was practically empty. She only had her purse with her, since she'd not been able to even lift a carry-on bag, and so the mission president had helped her check all of her luggage. She finally walked down the long ramp to the gate, with no idea what to expect.

Would the message have gotten through to her family in time? Would someone be here to get her? Or would she have to get a cab and a hotel room? She prayed that she didn't have to call home and surprise her family with her arrival on the Australian continent. She would prefer that someone else had already taken care of that dirty deed.

Emma stepped into the airport and saw Jess waiting there, a mixture of emotions in his eyes that mirrored her own. She was so glad to see him, but not under these circumstances. She saw his eyes take her in as she approached him, and she could almost feel the wheels in his mind turning. It would be impossible for him not to notice the changes in her. But would he recognize the extra pounds on her as water retention, or just assume that she had eaten a little too well on her mission? He couldn't help but notice her pallor, but whatever he did or didn't notice, she felt hideous and exhausted.

Feeling his arms come around her, she wasn't prepared for the emotion she'd been holding back through the journey to suddenly come bursting out. He did well at shielding her from curious eyes as she wept against his chest. When she had finally calmed down, he took her face into his hands, saying, "Let's go home."

She nodded and they walked together toward the baggage claim area. She knew that he sensed her weakness and fatigue by the way she couldn't keep from leaning into him as they walked. But he said nothing beyond, "Are you okay?" when she had to stop walking and catch her breath.

"I'll be fine," she said. "Just give me a minute."

It wasn't until they were in the familiar confines of one of the family planes that she said, "Who called?"

"The mission president."

"What did he say?"

"He said you were coming home for health reasons, and he told us when you would be arriving. That's it."

Emma sighed. She had hoped that the family would already know, which would spare her from having to break the news.

"So," Jess said, "are you going to tell me?"

"You know what? I'm exhausted. I don't want to have to repeat it all over again when we get home, so I'm afraid you're going to have to wait and hear it with the rest of them."

She sensed his frustration but he said nothing. He only reached for her hand and squeezed it before she moved to one of the back seats of the plane where she could rest more comfortably. Her next awareness was Jess's voice saying loudly, "We're home, Sleeping Beauty. You'd better snap out of it."

Once the plane had landed, Jess helped her step down, allowing her to lean her weight against him. He motioned to their left and she looked up to see Tamra and her mother approaching. Knowing how late it was, she assumed the children were in bed and Rhea was with them. Following tearful embraces, she was relieved when Emily said, "You must be exhausted. Let's get you home to bed and we can talk in the morning."

Emma drifted to sleep through the short drive to the house, and she needed help to get into the house. When she got to the foot of the stairs, she had no choice but to say, "I'm just too tired to get up the stairs. Can I sleep in the—"

Jess interrupted by scooping her into his arms to carry her up the stairs. In a voice gruff with worry he muttered, "You're scaring me senseless, Emma."

"No need for that," she said. "I'm just . . . tired. It was a long trip. I'll feel better in the morning."

Emma's last awareness before she drifted to sleep was her mother's voice saying, "I called your sisters. They're praying for you. You sleep well."

When Emma came awake, the room was filled with the light of midday, and her mother was sitting in a chair near the bed. An unopened book lay on her lap, and her expression betrayed her concern.

"Good morning," Emily said gently. "Did you rest well?"

"For the most part," Emma said. She turned to survey the familiarity of the room and sighed.

"Are you hungry?"

"Sort of, but I really don't want to eat anything."

Following a moment of silence, Emily cleared her throat carefully and Emma felt it coming. "We need to talk, honey. We need to know what's going on."

"I know."

"Did you want to take a shower or eat something before we—"

"No, we need to talk now, I think. It really can't wait. But I don't want to have to repeat it, so if you want Jess and Tamra to hear it, you'd better get them."

"Very well," Emily said and immediately left the room. In the few minutes it took her to return with Jess and Tamra, Emma prayed very hard and attempted to gather her words.

Jess entered the room and bent over the bed to kiss her forehead. "Good morning," he said.

"Good morning," she replied, adjusting her pillows so she could lean against the headboard.

When Jess, Tamra, and Emily were all seated, Jess said, "Okay, let's have it."

"All right, but . . . this is hard for me so I ask that you be . . . patient."

"Of course," Emily said tenderly.

"And I fear you will be angry with me over certain aspects of this situation, and for that I ask your forgiveness in advance."

"Angry?" Jess asked. "Why would we be angry?"

Emma looked at him directly. "Because I have known about this problem for a very long time, and I chose not to tell anyone in my family." She watched Jess and her mother exchange a harsh glance.

"What have you known about?" Emily asked, her voice dark with dread.

"I have a kidney disease, Mother."

She gauged their stunned expressions, but no one said a word until Jess blurted, "And *why* didn't you tell us?" The predicted anger was evident in his eyes, but he kept his voice even.

"Because," she countered firmly, "I started having problems right around the time Dad was diagnosed with terminal cancer. And no matter how I tried, I couldn't find a good time to bring it up. And the more time that passed, the easier it became to just handle it on my own. I was put on some medications and the whole thing became regulated. I was feeling fine and doing well. When I applied to go on a mission, I really didn't think they'd let me go. Every step of the way I kept expecting to be told no because of the problem, instead they just sent me to the same city where I had already been seeing a specialist. I continued my regular checkups with him through my mission, and everything was fine until . . ."

"Until?" Jess pressed, sounding angry.

"I don't know exactly; some weeks ago I started having problems, symptoms that I knew weren't good. I'm afraid I wanted so badly to not be sent home that I put off doing something about it. I mean, I met my usual appointment, but maybe I should have gone in sooner. I don't know, I just . . ." She felt tears threatening and fought them back. She'd cried far too much since it had become evident that she would be going home, her mission cut short.

"Exactly what are we dealing with?" Emily asked in a voice that made it clear she was barely keeping her emotion under control.

"Truthfully, I don't know *exactly* what I'm dealing with. The doctor in Salt Lake contacted a doctor here. I have an appointment the day after Christmas. Until then I have to be very careful what I eat and drink."

"Okay," Jess said, "you don't know *exactly* what you're dealing with, but what *do* you know?"

Emma sighed. She really hated this, but she had to get it over with. "I'm not going to bore you with the medical terms that I have actually become rather fluent at using. I will simply tell you that my kidneys are functioning far below what is normal."

"Forgive our ignorance," Tamra said, "but what exactly are the symptoms of that?"

Emma sighed again. "Well, everything I eat or drink tastes horrible because of the impurities in my blood. So I haven't been eating much."

"Is that why you're so weak and tired?" Jess asked.

"Yes. And I've also become anemic as a result of the condition."

"Forgive me for being blunt, honey," Emily said, "but you've obviously gained weight. If you haven't been eating well, then . . ."

"That's not healthy weight, Mother." She glanced down, knowing if she explained this they were going to realize how bad it was, and they would likely panic the way she had panicked a few days ago when she was told what was happening to her body.

"Well, what is it?" Jess demanded.

Emma drew the courage and just said it. "Much of the fluid and toxins that would normally be gathered by my kidneys and sent to my bladder are actually accumulating in my bloodstream. That's why I'm so bloated."

Emily made a noise of disbelief before her hand went over her mouth. Jess hung his head and took short, sharp breaths. Tamra just stared at Emma in horror.

"So now what?" Emily asked, her emotion breaking through into conspicuous tears. "Is there some . . . medication or something that can remedy this?"

Emma knew what the remedy was, but she couldn't bring herself to bring that word up right now. She simply said, "I'm sure there is. I just have to see the doctor in a few days."

"Should you see him sooner?" Jess asked. "Maybe we should take you to the hospital and get something now. Maybe we should—"

"No, Jess. I'll be fine. I just have to be careful what I take in, because I'm not having much output. I know what I need to do, and I'll be fine. So, let's just do our best to enjoy Christmas and not make a big deal out of this, okay? I don't want everybody fussing and fretting. If I need help with something, I promise I will let you know."

With less emotion Emily asked, "Is there something you need right now? Can I get you anything?"

"No, thank you, Mother. I'm fine."

Emily looked as if she didn't believe her, but she only nodded and hurried from the room. Emma tossed back the covers and stood carefully.

"What are you doing?" Jess demanded.

"I'm not crippled, Jess. I was exhausted last night; I'm not that bad off now. I'm going to go talk to my mother, because I'd bet money she's falling apart right now. I'm sure the two of you have work and children that could give you something else to do besides fuss over me."

Emma wished it hadn't come out sounding so unfeeling when she saw their stunned expressions. But she just didn't have the energy, physically or emotionally, to tiptoe around everybody else's feelings. She knew they were just concerned, and understandably upset, but there was nothing she could do about it.

Emma slipped into her mother's bedroom without knocking and was momentarily taken aback. She'd expected to find her upset, but Emily was kneeling beside the bed, her hands clasped and stretched over her head, her face pressed into the bedspread, sobbing uncontrollably. Emma had simply never seen her mother so upset. She wondered for a moment if she should leave her in peace, but she felt compelled to intrude and sat on the floor beside her, touching her shoulder gently. Emily looked up, startled, then she pulled Emma into her arms and held her as tightly as if she might never have the chance to do so again.

"Oh, forgive me," Emily said without relinquishing her embrace. "I shouldn't get so upset. I just . . ."

"Well, it would be difficult for me to think that such a revelation wouldn't upset you," Emma said. "At least I know I'm not the only one who fell apart."

Emily eased back and took Emma's face into her hands. "I do wish you would have told us. We're family. Whatever we come up against, we must be in it together."

"I know." Emma glanced down, feeling ashamed. "It was just . . . the timing, I guess. And then when the medication was keeping everything under control, I just didn't think it was that big of a deal. I never dreamed it would get this bad."

Emily hugged her tightly again, and they sat on the floor for a long while just talking about the circumstances and crying on each other's shoulders. They were winding down when Tamra came timidly into the room with a bed tray.

"Forgive me," she said. "I know you told us that everything tastes horrible, but . . . I just think you've got to eat something. It's just some toast and herb tea. If that's taboo then I can get something else. This is what always worked for me when I was pregnant and so sick and nothing tasted good."

"Thank you," Emma said and had to admit, "It looks good, actually."

Tamra sat on the floor with them and they talked a while longer, until Emma asked, "Where's Jess? Is he okay?"

"I think he's pretty upset," Tamra said. "But I think he just needs some time to himself to let your news sink in. He'll be up to talking about it later."

"I'm so glad he has you, my dear," Emily said to Tamra.

"I'm just glad we all have each other," Tamra said and Emma silently agreed. Now that the disease had gotten so out of control, she couldn't even imagine what she would do without her family. Her pride and courage had waned quickly when it couldn't be solved with a prescription and regular office visits.

Emma finally admitted that she needed a shower, and Emily agreed to stay close by with the bathroom door left ajar in case she got too weak or had any problems. She felt better being clean and refreshed, but terribly exhausted. But Emily seemed hesitant to leave her alone at all. At Tamra's suggestion, Emma agreed to keep Tamra's mobile phone with her, and Tamra or Emily would keep the cordless house phone close by so that Emma could simply call if she needed something, without exerting any energy. Even the intercom system in the house could be difficult to use if she didn't have the strength to cross the room.

Emma was glad she'd gotten cleaned up when two members of the stake presidency came to the house to talk with her and see that she was officially released from her mission. A while after they left, Emily mentioned that she wished they would have thought to ask them help Jess give Emma a blessing. Five minutes after she mentioned it, Murphy was at the door in response to Jess's phone call. Together they gave her a blessing in which she was told that the Lord was mindful of her struggles, and that her body would be able to endure the strain being put upon it. Once the "amen" was spoken, Emma declared exhaustion and Jess carried her up the stairs and put her to bed.

Emma slept on and off through that day and into the next. In between her resting, she talked more with her family about the situation and gave her mother a copy of the list of foods she couldn't eat. She kept the other literature she had out of sight. Until they got the holiday behind them, she didn't want anyone going into full-fledged panic. She felt panicked enough for all of them.

Between her naps Emma also had phone conversations with her sisters. They too were upset and concerned, but she pled exhaustion and kept their conversations from going on too long. By the afternoon of her second day home—the day before Christmas Eve—Emma was so sick of her bedroom and sitting room she wanted to scream. She'd spent a little time in the nursery, enjoying her observations of the children, but there was no place to lie down comfortably there. She finally lowered her pride and asked Jess if he would carry her down the stairs, since she just didn't have the strength to make it down on her own. Everyone pitched in to make her comfortable in the library with some pillows and blankets, and she slept on the couch there until Emily asked her if she would like to join the family for supper.

"You don't have to eat much if you don't feel like it," Emily said. "Rhea cooked lasagna, but we did fix some things you can eat, if you're up to it."

"Thank you," she said, sitting up. "I'll be there soon."

A few minutes later she found the family gathered in the kitchen and she eased carefully onto a chair beside the table. She enjoyed the familiar noise and banter going on around her, and realized she felt better when she was around the family, rather than all alone. If she had to find a silver lining in all of this, it was nice to be home, among her family. She knew that with their love and support she would get through this, somehow.

* * *

Scott arrived at the station filled with a childlike anticipation. He concluded that the only real problem was that he'd not gotten used to celebrating Christmas in the middle of summer. But given a few years, he felt sure he would adjust to the reversal of seasons. He parked his car in the usual spot and got out. He opened the trunk and flung his laptop bag and camera case over one shoulder, and his overnight bag over the other. He picked up the garment bag that held his dress clothes on hangers and closed the trunk. He stepped in the house and immediately knew from the sounds and smells that it was supper time, and he had to admit he was hungry.

"Is that you, Scotty?" Rhea called from the kitchen.

Emma drew her attention away from her meal, wondering who 'Scotty' was. Then she realized that whoever might be visiting as a friend to Rhea—or anyone else, for that matter—was simply of no consequence to her. She proceeded to eat without enthusiasm, indifferent to what was going on around her.

"It's me," a male voice called from the hall. "And I smell lasagna." His accent was American.

"Oh, come and eat before you unpack," Emily said, coming to her feet. She moved toward the doorway just as a tall, dark figure appeared there. From the corner of her eye Emma was aware of this man putting down some small pieces of luggage and hanging a garment bag on the door hinge. He turned and laughed as Emily hugged him and pressed a kiss to his cheek.

"Oh, it's good to see you," Emily said, and Emma looked up. Her mother's enthusiasm perked her interest only slightly as she wondered what lost soul they might have taken in during her absence. And they'd neglected to tell her about it through their exchange of letters.

"It's good to see you, too," he said, briefly lifting Emily off the floor with his embrace. Then he set her down and his face came fully into view. Emma's indifference fled like a mouse at the appearance of a very large cat. She couldn't hold back an audible gasp, which sent his eyes directly to hers. For a moment the world seemed to freeze, even though she was vaguely aware of laughter and conversation continuing in the room. But it all became hazy and distant as she exchanged a long, searching stare with Scott Ivie. She didn't know what was going on, but it was plainly evident that in her absence this man had moved into her home and made himself a part of the family. And it made her angry. She didn't bother stopping to analyze *why* it made her angry. She simply knew that she was angry.

When Scott realized that Emma was sitting at the table, his heart raced then came to a dead stop and fell to the pit of his stomach. *Something was wrong!* She wasn't due to come home for several months yet, and when he'd left here three days ago, there had been no indication that she would be coming home. In fact the conversation had been more focused on how they would miss Emma through the holidays. And just seeing her now made him realize that his memories of her had not been distorted by time. She was absolutely the most beautiful woman he'd ever seen, although she looked decidedly different, except that he couldn't quite pinpoint how beyond the fact that she simply didn't look healthy. But just being in the same room with her made his mouth go dry and his knees weak—in spite of the apparent anger in her eyes. She wasn't happy with seeing him here and he knew it. But why?

She looked abruptly away and broke the momentary spell between them just as Emily said, "Oh, Scott, you remember Emma."

"Of course," he said, taking a seat.

"And Emma, you must remember Scott. He's—"

"I remember," she said and rose from the table. "I'm not feeling well. I'm going to lie down."

"But you hardly touched your dinner," Rhea protested.

"I can't eat it," Emma said. "Nothing tastes good; I'm sorry."

She left the room without another word. And the only explanation Scott got from the family was Jess saying, "Don't mind her. She's been in a bad mood since she got home."

Scott wanted to ask a dozen questions, but he focused on his meal as Emily changed the subject by saying, "Tell us how your trip went."

When supper was over, Scott thanked the women for a wonderful meal and promised to do the dishes tomorrow before he gathered his luggage and headed toward the stairs. He felt sick with concern, not only for Emma, but for the apparent anger that seemed to have put a rift between them wider than the one that had existed while living on different continents. He was startled to see her in the hall, and he wondered if the anger in her eyes was directed toward him, or circumstances he was unaware of.

"What are you doing here?" she asked without the slightest hint of kindness in her voice.

"I was going to ask you the same," he said coolly. "You weren't due back for months."

"This is my home, Mr. Ivie. And my reasons for being here are simply none of your business. But what are *you* doing here?"

Scott attempted to swallow his frustration. In an even voice, he said, "I came to visit, and your family invited me to stay. It was an offer I couldn't refuse."

"I can only imagine," she said, her voice thick with sarcasm as she moved past him to return to the kitchen where the family was still gathered. Apparently she wanted to be in there, as long as he wasn't. He watched her move away, leaving a dark cloud in her wake.

* * *

Emma attempted without success to diffuse the anger boiling inside of her. She wanted to pace the library where she was sitting, but she didn't have the strength. Once Scott had left the kitchen, she'd gone back in there, asking discreet questions about his being here, and getting answers that had only made her more angry. Now, the more she thought about it, the angrier she became. She finally dialed the mobile phone and asked her mother if she and Jess could come to the library for a few minutes. They entered the room as quickly as if she were royalty and they were waiting to meet her every whim.

"What is it?" Emily asked. "You seem upset."

"Yes, I'm upset," Emma admitted. "I . . . I . . ." She told herself to take a deep breath and calm down, if only so she wouldn't make a fool of herself, which would require having to explain something she didn't even understand—and didn't particularly want to.

"Why did someone not bother to write and tell me that this man had moved into our home and taken over?"

"Taken over what?" Jess asked, sounding appalled.

"You told me yourself that he is now in charge of the entire horse operation."

"Yes, and doing a fine job of it," Emily said.

"I'm really sorry, Em," Jess said. "I just . . . thought Mother would tell you about him."

"And I thought Jess had told you everything," Emily said. "We should have communicated better."

"Yes, you should have," Emma insisted.

"Forgive me," Emily said, "but I don't understand why you're so upset. He's far from the first person we've had staying in our home for long periods of time."

"But," Emma protested, "it's like . . . he's just made himself a part of the family, and it's as if he . . ."

"Well, he is like a part of the family," Jess defended hotly. "But it's the other way around. *We* made him a part of the family. I realize you don't feel well and you have a lot to deal with right now, but that doesn't give you the right to be angry over something that you don't begin to understand. I was wrong to not let you know what was happening. I assumed you knew. But he's living here and you're going to have to get used to it."

Jess left the room in a flurry and Emma was left feeling stunned. She could rarely recall Jess being that abrasive with her. She turned to her mother, perhaps hoping for some apology on behalf of Jess's behavior, some comment of compassion for Emma's anger. But she lifted her chin and said gently, "Scott is a good man, Emma. He's filled a void in our home that's been here since we lost James."

"James?" Emma countered. "You're comparing him to my brother?"

"Not comparing, Emma," Emily said in a calm voice that made Emma feel foolish for sounding so hotheaded. "It's just that . . . he needed us, and we needed him. You must consider how all of this is for Jess. He lost his brother, his best friend, and his father to death in not so many years. Scott has been a huge blessing in Jess's life; in all of our lives, actually. I'm sure that given some time you'll become accustomed to his presence. In the meantime, just take care of yourself and don't worry about it. I'm sure it's not good for you to get so worked up."

Emily left the room as well, and Emma felt completely deflated. Not only had a complete stranger come into her home and made himself a part of the family, and the family businesses, but he had won her mother and brother over so completely that they had no compassion whatsoever for how difficult this was for her.

Emma felt the anger consume her to a point that her heart rate increased and the blood rushed from her head. She was glad to have been sitting on the couch when she came to and found her face against the blanket that had been left there. The realization that she'd lost consciousness frightened her and she knew that she had to get hold of herself. She knew she was prone to getting angry easily, but in her home she'd never been allowed to fly off and be critical without facing severe repercussions. Only once in many years had she felt this angry, and that was over an issue with one of her companions. And even though Emma had felt justified in her anger, she'd had the good sense to get down on her knees and pray until she gained control of her emotions. She concluded that she had to be humble enough to do the same thing now. Remaining where she was, Emma closed her eyes and prayed long and hard that she could be free of this consuming anger. She recalled her mother teaching her many times that anger was a secondary emotion, and in order to be free of the anger, one had to recognize what was at its source. She asked herself that question. Was it fear? Hurt? Frustration? Perhaps some of all three, even though she felt too weary to analyze it too deeply. She only knew that tears came to her eyes as she contemplated how horrible she felt—and looked. She'd never felt so homely and unattractive in her life. She refused to admit that her tears had anything to do with her anger, but she did resolve that she had too much on her mind to even give Scott Ivie any thought. She resigned herself to achieve tolerance for the sake of her other family members. But she didn't have to like him.

Chapter Seven

An hour after supper was over, Scott found Jess in the lounge room, reading. "Am I interrupting?" he asked.

"No, of course not." Jess pulled his feet down from the coffee table and patted the couch. "What's up, my friend?" he asked, but there was no denying a darkness in Jess's countenance that hadn't been there a few days earlier.

Scott closed the door before he sat down.

"Something wrong?" Jess asked when Scott said nothing.

"Apparently there is. Forgive me if I'm prying, but—"

"You're practically family, Scott. You can ask me anything."

Scott tried to keep that *practically family* thing in mind. If only Emma felt that way. He cleared his throat and said, "I was just . . . surprised to come home and find Emma here." He looked directly at Jess. "May I ask what happened?"

"Didn't Mom tell you?"

"No, I'm afraid not."

"Oh, I'm sorry." Jess set his book aside. "It seems my mother and I are causing all kinds of trouble by assuming the other one is doing all the talking. I just believed that she would tell you, and she probably assumed that I would." His countenance darkened further and Scott's nerves increased as he wondered what had gone wrong.

"Apparently she has a kidney disease," Jess said as if he could barely choke the words out. Scott leaned his forearms onto his thighs and pressed his clasped knuckles to his lips, attempting to conceal the emotion overtaking him. "She told us that she's known about it for a long time, but it first manifested itself when our father had cancer, and she didn't want to burden anyone with worrying about her. When she applied to go on a mission, she was sure they wouldn't take her, but they did. She was sent to downtown Salt Lake so she could be close to the proper medical attention, and everything was fine until a few weeks ago when she became suddenly worse. So, they sent her home. I picked her up in Sydney the day you left." He went on to explain some of the symptoms, which helped Scott understand why she looked different than he'd remembered her. But the sick feeling inside of him increased as the list of symptoms and possible problems went on. Jess finished by saying, "She has an appointment with a specialist the day after Christmas, and then we'll know more what we're dealing with."

The silence between them was filled with grief. Scott finally said, "I'm so sorry. This must be difficult for you—for all of you."

"Yes, it is; I admit. But we'll get through it somehow. We've certainly been through worse."

Scott took a few minutes to try and grasp what he'd just been told. Jess seemed to be doing the same, even though he'd known for days. Something struck Scott and he had to ask, "What kind of trouble have you and your mother been getting into?"

Jess looked momentarily disoriented, then said, "Oh, Emma just . . . well, apparently I thought Mom had told her all about your being here. And Mom thought I had, so . . . ."

"She didn't know?" Scott asked, wishing he hadn't sounded so upset.

"I'm afraid not," Jess said. "I apologize if that causes any problems for you."

"Well, it's obvious she's not happy about my being here, but . . . it's her home more than it's mine, and—"

"It's your home, Scott. End of comparisons. Personally, I just think Emma is upset about what's going on and she's just . . . in a bad mood. Hopefully that will level off when she gets to the doctor and gets this thing under control."

Scott nodded, but he couldn't think of anything to say. He was having trouble understanding why he felt more depressed than he had since before he'd met Emma Hamilton on Temple Square.

* * *

Scott awoke early on the morning of Christmas Eve, having slept very little, and realized that his excitement for the holiday had all but evaporated. He felt completely heartsick over the revelation of Emma's illness, especially as he pondered how it weighed upon these people he had grown to love. And for himself, he could not deny his own heartache on Emma's behalf. He couldn't even imagine how horrible it must be for her to be facing such a serious illness. And to have had her mission cut short as well had to be doubly trying. He'd not had the opportunity to serve a mission himself, but he could well imagine the spiritual and emotional conviction that would be involved. He didn't have to wonder why Emma felt short tempered. Her grief and frustration were likely beyond description.

As he lay for what seemed hours just pondering the situation and how it made him feel, Scott could not deny that his grief went far beyond his compassion for this family he'd come to care for. His grief was deep and personal. In the deepest recesses of his heart, he had to admit that he had fallen for Emma the first time he'd met her. She had clung to his memory and worked her way into his heart, even though they were complete strangers in most respects. He had to face the reality now that his expectations of their reunion had been shattered. Scott had pondered how it might be when she returned. He had often thought that he would write her a letter or two, just to express his appreciation for her serving a mission, and the blessings it had brought into his life. He'd wanted to write and tell her what an incredible family she had, and at the very least, to let her know that he was looking forward to seeing her again, and he might have even said that he was looking forward to getting to know her better. But he had procrastinated the idea, believing there were months left before her return. He'd imagined that with a couple of letters exchanged, she might actually smile when she saw him. Or maybe she'd even want to talk, and he would have eventually asked her out to dinner. In his mind their relationship would evolve naturally and easily. But now she had been catapulted from one world into another, facing a chronic illness, and, for some reason, angered by his presence in her home. He could certainly give her the benefit of the doubt on that count.

To come home with such a heavy load and find the dynamics of the household had changed would naturally throw her off. And realizing that a communication breakdown had left her unprepared to find a strange man living in her home, his understanding deepened. He could understand, but the resulting situation still threatened to crack his heart down the middle. He was far more emotionally involved than he wanted to be, but his involvement had a certain distance to it in a technical sense. In spite of how thoroughly he'd been accepted by the Hamilton family, this problem revolved around Emma, and she wanted nothing to do with him. What little time he'd spent in her presence, he felt like an outsider looking in, and he hated it.

When his thoughts really began to overtake him, Scott forced himself to get up and take a shower. He didn't have anything particular in mind to do today. Emily had let him know that their celebrations would begin in the afternoon, and she had let him know what to expect as far as their traditions went. If only he could feel prepared in regard to this sudden upheaval in the family dynamics.

After a quick shower, Scott found Emily, Tamra, and Rhea all in the kitchen working busily, chatting and laughing in a way that he loved.

"Sorry, no cooked breakfast today," Emily said.

"It's not a problem," Scott said, kissing her cheek in a morning greeting that had become familiar. "I was a toast and juice man before you took me in and spoiled me."

"And your herbal tea, of course," Emily said, pouring him a cup of hot water.

"Of course," he chuckled and thanked her before he went to the refrigerator and dug out what he needed. Familiar noises let him know that the children were playing in a room just off the kitchen where they often did. As he was inserting the bread into the toaster, he noticed that Emma was sitting at the table, previously hidden from his view.

"Good morning, Sister Hamilton," he said, unable to keep from staring at her for a few long seconds. But he couldn't bring himself to call her Emma when their relationship felt so formal.

"Good morning, Mr. Ivie," she said with a distinct glare that seemed to be some kind of response to his briefly staring at her. He felt miffed by her use of his name. The formality was excusable, given that he'd started that. But the fact that she couldn't even call him *Brother* Ivie seemed to be some kind of a jab. And there was no denying the subtle tension in her voice that seemed lost on the others in the room.

"Did you sleep well?" Emily asked him as his toast popped up.

"Not really. How about you?"

"The same," she said.

"Must be all this excitement for Christmas," he said with the barest hint of sarcasm. Emily gave him a sideways glance that only he seemed to catch, and he felt sure that they both knew their lack of sleep was not related to the holiday.

As Scott sat at the table to eat his toast, Emma excused herself and left the room. "I don't think she likes me," Scott said.

"She doesn't like much of anything right now," Emily said. "You mustn't take it personal."

Scott didn't comment, but he *knew* it was personal. Perhaps he had become the only available scapegoat for her anger, since she loved everyone else in the household. Whatever her reasons, it was most definitely personal.

Once Scott was done eating and had cleaned up after himself, he offered to help the ladies, but they shooed him out of the kitchen, insisting that they were managing just fine.

"Keep Jess company," Tamra said. "I think he's in the library."

"I think I'll do that," Scott said and walked up the hall to find Jess leaning back in the corner of one of the long couches, reading a newspaper.

"Good morning," Scott said.

"Oh, hi," Jess said, tipping the corner of the paper down. "I'm done with the business section if you want it."

"Thanks," Scott said and sat down in the opposite corner of the same couch so that they could easily pass sections of the paper back and forth.

A short while later Scott heard a noise and peered over the paper to see Emma entering the room. He pretended not to notice that she had seen him there and scowled. Taking note of the blankets and pillows on the opposite couch, he realized now that she had probably been resting in this room frequently in order to avoid going up and down the stairs. Her weakness was startlingly evident and he was hard pressed to not jump out of his chair and carry her from the door to the couch where she was obviously headed. Seeing how Jess watched her every step, he could well imagine him feeling the same way. He likely held back for fear of wounding her pride—or sparking her anger. Perhaps both.

"Sorry to bother you boys," she said curtly. "I didn't realize you were in here. I need to rest and I don't have the strength to get anywhere else right now."

"You're not bothering us," Jess said. "Can I get you anything?"

"No, I'm fine," she added and settled onto the pillows, snuggling beneath the blanket.

Not ten minutes later Tamra came to the room, asking Jess if he would help with the children, since they were getting out of hand and the women were in the middle of some projects.

"Duty calls," Jess said quietly to Scott as he left the room.

Scott watched him go, then realized that Emma was sleeping, only a few feet away. He took full advantage of the opportunity to just watch her, contemplating everything he felt for this woman he hardly knew. And yet he felt as if he did. He felt as if they should be the best of friends, intimately close in every aspect of their lives. Could that be the reason her blatant animosity toward him hurt so deeply?

As Emma slept on, Scott's mind wandered. He couldn't help indulging in the fantasy that she would eventually get beyond her prejudice toward him and they might have a chance for the future. The images in his mind felt right and good, but when she began to stir and he felt afraid to face her, he had to look at the stark reality that she wanted nothing to do with him. For a moment he felt tempted to put his newspaper in place and pretend to be reading. But something deeper and stronger compelled him to hold his gaze. He relished in watching her come slowly awake, and he could almost believe she'd been having a pleasant dream, then her eyes caught him and the serenity in her expression shattered.

"What are you doing here?" she demanded, clutching the blanket more closely around her as if it could save her from his gaze.

"Begging your pardon, Sister Hamilton, but I was here first."

"But . . . why are you staring at me?"

Scott spoke as sincerely as he could manage, feeling on trial as he did. "There was nothing else in the room so lovely to look at."

For a brief moment he caught the tiniest glimmer of something in her eyes that contradicted her anger. His compliment had touched something in her, something eager and vaguely warm. But it had quickly become squelched by . . . what? Anger? Doubt? *Fear?* Perhaps a combination. Still, Scott knew what he'd seen, however briefly, and he clung to it.

"I've never looked so horrible in my entire life," she said, perhaps giving a clue to her animosity.

"I haven't known you your whole life," he said, "so perhaps I can't make an educated comparison, but personally I think you look awfully beautiful."

Scott knew he was probably only setting himself up for more darts to be thrown from those eyes. Giving such bold compliments to a woman who made no effort to graciously conceal her dislike for him was likely foolish at best. But he just couldn't seem to help himself. Emma glared at him as if she simply didn't trust him, but she made no comment before she came carefully to her feet and moved toward the door.

"Don't leave on my account," he said.

"I'm not," she insisted, but the weakness that was made evident by every step she took made it difficult for him to not bolt out of his seat and carry her wherever she wanted to go. But if she wouldn't allow her brother to help her, she certainly wouldn't allow him anywhere near her.

A few hours later, Scott was relieved to have the Christmas celebrations officially underway. Being with the entire family, with structure to their activities, made it easier to let go of his difficult feelings. He quickly became caught up in the spirit of the traditions, and he could see that everyone else was doing the same—even Emma. It seemed that for the time being, they were all able to let go of their concerns and appreciate being together to celebrate this greatest of holidays.

Scott's experience with Christmas had few good memories. Instinctively he'd always believed that it was supposed to be better than what he'd known. He'd done his best to create positive and memorable experiences with Callie, but their celebrations had always lacked something. Once Scott had joined the Church he grew to understand what had been missing. He'd never fully put Christ into Christmas, and once he did, it had made a huge difference, even though Callie had never shared his enthusiasm. Still, he'd always wondered what it would be like to participate in a real family Christmas. Seeing that very thing unfold around him almost made him feel that he was caught up in a dream.

The highlight of Christmas Eve was the family all going together to the boys' home with boxes and baskets of food and gifts. They shared a huge meal with the boys and everyone worked together to clean it up before Father Christmas arrived, talking personally with each boy and giving them each a wrapped gift with their name on it. Jess told Scott quietly that the gifts were carefully selected so that each boy got one special thing from Father Christmas that they had wanted. For some boys, it was the best Christmas they had ever known. The boys also drew names to exchange gifts with each other, and that would take place the following morning.

Scott immersed himself in the sweet spirit of the celebration, personally feeling the joy he saw in the face of each boy. He also saw in each of them a little of himself. And for that reason he felt hard pressed to keep from crying several times.

Late that evening when Scott returned to his room, it occurred to him that he didn't have a gift for Emma. He wasn't by any means concerned that she would have something for him and he would feel obligated. In truth, he knew she wouldn't, and that was fine. The giving of gifts was not about keeping score or being even. He knew that Emma had sent a package from Utah that had arrived a couple of weeks ago with gifts for her family members, and those gifts were already beneath the tree. But Scott wanted to give her something; he simply felt like he should. Of course, it was nearly midnight on Christmas Eve. He couldn't just run out and buy her something. His only option was to give her something that belonged to him, something with meaning.

He thought long and hard, praying as he looked through his belongings. Perusing the contents of a dresser drawer that was filled with odds and ends, he came across a little red box. He felt drawn to it, even though he couldn't recall its contents. When he opened it, there was nothing inside but a cushion of white tissue paper that had once held . . . He turned abruptly and caught sight of the teardrop-shaped crystal, hanging in the window on a piece of fishing line that made it appear to be floating in the air.

"Perfect," he muttered to himself and took it carefully down, returning it to the box it had come from. He managed to quietly make his way to the spare room that Emily had dubbed "the North Pole." It was where the packaging and wrapping of all the gifts had taken place, and there was an ample supply of everything he needed to make the gift look the way he wanted it to. Before he went to sleep, he tiptoed down the stairs and put the gift beneath the tree. Then he went back upstairs and went to bed, praying that this Christmas day would be a good one—for all of them.

* * *

The gift-opening frenzy of Christmas morning was truly a delight for Scott. He'd never been around children for Christmas and they were truly a pleasure to watch as they absorbed the magic of the holiday with sparkling eyes. Scott was excessively mindful of Emma, but did his best to appear indifferent toward her. She looked more bloated and pale than she had yesterday, and he was decidedly worried about her. She lay on the couch, minimally participating in the festivities, with her mother or Tamra actually helping her open most of her gifts because she simply didn't have the strength.

The highlight of the morning was the pleasure he felt in the gifts he'd carefully chosen for his new family. Their pleasure was evident, even though he knew they could afford to buy anything they wanted. That in itself strengthened the sentimental quality of a gift, and he was partial to being sentimental. The gifts they shared with him left him in awe of their love and generosity, but also their insight into the things that held meaning for him.

Scott had almost forgotten about his gift for Emma until Jess was digging under the tree to make certain they had found every package. "Oh, this is for you," he said, handing it to Emma. Jess tossed Scott a subtle smile while Emma looked at the tag from her reclining position on the couch.

When Emma looked at the little tag and realized the gift was from Scott, something tightened inside of her. "You didn't have to do that," she said, trying to sound cordial, but the edge in her voice couldn't be disguised.

"I know I didn't have to," Scott said so pleasantly that she wondered if he had any idea how much his presence annoyed her. "It's something I wanted you to have. After all, your serving a mission has brought unspeakable blessings into my life, and I'm grateful, more grateful than I could ever say. So . . . consider it a thank-you gift, a small token of my appreciation."

Emma took a deep breath and reminded herself to be gracious as she pulled the paper away from the little box, then opened it. Sitting on a bed of crumpled white tissue paper was a large, teardrop-shaped crystal. She'd seen such things in gift shops many times, but had never paid much attention. While she was trying to think of something civil to say, he explained, "When you hang it in your window, the sunlight will come through it and scatter around the room. I confess that I didn't purchase it for this occasion. It was given to me by a sweet sister in my ward in Utah when I was going through an especially difficult time. She told me an analogy that ended up having great meaning for me, and the symbolism helped get me through some terribly trying challenges. More than the crystal, I want to pass along its meaning."

Emma found herself feeling touched by his genuine sentiment, almost against her will. She felt compelled to lift her eyes to meet his as she asked, "If it has such meaning for you, why give it to me?"

He answered as if it were obvious. "Because I believe that when the Lord blesses us with something that enriches our lives and makes us better people, we are obligated to pass those blessings and gifts on to others."

Emma looked back to the crystal in the box, fearing she might cry and make a fool of herself if she didn't stay focused.

"Tell us its meaning," Emily prodded quietly.

"The direct sunlight that hits the crystal is like the light of Christ. The crystal is like our hearts, or our spirits. We can choose to close the curtain between that light and ourselves, or we can let that light penetrate us and became an instrument to spread the light and diffuse it into all that we do. As long as we don't close ourselves off, we will always be touched by the light."

"That's beautiful," Tamra said.

"It certainly is," Emily added.

Emma carefully swallowed her rising emotion and said, "Thank you. It's beautiful. That was very thoughtful of you."

Scott watched her closely and felt certain that she was touched by the gesture, but she closed the lid on the box as if she might never look at its contents again.

The remainder of the day sailed along like the manifestation of a dream that Scott had held in his heart since his childhood. He'd always wanted to believe that real families existed and celebrated holidays this way, but a part of him had wondered if it was just television propaganda. He felt the spirit of the holiday deeply, and his appreciation for the birth and life of the Savior filled his every cell. Were it not for his Emma-related heartache, he would consider himself the happiest man alive.

The following morning Scott went down to breakfast and found that moods were low and the tension in the room extremely high. Apparently some problems had arisen with a couple of boys at the home, and Jess needed to be there, but he was upset about not being able to go into town with Emma and his mother for the long-awaited doctor appointment.

"Could I handle it for you?" Scott asked, genuinely wanting to help, which prompted a glare from Emma. He just countered her with a bold stare then turned back to Jess. "I'd be glad to help any way I can."

"I appreciate it, Scott, I do," Jess said, "but I'm afraid I have to take care of this myself."

Scott almost offered to drive the women into town, but instinctively he knew that wasn't a good idea. Instead he just looked directly at Emily and said, "If there's anything I can do—anything at all—you simply have to ask."

"Thank you, Scott. I'm grateful to know you're here. But we'll be fine. It's far from the first time I've driven someone into town for an appointment."

Jess almost glared at his mother, as if to say that his having to wait here for the outcome of this particular appointment would be torturous. But Emily quickly settled the matter and insisted that they share a good breakfast. Scott was aware of Emma mostly rearranging her food on her plate. In fact, he didn't see her eat anything at all. His worry deepened. She looked horrible. Beautiful, but horrible.

Jess barely ate himself before he left for the boys' home, obviously not very happily. It didn't take much imagination to grasp how worried he must be. The moment Scott finished eating he insisted on washing the dishes so that Emily and Emma could be on their way, and Tamra and Rhea could focus on caring for the children, which in itself was a full-time job. When the kitchen was in fairly good order, Scott went to his office and tried to focus on his work, but there was nothing that couldn't be put off, and he found his mind wandering with concern as he glanced at the clock often.

About two hours after the women had left for their appointment, the phone rang. Scott let it ring a few times, not wanting to be intrusive if Tamra was waiting by the phone. When it kept ringing he picked it up.

"Scott?" Emily's voice was strained.

"Yes," he said, his heart pounding.

"I was praying you'd answer. I need your help. I know you meant it when you offered."

"I did; of course. Anything."

"I need Jess here." Tears broke through her voice. "They took one look at her and sent us to the hospital. I think it's bad, but they need time . . . they're doing some tests, but . . ." The emotion overtook her and he was barely able to understand her. "I can't do this alone. I need Jess here, but I don't want him driving. I can't explain why; I just . . . need you to bring Jess to the hospital." She took a deep breath. "Don't let him argue with you. Just do it."

"I will," he said. "I'll go get him now. Everything will be all right."

She told him where to find her, thanked him profusely and got off the phone. Scott rushed across the hall to the nursery to give a thirty-second explanation before he hurried out to his car, dialing Jess's office phone from his mobile as he ran down the stairs.

"Hello, Madge. It's Scott," he said when she answered. "I need to talk to Jess. It's urgent."

"What?" Jess said when the call connected, his voice panicked.

"I'm going to pick you up in about one minute. Your mother wants me to take you into town."

The edge in his voice deepened. "Why did she—"

"Don't ask questions, Jess. Just tell them you have to go, and get out the door. I'm almost there." He hung up the phone and drove around to the front of the boys' home. Jess was running down the stairs and Scott barely stopped long enough for him to jump in.

"What's going on?" Jess demanded. "Why didn't she just call me?"

"She said she didn't want you to drive."

"What's that supposed to mean?" Jess growled.

"I don't know, Jess. I'm just doing what our mother told me to do."

Scott sensed that Jess was consciously attempting to get control of his senses. In a voice that was slightly more calm, he admitted, "There's only one reason she wouldn't want me to drive. She's afraid if I was upset, I might not drive . . . rationally." Jess turned to look at Scott with a hard stare. "What else did she say? Why would she think I'd be upset?"

Scott glanced at Jess and then back to the road. "She didn't say much, but she was obviously upset."

"Okay, but what did she say?"

"She said they took one look at Emma and sent her to the hospital. They're doing some tests. She just said she needed you there. And maybe . . ."

"Maybe what?"

"Maybe part of her motivation in asking me to bring you was just an excuse."

"An excuse for what?" Jess demanded, sounding understandably testy.

"To have two priesthood holders available. I brought some oil."

Jess nodded and looked out the window, pressing his clenched fist to his lips. "I knew we should have taken her in before now," he said. "She's just so blasted *stubborn*. I assumed she knew what she was talking about when she said it would be okay until today, but maybe it's even worse than *she* realized."

"Maybe it is," Scott said, putting a hand on Jess's arm. "But everything's going to be all right."

Jess looked at him as if he desperately wanted to believe that. "You just keep telling me that."

Scott nodded firmly and drove on. They made good time and arrived at the hospital to find Emily pacing the waiting room. She made an emotional noise when she saw them and pressed herself into Jess's arms, holding to him desperately. "Thank you for coming," she said and greeted Scott the same way. He relished her tight embrace. "I just couldn't be alone," she added, stepping back.

"Tell us what's going on," Jess said.

"Walk with me," she said and moved down a long hall. "She should be settled into a room now. They've been doing some tests, and now they want to observe her for twelve hours to see how she's doing, and to monitor her urine output, but . . ." The lack of emotion Emily had shown since their arrival suddenly dwindled. She stopped walking and moved quickly to lean against the wall.

"What is it, Mother?" Jess asked, holding her hand.

"She told the doctor that there has been practically *no* output for days now."

"I don't understand," Jess said, looking confused. But Scott understood what Emily meant and his heart dropped like lead. He watched Emily squeeze her eyes shut as a steady stream of tears rolled down her face.

"Everything her kidneys should be filtering out of her bloodstream is still in her bloodstream, because her kidneys are barely working at all. They will likely be starting her on dialysis before they'll let her go home."

Scott noticed Jess teetering slightly and he reached out an arm to steady him.

"I need to sit down," Emily muttered and moved quickly toward another waiting area.

"Wouldn't hurt," Scott muttered, keeping a hand on Jess's arm as they followed her.

They all sank weakly into chairs and sat there for a few minutes in silence before Jess said in a shaky voice, "But . . . isn't dialysis . . . permanent? I mean . . . once she starts that, isn't it like . . . every couple of days . . . forever?"

Emily nodded and pressed a tissue over her mouth for a moment before she moved it and said, "They will be surgically inserting some kind of permanent catheter into one of the main arteries near her heart . . . at least I think that's what they said."

"I can't believe it," Jess muttered, pressing his head into his hands. "She'll never be able to live any kind of a normal life."

Scott listened to Jess's words and felt them pierce his very soul. But Emily's voice held a glimmer of hope as she said, "There is . . . a chance."

"What chance?" Jess demanded, looking up abruptly.

"She could have a transplant."

Jess scowled. "You mean like . . . having her name on some enormous list, waiting for somebody to end up brain-dead from an accident, so we hope and pray that somebody will get killed who actually has the same blood type."

"It's more than just the blood type," Emily said. "Finding a match is extremely difficult."

Jess closed his eyes and turned his head to the side as if he'd been struck with one too many blows. He blindly reached a hand toward Scott, as if to verify that he wasn't facing this alone. Scott held his hand tightly and realized that Jess was shaking, then he looked at his other hand and knew that he was shaking, too.

Jess sighed loudly and said, "Apparently you've just had a crash course on all of this."

"Yes, I suppose I have," Emily admitted, still struggling with her ongoing grief. "There is one other thing," she said and Jess looked at her as if he couldn't possibly bear one more blow. "I believe I knew this, but I'd forgotten that it was possible."

"What?" Jess asked, straightening his back at the hint of hope in Emily's voice.

"Kidneys are something we have two of. She can have a transplant from a living donor." She sniffled loudly. "I'd give her one of mine in a minute, but I'm not even the same blood type."

"How do you know that?" Jess asked.

"I just . . . know. She's my daughter. I know my blood type. I know hers."

"And mine?" Jess asked, scooting to the edge of his seat as if he would lay himself down this very moment to give Emma whatever she needed to survive this horrible disease.

Emily almost showed a smile. "You have the same blood type as Emma, but that's not the only factor, Jess. We have much to learn and we're going to have to be patient."

"But there is hope," Jess said, "that she can get beyond this?"

"Yes, there is hope," Emily said.

Chapter Eight

"Can we go see her now?" Jess asked, jumping to his feet, a fresh determination etched into his countenance.

"I believe so," Emily said, seeming more in control of her emotions now that she'd shared the burden of the news she'd been given.

Scott walked with them toward Emma's room, feeling all tied into knots. The grief and fear that consumed him was indescribable, combined with the compassion he felt for Emily and Jess. As much as Scott had grown to care for Emma, in a strange and distant sort of way, Jess and Emily were her family. He couldn't even imagine how they must be feeling. He only hoped that he could do some measure of good in helping them through this. They'd given him so much that he could never repay.

Scott's heart began to pound as they approached the door to Emma's room. He nearly followed Jess and Emily in, then he reminded himself that he was not family, and he needed to remember his place. He touched Jess on the arm and whispered, "I'll be out here if you need me."

Jess frowned and grabbed Scott's arm, dragging him into the room beside him. Scott's pounding heart dropped like a rock and he heard Jess draw a ragged breath. Emma looked practically dead. He could almost imagine how she'd fought to keep going, not wanting to mar her family's Christmas. And now that she'd been hospitalized and the severity of her condition made known, she had no strength left to uphold any pretenses. She opened her eyes and showed some response when Emily took her hand and spoke to her. Following some quiet conversation between them, Emily said, "Jess is here." She motioned him closer.

Jess approached and took Emma's hand. She smiled weakly at him. "I thought you had work to do."

"I got everything under control before I came. It's okay. I want to be with you."

"I'm screwing up everybody's life," she said.

"No," Jess pressed. "We're family; we're in this together." She smiled and he added, "Would you like us to give you a blessing?"

She nodded before she said, "Us?"

"Scott's with me," Jess said and Emma showed no reaction.

"That would be good," Emma said, then her voice cracked. "I'm scared, Jess."

"I know," his voice broke as well. "I am too. But it's going to be all right."

Jess motioned Scott closer to the bed and whispered, "Will you do the first part?"

Scott was more than willing, but he felt the need to ask Emma, "Is it all right with you if I help Jess give you a blessing?"

He didn't know if she was simply too ill to care, but she simply nodded with no apparent animosity toward him, whatsoever. Scott did the anointing without any difficulty beyond the nearly electric feeling that surged through him when he placed his hands on her head. Through the second part of the blessing, Jess spoke with a firm and steady voice as he told Emma that these experiences would be for her growth and the growth of those who loved her, that she would gain humility and learn to trust in the Lord. Emma was told that she would emerge strong and healthy, and the life she lived would be full and bright. Scott couldn't help noticing that there was no mention of exactly how long that life would be. Still, it was a beautiful blessing and the Spirit was strong in the room.

"Thank you," Emma said to Jess after the "amen" had been spoken. Then she turned to Scott and repeated quietly, "Thank you."

"A pleasure," he said, briefly taking her hand to give it a gentle squeeze.

Scott hovered at the perimeter of the room while Jess and Emily spoke quietly with Emma. He felt frustrated with the sense of being outside of this aspect of the family circle, yet privileged to be as much a part of it as he was.

The conversation remained light and simple until, without warning, Jess leaned over Emma and looked into her face, saying with conviction, "I'm going to give you one of my kidneys, Emma."

Scott was taken aback, knowing that many tests had to be done before Jess could know if that was possible. Emily evidently had the same response when she said with gentle reprimand, "Jess, honey, we don't know for sure if that's possible."

"It will be possible," he said firmly to his mother, then he turned to Emma again. "Don't you worry, Em. I'm going to give you a kidney, and everything's going to be all right."

Weakly Emma said, "I don't know . . . if you should. You have a family and . . . so many people who need you. If you . . ."

"They only need one of my kidneys," he said lightly. "You can have the other one, if you promise to take good care of it."

Emma showed a hint of a smile and tears leaked from the corners of her eyes. "I love you, Jess," she said.

"I love you too, Emma," he replied, his voice cracking with emotion.

"You don't have to give me a kidney to let me know you love me," she said.

"I know that, but it's what I'm supposed to do, and I'm happy to do it."

The conversation slid back into trivialities until a nurse came to check on Emma, and a few minutes later they wheeled her bed down the hall for the brief surgery she needed to install the permacath. With Emma in surgery, Emily went to a payphone to call her other daughters and give them the news. Jess offered to do it, but she insisted that she needed to talk with them and she might be a while. Jess and Scott wandered into a nearby waiting area where they'd been told the surgeon would seek them out when he was finished.

They sat in silence for a few minutes before Scott said, "Forgive me, but . . . why did you tell her you'd give her a kidney when there's so much that has to be done before you can know if—"

"I already know," Jess said firmly. "I just . . . had this feeling during the blessing that it's what I'm supposed to do."

Scott wanted to point out that being prompted to be willing, and being physically capable, were two very different things. But he said nothing. He wasn't about to question what the Spirit might have spoken to Jess, or Jess's interpretation of it.

Time dragged on silently until Scott heard Jess gasp loudly, as if he'd just remembered something terribly important that he'd forgotten to do.

"What?" Scott asked, expecting Jess to say he needed to make a phone call, or he'd have to make amends to someone for something that had been overlooked. But Jess met his eyes with blatant terror. He pressed his hands to his chest and his breathing became sharp and raspy.

"What is it?" Scott demanded, taking hold of his shoulders.

"Heaven help me," Jess managed to utter. "What have I done? What have I done?"

Scott glanced around, grateful to find that they were alone in the waiting room. "Jess, what is it? Talk to me."

It took Jess several minutes to calm down with Scott encouraging him to breathe deeply. "I feel like I'm having a heart attack," Jess said, a hand still pressed over his chest.

"I think they call it a panic attack, actually," Scott said. "So, why don't you tell me what brought on this sudden panic?"

Jess looked at him as if answering the question might jeopardize the friendship they'd come to share. Scott said gently, "There's nothing you could tell me that would make any difference. But whatever it is, I think you'd better talk about it, or I'm going to march you down the hall and tell them you *are* having a heart attack."

Jess's expression made it clear that he didn't want to undergo medical probing. Again he made a visible effort to calm himself before he said, "I nearly died in that accident—the one that killed my brother and his wife and my friend."

"Yes, I know."

Tears came to Jess's eyes. "What if I had? If I'm the one who can give a kidney to Emma, then . . . what if I *had* died?"

"Well, you didn't. You obviously weren't supposed to. And if you are the one who can give her a kidney, then obviously that's one of many reasons you were spared. Not to mention the fact that you are now a husband and father, with many people depending on you."

"Yes, but . . ." Jess became upset again, "there was another time that I almost died, and if I had . . . where would that have left Emma now? I tried to tell myself that it wouldn't hurt anybody, that they would all be better off without me. But if Emma . . ." Jess became so upset that he couldn't talk. Once again Scott coached him through the attack, helping him slow his breathing. When he could speak again, he said, "It was my fault, Scott, and if I had died, what would have happened to Emma?"

Scott felt confused and had to ask, "How did you almost die, Jess?"

Jess looked at him like a frightened child and huge, new tears rose in his eyes. "I took sleeping pills—twenty-five of them."

Scott sucked in his breath as he began to comprehend the full breadth of Jess's present heartache. "What if I had succeeded?" Jess asked, as if Scott should have the answer.

Scott uttered a silent prayer then said with conviction, "You didn't, and that's the important thing. You're here now, and you just need to be grateful that you are." Jess nodded and seemed to accept the answer. With some time and effort he calmed down considerably before Scott asked, "May I ask *why* you didn't succeed?"

Jess gave a humorless chuckle. "It was Tamra," he said and Scott felt surprised. To see them together now, and the relationship they shared, it was difficult to imagine that they'd endured such struggles. He recalled now that Tamra had shared with him some bits and pieces of the struggles that had led up to her marrying Jess, but she hadn't told him this story. She had probably figured it wasn't her place to share something so personal for Jess.

"According to what she told me, the Spirit practically kicked her down the hall to my room. I vaguely remember her slapping me and screaming at me before I completely lost consciousness. She called for a helicopter and my stomach was pumped on the way to the hospital."

"Then we can all be grateful that the Lord wasn't going to let you die, and that Tamra had the sense to listen to what He was telling her."

"Yes, we can be grateful," Jess said sadly. He remained calm after that, but Scott sensed that he was troubled. But then, he had plenty to be troubled about, given the present situation with his sister.

An hour later, Scott said to Jess, "I hope you don't mind if I stick around with you; if you'd prefer I could go and—"

"Mind?" Jess snorted a laugh. "Good heavens. I would be a blubbering idiot without you here to hold me up."

"Well, I'm glad to be here," Scott said. "Just let me know if I get too intrusive."

Jess snorted again before silence descended around them once more.

Scott and Jess eventually went home, but only after Emma had come successfully through the surgery and was stable. Emily would be staying with her, and Jess agreed to return first thing in the morning. "If Scott will drive me," Jess said almost lightly.

"Of course," Scott said. They both hugged Emily, then Scott waited for Jess to speak with Emma before they started home.

The following morning when they returned to the hospital, they entered Emma's room to find a completely different woman. Emma was sitting in a chair wearing a long bathrobe over her hospital gown. She was looking at a magazine, looking very much like the woman Scott recalled meeting on Temple Square. The extra water weight that had bloated her was completely gone. *She was so beautiful!*

Jess laughed as he greeted her, and it seemed that nothing had ever been wrong. Scott wanted to fall down on his knees and thank God for the creation of dialysis, if this was what it was capable of doing. Of course, he knew that her ongoing need for it would be difficult, and a transplant was the only way to free her from that need. Still, the fact that a person with such problems could have their life prolonged this way was truly a miracle.

"Hello, Mr. Ivie," she said to him, her tone indifferent. But he figured that was better than a cold glare. That too was a miracle.

* * *

Three days and three dialysis treatments later, Emma came home from the hospital. She was able to walk up the stairs on her own, and the entire family seemed to relax with this tangible evidence that Emma would be all right until a transplant donor could be found. Scott knew that Jess had already begun the testing process, along with everyone else in the family, as far as he knew. Even her sisters in the States were undergoing the process, which comprised many steps that would take weeks before a firm conclusion could be reached. Scott didn't even have to wonder if he was willing to do the same. Without telling anyone, he proceeded with the tests himself. Deep inside he believed that he wouldn't be a match, but he wished that he could be, and he wanted to at least try, so that he would know for sure. He wasn't certain why he didn't tell anybody he was being tested. Perhaps he didn't want anyone, especially Emma, thinking that it was just some heroic effort to win her over, or to further ingratiate himself with the family. Whatever the reason, he chose to keep it to himself.

As Emma continued to gain strength, Scott realized that her minimal congeniality in the hospital had been short-lived. He couldn't enter a room where she was present without receiving a harsh glare, as if she simply deemed him unworthy of being associated with her family. Scott always countered her with a firm stare, hoping to imply his confidence in being where he was, and he bit his tongue daily from confronting her about her attitude toward him. He kept reminding himself that she was going through a great deal, and he'd do well to bide his time and mind his business.

Late in January he had no choice but to make a trip to Brisbane, but he found he was dreading it more than usual. He tried not to think about it and just forced himself to pack and get ready to go.

He rose early and went down to the kitchen with his bags to get some toast for the road. He had plenty of time to get there, but he figured the sooner he got there, the sooner he could come home. He found Emily in the kitchen with breakfast waiting for him.

"I knew you'd be leaving early," she said, setting aside the book she'd been reading before she stood to dish up a plate for him from the pans that had kept the food warm on the stove.

"You are far too good to me," he said as she set the plate in front of him, along with a cup of herbal tea.

"I was thinking the same about you," she said and sat beside him. He said a blessing and they ate together, sharing small talk. When he was finished he stood and rinsed his dishes at the sink before he thanked Emily again for breakfast and moved toward the door.

"Scott," she said and he turned back. "The hospital lab called late afternoon yesterday while you were in the stables; they left a message for you." Scott froze but couldn't look at her. "I should have told you sooner, but . . . I needed some time, I suppose." Her tone softened as she added, "You were being tested, too." It was not a question.

"That's right," Scott said, mostly looking at the floor.

"Why didn't you say something?"

"I just . . . wanted to do it, but I didn't want to make a big deal of it."

"Being willing to give your kidney to a stranger is a big deal."

"She's not a stranger," Scott said firmly, finally meeting her eyes. "And I would give much more than that if it were possible."

He saw tears rise in Emily's eyes before she glanced down, saying, "Well, it's not possible."

Scott absorbed what she'd said before he asked, "They said that?"

"Yes. You can call them for details if you want. But they said you're not a match—not even close." She smiled before her tears overtook her.

"What is it?" he asked, putting his arms around her.

"Just . . . so many things. It's all so frightening and overwhelming, but . . . I'm so grateful."

"Tell me what you're grateful for," he said while she cried against his shoulder.

"Well, first of all," she said, looking up at him, "I'm grateful for you. Your love . . . your support. You will never know what it's meant to me through this. And I can't tell you what it means to me to know that you were willing to give of yourself for Emma that way."

Scott tried to ward off his embarrassment. "It's not a big deal."

"It's a big deal to me," Emily said and immediately dissolved into sobs.

Scott guided her to a chair and sat beside her, keeping his arm around her. "What else is going on?" he asked, knowing that something was.

She fought for control of her tears and finally managed to say, "Jess is a perfect match; they said they don't come any better matched than that."

Scott took in the news, wondering why a part of him felt almost envious of being able to do such a thing for Emma.

Emily went on to say, "A part of me is so grateful that I can't even begin to express it."

"That's understandable," Scott said. "What's the other part?"

She sniffled loudly and wiped her face with a clean dishtowel that had been on the table. "The other part of me doesn't want to see Jess go through this. I know the risks are few, but there are risks, and at best, it will be a strain on him until he recovers. It's just . . . difficult to see one of my children suffering, but more difficult, in a way, to see one suffer for the sake of another."

Scott thought about it for a minute before he said, "Do you want to know what I see?" Emily looked curious as she nodded and he went on. "I see a great tribute to you in the kind of children that you raised—that they would be willing to give so much for each other."

Emily smiled as if she truly felt better. "Thanks for listening," she said. "You're always so good to listen and let me cry, and you always manage to say the right things."

Scott glanced down humbly, saying, "I was thinking the same about you."

He came to his feet and asked, "Is there anything I can do before I go?"

"No, I'll be fine. Thank you. Have a safe trip."

Scott walked out of the house, hating the fact that he had to go at all. Through the drive he contemplated how many times he'd made the long drive to Brisbane and back. The difference now was that he hated every minute of it. He just wasn't sure what to do about it.

* * *

Emma watched from her bedroom window as Scott loaded his bags into the trunk of his car, then he got in and drove away. She pulled her bathrobe more tightly around her and hoped he'd be gone a long time. Just the thought of his absence eased her anxiety, although she wasn't quite sure why.

She was still standing at the window when a knock came at her door and she called out an answer. Jess and her mother came into the room. Jess looked happy; her mother was unreadable beyond the usual concern showing in her face.

"Good morning," she said and they responded with the same. "To what do I owe this unusual visit?" she asked.

"I have something to tell you," Jess said.

"Okay, I'm listening," Emma said, moving to a chair.

Jess scooted a chair close to hers so that he could face her. Emily sat on the edge of the bed, keeping a distance that implied she was simply an observer of this particular conversation.

"What is it?" Emma asked when Jess said nothing.

"The tests have all come back," he said and once again broke into a smile. "I'm a perfect match, Emma. Once you build your health up a little more, I can give you one of my kidneys."

Emma said nothing and Jess went on to say, "I thought you'd be happy about this."

"I am," she said in a tone of voice that sounded hypocritical. She struggled to find the words to explain while he watched her expectantly. "I can't begin to tell you what this means to me, Jess. I'm grateful. I just . . . wish there was another way; that you didn't have to go through this. I mean . . . maybe I should just wait for a fatal donor or—"

"That could take years," Jess protested. His voice softened and he took both her hands into his. "This is what I'm supposed to do, Emma. I've felt it in my heart since I gave you that priesthood blessing. I've prayed and fasted, and so has Tamra. It's the right thing to do, simple as that."

"But what if . . . something goes wrong, or . . ."

"It's the right thing to do," he repeated, "and we will take it on the best we can."

They both turned in surprise when Emily stood and moved quickly toward the door. "I need to be alone," was all she said before she rushed out of the room. Emma exchanged a concerned gaze with Jess before they agreed that they should just let her have the time that she'd requested.

Through the next couple of days, Emily spent a great deal of time alone, and when she was around, she just didn't seem like herself. Emma felt concerned for her, but she didn't know what to say when any inquiries were answered with, "I'm fine. Just take care of yourself and stop worrying about me."

Jess seemed terribly pleased that he would be able to give a part of himself to free Emma from the need for a lifetime of dialysis, but Emma had trouble feeling good about it. She wondered what it was that made her feel somehow unworthy of such a gift. Through much prayer and pondering, she recognized that this was the only feasible option, and that it was the right course to take. Still, she didn't particularly like it.

* * *

Scott returned home grateful beyond words to have the trip behind him. He found that all was well with the family except that Emily seemed more down than usual. And Emma was still prone to glaring at him, which he figured meant her health must be tolerable.

Over the next couple of days, Scott contemplated the situation of his occupation and the growing discomfort he felt. He engaged in some serious prayer, then a seemingly simple event occurred that made everything fall into place, and he knew what he should do. The minute he became absolutely certain it was the right course, he called his boss in the States, grateful that the timing made it possible to do so and find him at his desk and not in bed. After they shared a long, heartfelt conversation, he went to the boys' home to find Jess. He wasn't in his office, but he quickly found him upstairs talking with a member of the staff. He waited for them to finish then asked, "Can we talk? It's business."

"Sure," Jess said and they went back to Jess's office. With the door closed they sat on opposite sides of the desk. "What can I do for you?" Jess asked.

"I guess you know we lost another stable hand."

"No, I didn't, actually," Jess said, looking distressed. "Why?"

"Some family-related struggles that necessitated him moving elsewhere."

"I guess I need to learn to stop worrying about those things; you keep everything under control in that department."

"So, you think I'm doing okay with my job?" Scott asked.

"More than okay."

"In that case, I would like to forego hiring another stable hand and just take over his job—along with the one I have, of course."

Jess looked at him deeply. "What are you saying . . . exactly?"

"I'm saying that I would like to work for you full time. I hope it's okay, because I already called my boss and told him to get somebody to replace me."

"You're kidding." Jess let out a surprised chuckle.

"I'm quite serious."

"Just like that?"

"Just like that. It's not right for me anymore, Jess. I belong here. I feel it in my heart."

Jess leaned back and sighed, his expression pleasant, almost relieved. "And what did your boss say?"

"Well, he's not happy about losing me, which I guess is good for my ego. But he understands. There are plenty of eager and qualified people who would kill for my job. I agreed to do some occasional contract work for them, and to do whatever I could to help with the transition. So, if you're okay with taking me on full time, I'm your man. If not, I'll call my boss back and—"

"Not on your life," Jess said. "This is what I've wanted since the first day you got here."

"Really?" Scott asked and laughed. "Well, then I guess we could call this a win/win situation."

Jess laughed as well. "We certainly could."

Once Scott left Jess's office, he felt compelled to find Emily and tell her what he considered the good news. He'd developed a habit of sharing so much with this surrogate mother that he wondered how he had ever gotten along without her. When she wasn't in any of the usual places upstairs, he checked the kitchen and lounge room to find them empty. He wondered if she'd gone outside for some reason, then he peeked into the library and found her there. But his heart sank when he realized she was crying. With her face buried in her hands she didn't see him enter, so he closed the door somewhat loudly to alert her to his presence. She looked up startled, then outright relief showed in her face when she realized it was him. He wondered why she would prefer to be found by him as opposed to anybody else in the household. Was there something upsetting her that she was trying to keep from her children?

"Forgive me," he said. "Perhaps I should have gone away and pretended that I hadn't seen you, but . . . I couldn't."

"No, it's all right," she said, wiping at her face with a tissue. "Come, sit with me," she added, and he noted a significant pile of wadded tissues on the floor. She'd been crying long and hard.

"Do you want to talk about it?" he asked, sitting beside her.

"I don't know what to say," she said. "I'm just . . . having such a hard time with this, and I'm not sure why. I mean . . . I lost my first husband to an accident. And when Emma was born, her twin brother died right away. We lost James and Krista in that accident that nearly killed Jess, and we lost his friend Byron, who was nearly like one of my own. And then we lost Michael." She chuckled and blew her nose. "You'd think I'd be used to grief. You'd think I'd know how to handle it better than this. Through each of those experiences I cried, and mourned, and grieved, even though I did most of it behind closed doors, away from others. Eventually I found peace and was able to move on, but . . ." Her tears surfaced again. "I've tried to have faith. I just can't feel anything but . . . afraid. I'm just not prepared to lose another one of my children. I keep praying that I can have faith and just accept the Lord's will and trust in Him, but I just can't find peace in being able to let Emma go. And what if something goes wrong with Jess as a result of this? How could I bear it?" Her tears turned to sobs. "I couldn't. I just couldn't."

Scott put his arms around her and let her cry. He had always seen her as the pillar of this family, the strong and secure one. And it was likely that her family saw her the same way. But it was evident that even Emily Hamilton had a breaking point.

"I don't know what to say," he muttered. "If you don't have the answers, I certainly don't." Her crying quieted but she kept her head against his shoulder. "Your grief is understandable, Emily. I think most people would have crumbled long ago, given what you've lived through. I do believe it's true when the scriptures tell us that the Lord will not give us more than we can handle. Although I know that it doesn't feel that way at times. But I've seen evidence of how he somehow manages to give us gifts that compensate for the losses, if we remain faithful."

Following many long minutes of silence, Emily straightened her back and looked directly at him. "Thank you," she said.

"I didn't do anything," he chuckled humbly.

"Yes, you did. You just reminded me of some things that I'd lost sight of, and you've made me realize that I have been given much to compensate for my losses." She touched his face and said, "He sent me a son who needed me, but when I took you in, I had no idea how much I needed you, too."

Scott attempted to lighten the mood and divert the attention from himself. "Don't start saying things like that or you'll have me crying too."

Emily smiled and added, "You're so much like James, in a way."

"And what way is that?" Scott asked.

"He had such perfect faith. Oh, he was not beyond getting discouraged or confused at times, but eventually he would sort it out, and his answers were always right on. He just seemed to know at his very core that God was watching out for us and we were in His hands."

"And if we believe that, then we have to know that all will be well in the end."

"Yes," Emily glanced down sadly, "I don't have any trouble believing all will be well in the end. It's what we have to go through as we endure to the end that gets to me, I suppose. I know I have to keep putting one foot in front of the other, but sometimes I just feel so . . ."

"Tired?" he asked.

"Yes, tired," she admitted.

"May I share something with you?" he asked.

"Of course."

"I struggled tremendously when Callie left me because of the changes I'd made in my life to join the Church, but I kept hearing the phrase: 'faith in every footstep.' I knew it applied to the pioneer heritage of the Church, but after I'd heard it half a dozen times, I began pondering how it might apply to me. Surprisingly enough, I came to a rather firm conclusion, rather quickly."

"Tell me," she said, interest showing in her eyes.

"Well, as I understand it, the Saints left behind most of what they had to cross the plains, many of them suffering greatly, even burying loved ones in shallow graves. The sacrifices were unspeakable. We in this day and age are not asked to make such tangible sacrifices; our trials are not so black and white. Those people had a choice: either follow the prophet and go, or cling to their comforts and stay. We have a choice: either follow the prophet and keep moving forward, or cling to our comforts and stay put. For us it's not physically required to leave our homes, but perhaps it's a series of emotional sacrifices we are called upon to make. For me, I knew I had to make significant lifestyle changes if I truly hoped to progress in the gospel, because otherwise I never could have moved forward. For you it's been losing loved ones prematurely. We say that we could never have endured the hardships of the pioneers, but I wonder if they could have endured the complicated world we live in, assaulted by Satan's evil on every side. I'm certain that most of those people reached a point where they just wanted to sit down on the trail and say, 'I'm not going another step.' But somehow they kept going. For us, we don't have to literally keep walking, but we do have to keep going. And that's why we need faith in every footstep." He took hold of Emily's hand and squeezed. "I don't think you're so much lacking in faith as you're just weary. Maybe you're looking too hard for answers that are simply not ready to be given. I think if you just press forward, one step at a time, eventually the light will come through." He smiled and added, "Perhaps we each, in our own way, have to climb our metaphorical Rocky Ridge, and cross the Sweetwater, and eventually we will all reach a point where we can say, 'This is the place.'"

Emily actually smiled at him as he finished. "That's incredible," she said. "I've never heard it put quite that way before, but it makes such perfect sense."

"Well, I can't take credit for the idea. I've no doubt the Spirit has taught me all I know that's worth knowing."

"Which is the case with all of us, I'm sure. Since you mentioned the Sweetwater, may I tell you my feelings on that?"

"Please do," he said eagerly.

"Well, as I understand it, when the Saints reached the Sweetwater river, many had reached their limits; they just couldn't go any further. And that's when those brave and faithful young men showed up and carried them across the river, one at a time. I think I've had many times in my life when I just thought I couldn't go any further, and God has sent someone to carry me across the river."

While Scott was waiting for her to go on, he realized she was finished. She looked at him deeply and he wondered where her thoughts were until she said, "Thank you . . . for carrying me across this river."

Scott felt so touched that tears burned behind his eyes, but it didn't take much thought for him to admit, "You carried me across my own Sweetwater a long time ago, Emily. There is nothing I could ever do to repay the love and belonging you have given me here."

Emily let out a genuine laugh and hugged him tightly. "And here I thought I was selfishly keeping you around because you filled something in me."

Scott recalled his reason for seeking her out and said, "So, I take it you'd be okay with my staying around even more." She looked pleasantly expectant until he added, "I quit my job in Brisbane. I'm taking Jess's offer to oversee the horse operation completely."

Emily laughed as if she'd just been awarded some great prize. And Scott laughed with her. They talked a few more minutes before she noticed the time and they went together to the kitchen to find Emma and Tamra just putting supper on the table. It turned out that Emma had done most of the cooking, and when Scott complimented her, she simply said, "I learned everything I know from my father."

"He was a good cook," Tamra said. "No doubt about that."

Later in the meal Jess spilled the news about Scott's change in profession, and everyone was genuinely thrilled—except for Emma. The glare she gave him over the table threatened to turn him to stone. But he just smiled at her in return, holding her eyes firmly until she darted her gaze away. *Faith in every footstep,* he reminded himself as he turned to glance at Emily. She smiled in a way that made him wonder if she suspected his feelings for Emma. Either way, he knew she understood his heart, and as long as one woman around here did, he would make it through.

Chapter Nine

Scott wasn't certain what shifted inside of him, but sitting at breakfast on a rainy morning, he felt decidedly angry with the way Emma Hamilton glared at him. He bit back a sassy retort, knowing that acting on such feelings would get him nowhere. He tried to analyze his feelings through the day while he was in and out of the stables and seeing to his work, but he came to no firm conclusions. He only knew that while he'd felt content to just sit back and let time take its course with the hope that she'd come around one day, he now felt an urgency inside of him that if he didn't do something about it, nobody would.

After supper and a couple of typical long glares from her, he wondered if he wanted to kiss her or shake some sense into her. When the house became quiet later that evening, he found Jess in the lounge room. Needing to vent, he plopped down into a chair and sighed loudly.

"What's up?" Jess asked, peering over the top of his newspaper.

"Your sister is charming," he said with sarcasm.

"Yeah, she's been on one since she came home—that's for sure."

"Well whatever she's on, she's a heck of a lot more civil with you than she is with me."

Jess actually grinned. "Really?"

"You find that funny?"

"Maybe. What does she do?"

"She *glares* at me. She's apparently not afraid to look me right in the eye, and not embarrassed at the obvious fact that she hates me. Every time I'm in the same room with her, she just glares at me."

"What do you do?"

"I just stare back at her."

"She glares, you stare. Sounds like some ancient mating ritual."

Scott wasn't amused. "Yeah, well, I think it's more like the female spider that devours the male, if given half a chance."

Jess simply chuckled and said, "You're on your own, buddy. I hate spiders."

"Some friend you are," Scott said, only slightly serious.

Jess looked at him again and said, "Care for a late-night ride?"

"I would love it," Scott said and they headed out to the stables, pausing only long enough to let the women know where they were going. The evening air felt invigorating and Scott hoped that with any luck, a good hard ride would rid his head of Emma Hamilton.

* * *

Emma was sitting on the veranda, enjoying the night air, when she saw a couple of horses go into the stables. From the distance, through the darkness, it was impossible to tell who was riding them. But a short while later Jess and Scott approached the house, laughing like a couple of teenagers.

"Nice ride?" she asked, making them aware of her presence.

"Yes, actually," Jess said. "What are you doing up this late?"

"I couldn't sleep."

"Mind if we join you?" Jess asked.

"Count me out," Scott said tersely, then he added more kindly, "I'm exhausted; I'll see you in the morning."

"Goodnight," Jess said to Scott before he disappeared into the house. Jess sat beside Emma and put his booted feet up on the veranda rail. "So, how's it going?"

"Fine, how about you?"

"Good. How are you feeling?"

"Some days are better than others," she said. "How are you?"

"Good and strong," he said. "Just counting down the days until I can give you half of my plumbing."

"I can't wait," she said with subtle sarcasm.

"Hey," he said, "I get the impression you don't like Scott."

"Whatever gave you that idea?" she asked with the same sarcasm.

He hesitated, then said, "Just an impression."

"Well, don't bother analyzing it too deeply. It makes no difference to me if your buddy is around constantly."

Jess's tone became defensive. "It makes a difference to me if you are rude to him."

"I have no idea what you're talking about," Emma said and went into the house. The last thing she wanted to do was talk about Scott Ivie.

The following day Emma returned from her treatment and went straight to the upstairs hall of the house. It was large and spacious and unnaturally elegant in contrast to the rest of the house. The room was empty beyond an entertainment system in the corner, and a few chairs placed along the walls. The room was often used for dancing during family social events—at least if Jess was in attendance. Emma and her sisters had often exercised in this room. At the moment she wished she had the energy to do some serious aerobic dancing. Perhaps it would release some of this nervous energy she felt. And maybe it would get Scott Ivie out of her head. Even though she felt pretty good at the moment, she knew her energy levels were far from optimum. Still, she found a particular song that, for some reason, she'd found running through her head. It was the only song on that particular CD that she really liked, so she programmed the machine to play that song over and over, then she turned the stereo up loud and laid down in the middle of the floor, feeling the high-energy beat move through the floor. She was grateful to know that Tamra had the children outside and no one was trying to sleep; otherwise she would have needed to keep the volume down.

Emma closed her eyes and began to relax, as if the music itself gave an outlet for her frustrations. As the repeating lyrics began to penetrate her conscious mind she realized why this song had been sticking with her. At first her brain refused to admit that the words expressed how she really felt, but after she'd listened to the song more than a dozen times, she finally had to accept that she *did* feel that way. And it made her angry. *Why* did she have to feel that way about someone who had moved in and taken over the household in her absence? Scott Ivie was too good to be true, plain and simple. And she simply couldn't believe that he was really what he let on. When the thought crossed her mind that perhaps he *was* what he appeared to be, and the problem was more with her, she quickly brushed it aside, not willing to even consider the possibility.

"Is this the only song we own?" Jess shouted, startling her.

Emma opened her eyes to see him standing above her, his hands on his hips.

"Yes!" she shouted back. "If you touch it I will hurt you."

"Paula Abdul is good, but . . ." She glared at him and he changed his tone. "You like this song, I take it."

"Right now I do."

"That's apparent. The whole household knows it quite well now, and this is a pretty big house."

"You know what?" she shouted. "I don't care!"

She expected him to scold her about the obvious anger she was feeling, but he only held out his hand toward her. "What?" she demanded.

"Let's dance," he said and she knew what that meant. Jess had dearly loved his college dance classes, and he prided himself on knowing all the classic steps. Dancing with him was like a carnival ride, and she just didn't have the energy or the desire for that much fun.

"I don't have the strength to dance," she snarled. "Why do you think I'm lying on the floor?"

"We'll take it easy," he said. "You're supposed to exercise. Come on."

Emma scowled at her brother and put her hand into his. He helped her to her feet and easily guided her into the swing, but he did it with a halftime beat, moving slowly and without expending the high energy that he usually did.

"There, that's not so bad," he said and laughed. He led her through a haphazard tango and made her laugh.

"Hey," Jess said loud enough to be heard above the music, "I think we could do the lip-sync thing; I've about got this song down pat."

"Okay, go for it," she said, taken back to childhood memories that were a pleasant distraction. Jess had been the king of lip-syncing other people's music during his youth, and Emma being his baby sister, filled with hero worship, had quickly taken up the habit right along with him. It was something they'd done together countless times just for the laughs. They had come up with some pretty silly dance moves they could do in perfect synchronization, and within a few seconds they were moving side by side like Gladys Knight and the Pips. She was careful to keep her movements low key so she didn't tire herself, but she had to admit she was having fun. As she and Jess turned to face each other, mouthing the words with intensity, she actually felt some of her pent-up frustration coming out.

Scott followed the sound of loud music and found his way to the upstairs hall. He leaned in the doorway from the hall that led to his room and thoroughly enjoyed watching Jess and Emma put on a performance that he considered pretty impressive. He could tell they were holding back, likely for the sake of Emma's poor health, but the intensity and accuracy with which they mouthed that song made it impossible for him to keep from smiling. He recognized the song as one he'd always liked. *Straight Up,* it was called; he knew that from a time when he'd regularly heard it on the radio, but he couldn't remember the name of the female artist. But it certainly had an effect with Emma Hamilton pretending to sing it. He folded his arms over his chest, wishing he'd brought his camera.

Scott enjoyed himself so thoroughly that he was startled when the lyrics of the chorus jumped from Emma's lips into his heart. Could it be possible that his ongoing prayers for some measure of hope would be answered through this seemingly insignificant song? Still, he couldn't deny what he felt when he heard the words, *Straight up now tell me do you really wanna love me forever . . . Straight up now tell me is it gonna be you and me together, or are you just having fun?* He wanted to just stand there and listen to the entire song again, and absorb the way it made him feel, but he saw Emma catch his eye and her entire countenance fell the same moment his heart did.

When Emma caught a glimpse of Scott leaning in the doorway to one of the halls, her heart quickened. She almost hated him for the effect he had on her. Embarrassed beyond belief, Emma turned her back abruptly, but she didn't want her brother to pick up on her animosity and give him something to drill her about. She took hold of Jess's hand to go back to their dancing, but as he turned her around he caught sight of Scott and hollered, "Hey, Scotty. Join the party."

Oh, that's just great, Emma silently responded with sarcasm, but she kept her expression steady. Scott grinned and sauntered toward them while they were engaged in a slow, easy version of the swing.

She was startled when Scott stood beside Jess and easily imitated his steps. The men began to laugh but Emma felt thoroughly uncomfortable. She tried to let go of Jess's hands but he held them tightly, even as she said, "I don't have the energy to dance with one man, let alone two."

"Ah, you need a *little* exercise," Jess said. And then she wanted to physically throttle her brother as he put one of her hands into Scott's, and the next thing she knew she was dancing with him. She figured she had two choices. She could turn and leave and have her brother calling her a liar according to last night's conversation, and demanding to know what was going on, or she could endure this little dance with Scott Ivie and be done with it.

When he smoothly guided her into a tango and it became evident that Scott knew what he was doing, Emma said, "Don't tell me you have this in common with my brother as well. You're a little too much like him."

"There's one big difference," Scott said and Emma was glad that Jess had moved to a chair, out of hearing range.

"What's that?"

Scott wasn't sure where this sudden burst of confidence had come from, but he was quick to say, "You *like* your brother."

"We're related," she countered quickly.

"So, if we were related you would be more tolerant of me?"

"If we were related I would *expect* you to be living in my home."

He actually smiled and she hated him. "Well, you know what, Sister Hamilton, I have no desire to be your brother."

The song ended and Emma tried to move away but he held her hands tightly, whispering while the room was silent for only a few seconds before the song began again, "Sing it to me."

Emma felt momentarily baffled, but for reasons she could never explain, she found it easy to look into his eyes and mouth the words. She realized then that she had become well accustomed to looking into his eyes, and having him look straight back at her. He held one of her hands in his, and another around her back, barely moving in a simple two-step, while she silently propelled the words at him. Realizing that she'd been thinking of him while she'd absorbed the lyrics earlier, the experience suddenly felt completely surreal.

Lost in a dream. I don't know which way to go. Let me say that if you are all that you seem, then baby I'm moving way too slow . . . Let me say that I keep getting chills when I think your love is true . . . Straight up now, tell me do you really wanna love me forever?

Through a brief musical interim, he spun her gently and she panicked to realize that Jess had left the room. Ooh, when she saw her brother again . . .

The turning stopped but her head kept spinning, a sensation that became intensified when she felt Scott's lips close to her ear, saying in a husky voice, "Do you want me to tell you, straight up?"

She briefly felt a heart-pumping elation at the implication, but she replaced it so quickly with her habitual anger that the blood rushed from her head. Everything went blurry, then black. The last thing she remembered was Scott's arms tightening around her as he said, "Whoa," in a panicked voice.

Emma came awake to hear the same song still playing. She forced her eyes to focus and saw Scott's face close to hers, looking concerned. While she attempted to orient herself to her surroundings, she heard the words reverberate through the room, *I keep getting chills when I think your love is true.* A chill rushed over her as if to echo the idea.

"You okay?" he asked and she realized she was lying on the floor. He had one hand beneath her head and the other against her face, and surprisingly enough, she felt no desire to protest. But the music suddenly felt too loud and annoying—with lyrics that hit far too close to points inside of her she didn't want to look at.

"Could you . . . turn the music off?" she asked, squeezing her eyes closed again in an effort to be free of a hovering dizzy sensation.

He carefully laid her head back on the floor and a moment later the room became eerily still except for the sound of his boots on the wood floor as he walked back toward her. She actually felt relieved when he lifted her head again. He sat on the floor and set her head in his lap, absently pushing her hair back from her face.

"Are you going to be all right?" he asked.

"I think so," she muttered without opening her eyes.

"Should I be getting some help or—"

"No!" she insisted, then more quietly, "I don't want them to worry. I'll be fine. I think I just overdid it."

Emma became distracted by the feel of his fingers as they continued to move over her face and into her hair, as if he had a right to do so.

But in this barely coherent state, she found that she actually liked it. His touch was soothing, his nearness somehow secure. She chose not to think about the anger she felt toward him, and simply enjoy the moment, almost wanting to prolong the need to let her head settle.

She finally opened her eyes and shifted her head to look up at him, not surprised—but somehow annoyed—by the way her heart quickened and her mouth went dry. With a subtle smirk he said, "Whatever you're remembering I said or did that ticked you off, I want you to know you were only dreaming."

"If only you could be so lucky," she said.

"If only," he added with sarcasm.

"I think I can stand up now," she said, lifting her head.

Scott didn't want to admit to his disappointment as she moved away from him and attempted to stand. But she teetered as soon as she got to her feet and he quickly shot his arm around her to hold her steady. He loved having her so close, and the simple feeling of having her need him was absolutely incredible.

He helped her back to her room and to her bed. "I'm sure I'll be fine once I rest," she said while he resisted the urge to kiss her, right here and now.

"Is there anything I can get for you?"

"No, thank you," she said without looking at him. "You've been very kind," she added as if she begrudged it.

Scott walked toward the door until she said, "You won't tell anyone, will you? I don't want them to worry."

"Should they be worried?" he asked, not wanting to ignore something that could be detrimental to her health.

"No, of course not. It's happened before. I just . . . overdid it."

Scott left the room, using every ounce of self-discipline to keep himself from falling to his knees and begging her to believe that he was a decent human being. The following day he was pleased to see her up and about, and he wasn't surprised by her cool indifference toward him. Three days later she had taken up her old habit of glaring at him whenever he entered a room. She'd apparently had time to forget the somewhat tender moment they had shared. But at least he felt some degree of hope. He believed there was something inside of Emma that, with some prodding, just might come around.

* * *

Emma knew she didn't dare attempt to ride, especially on her own. And everyone was so busy. But she felt compelled to go to the stables and took it upon herself to curry one of her favorite mares, talking quietly to her as she went about the chore. She turned when she heard someone enter the stable, and she quickly ducked back into the shadows when she realized it was Scott. He was wearing attire similar to that her father and brothers had always worn to ride, and she gave that reason the credit for her quickened heart. She watched him discreetly as he bridled and saddled a stallion with ease. Watching him gracefully mount and move the horse forward with natural expertise, she felt something stir inside of her that she didn't want to admit to, but couldn't deny.

Once he was gone, Emma returned to her chore, inwardly cursing this man for being in her life at all. She was barely finished when he returned and dismounted, and she wondered why he couldn't have chosen to take a *long* ride, today of all days.

Emma moved toward the door just as he dismounted, figuring it was best to just leave as quickly as possible.

"Hello," he said brightly.

She nodded but said nothing.

"How are you feeling?" he asked but she pretended not to hear him. She simply wasn't prepared to have him take a giant step toward her, taking her arm into a firm grip. "Is it so difficult to answer a simple question?" he asked.

Emma looked up at him, attempting a well-practiced glare, but she found his face so close to hers that her head started to spin. Her heart quickened and what little blood she seemed to have in her head suddenly drained away.

Emma emerged from the blackness to find Scott Ivie sitting on the ground, holding her in his arms. He smiled as if he found the situation pleasant, and she couldn't find the will to protest. She closed her eyes to pretend that she was attempting to gain her bearings, when in reality she found it difficult to look at him while he was holding her at such a disadvantage. "I could swear you enjoy this," she said.

"Certain aspects of it, yes."

"You just enjoy seeing me helpless," she growled. "Either that or you like seeing me make a fool of myself."

"As far as admitting what exactly I enjoy about this, I think it would be wise for me to stand on the fifth amendment."

Emma attempted to sit up slowly. "Are you going to be all right?" he asked.

"Of course," she said, but as she attempted to get to her feet she teetered and would have fallen if he'd not been there to hold her up.

"Yes, of course," he said with sarcasm. "Why don't you let me help you get to the house before you—"

"No, I'm fine," she insisted, pulling away and teetering again.

"You're proud and stubborn, is what you are." Scott pulled her into his arms and carried her toward the house, laughing when she called him an arrogant boor.

"You're making a scene," she said when he ignored her protests to put her down. "Everybody and their dog will know you did this and . . . oh, my gosh. With any luck my family won't be looking out the window and they will never know. You've got to promise you won't tell my family. They'll just worry and get upset."

"I most certainly will tell your family," he said in a voice that stopped any argument she might come up with. "I'm worried and upset and I don't want to be that way alone. I'm not going to ignore something like this and have you fall over and die because we neglected to do anything about it."

Emma growled at him but said nothing as he carried her into the house, setting her down on a kitchen chair just as Emily turned from the stove to observe with wide eyes.

"What happened?" she demanded.

"She just passed out . . . again," Scott said. "She insists that it's nothing. I'm not so sure. I'll leave you to deal with the little imp."

"What did you call me?" Emma snarled as he walked toward the door.

"I'm sorry? Did you say something?" he asked, turning back toward her. His exaggerated innocence turned to a smirk before he left the room.

As soon as the side door of the house closed, Emma made a growling noise and said, "He really didn't have to tell you that. I told him you would just worry and get upset."

"Perhaps I have good cause to be worried."

"It only happens when he's around. He's like some kind of a curse." Emily smiled and Emma demanded, "What?" Emily positively grinned and her concern seemed completely absent. "What?" Emma insisted more loudly.

"This wouldn't have anything to do with a quickened heart rate and blood rushing from your head, would it?"

Emma glared at her, missing the point. "Well, that is what usually precedes someone passing out."

"And with most women, they have enough strength to withstand such an effect when a man they're attracted to walks into a room." Emma made a scoffing noise but couldn't find any words to protest that wouldn't make her look like a fool. "It certainly happened to me when I fell in love with your father," Emily added.

"I am not in love with him," Emma insisted. "He's arrogant and obnoxious."

Emily actually laughed. "If that's what you think, then we're not talking about the same man."

"Or maybe he's just on his best behavior when he's around you," Emma suggested, coming to her feet, grateful that her head felt steady.

"He's lived in our home for several months, Emma. No one is on some false best behavior that much. Credit me with more discernment than that."

Emma decided she hated this conversation and rushed out of the room, but she definitely heard her mother chuckle before she got to the foot of the stairs.

The following afternoon Emma returned from getting her treatment, very much looking forward to going riding with Jess. His offer had been an attempt to make peace with her after she'd laid into him for leaving her alone with Scott in the upstairs hall. Feeling rather well, she hurried to change into her riding attire and went to the stable, praying that Jess would be there, and that Scott Ivie would be nowhere around. When she walked in and saw exactly the opposite of what she'd been hoping for, she cursed inwardly. She considered turning her back and leaving to go find Jess, but he looked up and saw her before she could slip away.

Scott looked up to see Emma enter the stable and his heart skipped a beat. She was wearing an adorable pair of riding breeches and classic, well-worn boots, and a white shirt topped with a tapestry-front vest.

"Hello," he said, wondering if she would blatantly ignore him as she'd done yesterday.

"Hello," she replied.

"May I help you with something?"

"I'm meeting Jess here," she said. "Thank you." Emma moved toward the closest horse in its stall and began patting its nose, if only to distract herself from his presence. She gasped when she realized he had moved close beside her.

"You know," he said, his voice low and husky, "I think if you stopped to figure out why you're angry with me, you might realize that you're not really angry with me at all."

"I have no idea what you're talking about," she insisted, raising her eyes to throw him the usual glare. And then she felt it. That same old heart-racing, lightheaded feeling that happened whenever he was close by. If she'd been sitting down she'd have stuck her head between her knees. As it was, she could only recall her mother's laughter before she passed out.

Her next awareness was hearing Scott say, "You're getting pretty good at this."

"It only happens when you're around," she said, hoping he'd get the point of how angry he made her.

But he laughed and said, "I had no idea I affected you so deeply."

Emma looked up at him and found herself wondering if her mother was right. The very idea seemed so ludicrous, but feeling her heart quicken all over again, she couldn't help but ponder the idea, if only for a moment. The way his eyes delved into hers left her feeling weak and strong, hot and cold, helpless and powerful, all at the same time.

Scott watched Emma's eyes almost glaze over, as if she were intoxicated. Perhaps being barely conscious made her briefly forget how much she hated him. Whatever the reason, he couldn't deny that he enjoyed these moments. He was waiting for her to snap out of it and say something rude when she said in a voice that was almost tender, "Tell me."

"Tell you what?" he asked, certain she was delirious.

"The first time this happened, the last thing I remember you saying to me before I blacked out was, 'Do you went me to tell you, straight up?' So, the answer is yes, I want you to tell me."

Scott was so taken aback that he could hardly put together a coherent thought. He tried to recall what he'd been thinking and feeling at the time. Sensing her impatience, but needing more time to contemplate his answer, he said, "It had something to do with that silly song, but I'm afraid the lyrics aren't quite so fresh in my mind now as they were then."

He could see in her eyes that she remembered the lyrics well, but she didn't want to discuss them. She looked away and closed her eyes. In spite of what he wanted to tell her, he went with his deeper instincts and said, "Tell you what, Sister Hamilton, I'll answer the question, straight up, when you can look me in the eye without glaring at me and ask me a question that makes sense."

She made a noise of frustration and said, "You are positively the most arrogant man I have ever known."

Scott actually laughed, which he sensed made her angry. Still, she kept her head in his lap, and her hand tightly holding to his arm. He decided against pointing out her hypocrisy in moments when she needed someone to scrape her up off the ground. Instead, he just enjoyed the moment while it lasted.

Emma was back on her feet before Jess arrived. Listening to the men's conversation while they saddled the horses, she was hoping beyond hope that Scott would say nothing about her fainting again. Jess was helping Emma mount when Scott said, "Keep an eye on her. If she passes out again, you'll be the only one there to scrape her up."

"Again?" Jess echoed, glaring at Emma.

"I'm just fine," she said and trotted out the main stable door.

"Your sister grows more charming by the day," Scott said to Jess, who frowned and rode out, quickly following Emma. Scott moved to the doorway and watched them go, deciding he'd had about enough of this game she was playing. He could only hope that confronting her would do more than make her more angry. That's just what he needed, to scorn a woman who already considered herself scorned. If only he could figure out why.

* * *

Emma stepped out onto the veranda and leaned against one of the posts. She sighed and looked up at the black sky, littered with stars that looked close enough to touch. She was almost beginning to relax when a voice from the darkness startled her. "Hello there, Sister Hamilton. A fine night, is it not?"

"It is," she said, glancing at him only long enough to see that he was leaning back in a chair, shadowed by the darkness, his booted feet stacked on the veranda rail.

She said nothing more and the silence became thick. While she was searching for words to preface her escape, he said, "Perhaps you should join me. The view is marvelous."

"I'm well accustomed to the view, Mr. Ivie," she said, taking a step toward the door to go back in the house.

"Yet, you're looking at it now," he said. "So I must assume that your apparent desire to *not* enjoy the view any longer would be due to the prospective company."

Emma couldn't keep the defensiveness out of her voice. "I had the desire to be alone."

She could feel his eyes boring into her, even though she couldn't see them. She could almost imagine him calling her a liar. Certain that even he would not be so bold, she was taken aback when he said, "Forgive me, Sister Hamilton, but I would bet a month's wage that if any other member of this household were sitting here, you would take up a chair and make yourself comfortable."

Emma's heart quickened when she couldn't deny within herself that he was right. She was grateful that he couldn't see her expression any more than she could see his. She searched for some clever retort but came up empty. When the silence grew too long, he finally said, "Maybe it's time we cleared the air between us, don't you think? And don't think you can imply that your coldness is my imagination. I'm not so stupid that I can't see the stark difference in the way you treat others, as opposed to the way you treat me. So if I've done something to wrong you, Sister Hamilton, I would truly like to know about it, because I have racked my brain trying to come up with an answer.

Was I not proper enough with you at Temple Square? Was my enthusiasm over our conversation inappropriate? Or perhaps my delivery of German pastries lacked some degree of finesse. Beyond that we had no encounter until you returned home, and that chip was on your shoulder the minute I walked in the door and saw you there. Given *that* little piece of evidence, I'm having to assume that you have some aversion to my presence here, period. Did I do something wrong, Sister Hamilton? Where is my offense? Tell me and be done with it."

Emma leaned her shoulder against the pole and looked out over the darkened lawn. She didn't like this conversation, but as long as they were having it, she concluded that she had to be honest. "Well, if you must know," she said curtly, "when I gave you my brother's email address, I was not expecting you to move in with him."

Scott swallowed carefully and counted to ten. "Allow me to clarify your meaning, Sister Hamilton. Are you implying then that I'm some kind of freeloader? Is that the kind of man you think I am? Are you assuming I took one look at this beautiful estate and thought, 'Oh, I could get free rent if I play my cards right?' Is that it?"

Emma felt internally mortified to realize he had pegged her thoughts very accurately, and to hear them spoken out loud that way made them sound so horrible. She said nothing.

"Your silence implies that you agree with me," he said, his voice picking up an edge. "So, if it's all right with you, I'll just clarify a few things. One of us ought to say *something*. The truth, Sister Hamilton, is that your brother begged me to come for a visit, and then begged me to stay. Your mother was quite emphatic, as well. It was their idea that I stay indefinitely. I offered to pay rent. In fact, I practically threatened Jess with it, but he wouldn't have it. I don't know whether it means anything to you or not, but knowing you served a mission, I have to believe that you would understand what I'm telling you when I say that I fasted and prayed about the decision to stay here, and I knew beyond any doubt that it was right. I am not here because I found a good deal on room and board. I am perfectly capable of providing for myself and have done so for many years, quite abundantly, in truth. I am here because I believe the Lord wants me to be here, and for the first time in my life I almost feel like I belong to a real family. The *almost* would come from the fact that *you* glare at me every time we're in a room together, which is only slightly better than the absolute indifference you show to me otherwise. So, now you know where I stand. You can take my word for it, or we could have a little trial and drag all of the facts out and spread them on the table. You could take a look at my bank statements, if you'd like. I could show you my paycheck stubs. You could cross-examine your brother . . . your mother, or maybe—"

"Okay, I think that's enough, Mr. Ivie."

"Enough for what?" he countered. "Enough to get you to stop glaring at me?"

"Goodnight, Mr. Ivie," she said tersely and went into the house.

"That went well," Scott said with sarcasm, and the darkness gave no answer. He resisted the urge to curse aloud and instead went for a walk around the house to ease to some degree this intense frustration that had nowhere to go.

Chapter Ten

Emma told herself she just needed to go to bed, but she doubted that sleep would be possible with the way her thoughts were churning. She went instead to the library in search of something to read. She was scanning the long shelves of books when her eye caught an unfamiliar album sitting close by. She opened the front cover and was immediately intrigued to see photos of her family members that must have been taken while she was on her mission. She ended up sitting on the couch, engrossed with the album for nearly an hour, marveling at the beauty of the photos, and their distinct artistic quality. She felt touched and amazed at how well they captured her loved ones in comfortable settings, acting naturally, talking and laughing. And her home and its beautiful surroundings were captured equally well. Turning the last page, she noticed a card tucked there. She opened it to read, "Here is my thesis of what a real family looks like. Thanks for including me in yours. With love, Scott."

Emma gasped aloud when she read the name, then she glanced through the pictures again, trying to imagine these beautiful photos as being seen through his eyes. Abruptly she set the album aside and hurried upstairs, praying that her mother hadn't yet gone to sleep. She was relieved to see light shining from beneath her bedroom door. After knocking at the door, she found Emily sitting up in bed, reading.

"Hello, dear," Emily said brightly, patting the bed beside her to indicate that Emma should sit down. "What's up? You look . . . glum."

Emma sat on the edge of the bed, then she lifted her feet and moved her head to her mother's shoulder. "What is it?" Emily asked more tenderly, putting a gentle arm around her.

Emma knew she could skirt the issue and avoid it. Her mother would give her some tender loving care and they could both go to sleep. Or could she? It was doubtful. Something deep inside lured Emma to believe that the time for skirting and avoiding the issue was over. She was being faced with real life, and Scott Ivie was there every time she turned around, confusing and upsetting her. She finally just forced the words out, "Mr. Ivie just had some strong words for me."

"Really?" Emily said, almost sounding pleased. "And what did he say?"

Emma repeated the gist of the conversation, followed by her reasons for feeling hesitant and mistrusting. Emily listened, then asked, "And what's *really* the problem, dear?"

"What do you mean?"

"What is it about him that makes you have such animosity?"

"I have animosity, all right. He's arrogant and obnoxious and he drives me crazy."

"Emma," Emily said in a gentle voice that got her attention, "listen to me when I tell you that Scott Ivie is one of the most spiritual, honest, and decent men I have ever known. And I have difficulty understanding how you can only see characteristics in him that no one else in this household has ever seen even a hint of."

"I don't know," Emma growled, sitting up straight.

"Oh, I think you know. You just don't want to admit it aloud. Or maybe you haven't quite let it into your conscious brain. But I believe if you think about it for a minute, you'll realize that you know."

Emma shook her head. "How do you do that? How do you manage to be practically psychic sometimes?"

"Only with my own children," she said. "And it's not psychic. I just know my children well enough to know how they think. Stop avoiding the subject and answer the question."

Emma thought about it long and hard, and her mother gave her the silence to do so. When the answer occurred to her, she realized that a part of her had known from the first time they'd met on Temple Square. And it scared her. Is that why she had stuffed the knowledge deep into the musty recesses of her brain?

"Well?" Emily finally said.

"I think he's in love with me, Mother."

While Emma expected some reaction of surprise or astonishment, or perhaps even concern, Emily just smiled and said, "Very much in love with you, I believe."

"But . . ."

"But what?"

"There are so many buts I don't know where to begin."

"Try."

"Well . . . what if he's not the right one for me?"

"And what if he is?" Emily asked in a voice that was quiet and intent. "Are you willing to risk losing the right one because of some silly fears that really have nothing to do with him?"

All of Emma's other questions fizzled. Her mother was right. And what else mattered if a man was truly the right one for her? The possibility seemed so incredible that she could hardly entertain it. Emily added in a gentle voice, "I know the situation in your life is not ideal, but if a man truly loves you, anything else is workable. You must get beyond the reasons that you're holding back and pushing him away." She smiled and added, "I fear you are slamming the door in his face before he's even had a chance to knock on it."

Emma hated the analogy, mostly because it was completely accurate. She was still contemplating it when Emily went on to say, "Trust me when I tell you that life is too brief and too precious to waste it with poor communication and trite contention. I know you're concerned about your health problems, but not one of us knows what the span of our life will be. No matter how long or short your life may be, Emma, you've got to take hold of life and live it; live it while you can. Live life to its fullest. Enjoy every moment." She paused and dabbed at tears gathering in her eyes. "I've had much cause for joy in my life, Emma. I love my children and grandchildren, and I've had many wonderful experiences. But there is nothing—*nothing*—so wonderful as the love of a good man. And he *is* a good man."

"You really think so?"

"No man is perfect, honey, but if nothing else, having him live in our home has allowed us to see him outside his best behavior. I consider myself a discerning person, and I have no reason to believe that he is not everything he lets on to be. You need to discern for yourself. The Spirit will guide you, and you'll know what's best. But first you have to let him into your heart."

"Scott or the Spirit?"

"Both."

Emma wasn't certain why she started to cry, but once the tears let loose, there was no holding them back. A torrent of emotion that she'd kept bottled inside of her suddenly refused to be held back any longer. Emily held her while she cried, whispering words of comfort and smoothing her hair with a gentle hand.

"What is it?" Emily asked when she had calmed somewhat.

Emma was surprised at the words that came to her tongue, when there had been so many different thoughts tumbling through her mind. She'd gotten beyond the pride of holding her feelings back, and simply let the words spill on a fresh bout of tears. "I've dreamed my whole life of what it would be like when I found the right man. And in he walks when I felt positively more sick and ugly than I've ever felt in my whole life. I'm not naive enough to believe that real life is going to compare to our fantasies, but this . . . this . . . is so . . . horrible and pathetic. You would think I'd be entitled to a little romance."

Emily hugged Emma tightly then looked into her eyes, wiping the tears from her face. "Listen to me, darling. I have come to learn that true romance is not the sentimental idealism we see in movies. After my first husband died, your father showed up on my front porch on a day when I looked horrible, I felt horrible, the house was horrible; I felt mortified. But given some time I realized that he hadn't given any of that a second thought. He'd come to see *me,* and he was willing to give all that he had to help me through my struggles. There's nothing more romantic than that. And through the years I have learned that true romance is when a man can look at you at your worst and still see the woman he loves. True romance is mutual respect, commitment, and trust—especially in the face of life's challenges. And I think if you get past the fears and delusions you're struggling with, I think you might just find some pretty powerful romance staring you in the face."

Emma looked hard into her mother's eyes, as if she could perceive a deeper layer of what Emily was trying to tell her. She felt her heart quicken and the blood rushed from her head. She quickly put her head down to keep from passing out, then she realized that this physical reaction usually had something to do with Scott Ivie.

Hearing her mother laugh softly, she demanded, "What's so funny?"

"Do you realize what you just said?"

"What did I say?"

"You admitted that you had found the right one."

Emma lifted her head slowly, not wanting to pass out. She scowled at her mother and tried to remember what, exactly, she *had* said. Emily just smiled and helped her out, "You said that you'd waited your whole life to find the right man, and when he walked in you were feeling sick and ugly." Emily touched Emma's face and her expression softened with compassion. "And in my personal opinion, I think that's what most of this has been about. I suspect you felt something right from the start, but with everything else that was going on, you just weren't prepared to feel it, or to know what to do with it. But eventually our heads have a way of catching up with our hearts."

Emma lay awake far into the night while her mother's words rumbled through her mind. She knew what she had to do, and it would have to begin with eating some crow. With any luck, Scott Ivie would prove to be a forgiving and patient man.

* * *

Scott was grateful to avoid Emma at breakfast. Her mother reported that she had slept in, and that was fine with him. But he nearly resented the sleep she was apparently getting, when he hadn't slept at all.

Feeling too uptight to even attempt getting to work that could wait anyway, Scott went straight to the stable. He eased the fine stallion out of his stall and set to work currying him. He didn't know why he found the ritual so soothing, but he did. And given that he was still in a foul mood over last night's encounter with Emma, he couldn't think of any better way to calm down and soothe his nerves.

Hearing noises behind him, he just proceeded with his self-appointed task, certain it was one of the hired hands going about his business—until a feminine voice broke the air.

"Good morning, Brother Ivie," Emma said.

"Sister Hamilton," he said without so much as glancing her direction.

He heard her sigh loudly. "I believe I owe you an apology."

When she said nothing more, he said, "I'm listening."

"Would you mind looking at me while I talk?" she asked curtly. "Otherwise I have to wonder if you really *are* listening."

Scott stopped what he was doing and turned slowly, hating the way his heart quickened just to see her. She was wearing a crinkly skirt, full of gathers, that hung almost to the top of her bare feet. She was beautiful and he almost hated her for it. He reminded himself that she had just told him she was prepared to apologize, but he was in no mood to hear patronizing words that would likely change nothing.

"I'm listening," he repeated, folding his arms over his chest. His first clue that something was different came when he saw something soft and humble in her eyes before they turned downward. His heart quickened as what he saw there reminded him of the girl he'd met in Salt Lake City. Perhaps last night's conversation had done some good after all.

Emma lifted her chin and looked straight at this man who had consumed her thoughts since the first time she'd laid eyes on him. And he'd confused her mind and invaded her heart since she'd come home to find that he'd become a part of her family. She took a deep breath and forced herself to just say what she'd come to say.

"First of all," she said firmly, "there are no excuses for my behavior, therefore I won't try to excuse it. Reasons perhaps, but no excuses. With that in mind, I simply want to say that I'm sorry. I apologize for jumping to conclusions and making silly assumptions. And while I was so caught up in being angry over my false conclusions and assumptions, I didn't bother to consider how ridiculous they were. So, thank you for pointing out what I was apparently too dense to figure out myself. I hope that you will forgive me, and . . . well, I was really hoping that we could just start over."

When he said nothing, didn't even move, Emma stepped forward and held out her hand. "Hello," she said, "I'm Emma Hamilton, Jess's sister." Still he said nothing and she added, "And you are?"

Emma's nervousness merged into a delightful kind of fear as she watched something intense fill his eyes. He tossed the curry comb to the ground and looked at her hand before he lifted his eyes back to hers and took her fingers tentatively between his. "I'm just a man. Nobody important."

"According to whose opinion?" she asked.

"Nobody's opinion really matters to me—except yours."

"Why is that?" she asked, feeling herself tremble from the inside out. The tremor finally made it to her hand and he glanced at it suddenly as if to question its sudden shaking. He slowly drew her hand to his lips and pressed a lingering kiss there, while his eyes remained glued to hers. When the kiss was finished he didn't let go of her hand. When she tugged gently to remove it, he only tightened his grasp.

"Before I answer that question," he said, his voice almost husky, "I want to know the reasons."

"What?" She felt confused.

"You said there were reasons; no excuses, just reasons. I want to know what they are."

Emma felt flustered and incapable of putting a coherent thought together. She forced her eyes away from his if only to clear her head. But even then, his hold on her hand, his very nearness, left her rattled. Still, she couldn't help noticing that she didn't feel like she was going to faint. She hoped that was a good sign.

"Okay," she finally said, "but . . . could we go someplace else?" She glanced over her shoulder. "Someplace where the hired hands won't be coming and going?"

"Sure," he said, finally letting go of her hand. "Did you want to walk, or should I saddle some horses?" Glancing at her bare feet and the skirt she was wearing, he added, "Or we could go the twenty-first century way and get in the car."

Emma felt tempted to back down and tell him they could talk later. She knew what she *wanted* to do, but habit tempted her to be reserved and cautious. She reminded herself of her mother's advice to live life to its fullest, and to enjoy every moment. One of her favorite excerpts from her great-grandmother's journals came to mind. A quick examination of what her heart was telling her finally pushed the words out of her mouth. "That horse will do just fine."

Scott glanced over his shoulder to the stallion he'd been currying. His heart quickened at the implication, but he wasn't about to make assumptions or take anything for granted. He looked back at Emma and asked, "And which horse would you like me to saddle for *you?*"

"That one will do fine . . . for both of us," she said. "There's plenty of room."

Scott couldn't hold back a smile, and he was pleased to see her smile in return as he turned to retrieve an appropriate saddle.

Emma watched him efficiently saddle the horse and felt something quiver inside of her. It was such a thoroughly masculine task, even though she was fairly adept at it herself. Still, it seemed a man could always tighten the straps more easily, and watching Scott do just that stirred something in her. He was obviously very comfortable with the task.

When the saddle was secure, Scott motioned her toward the horse. She stepped past him and put one of her bare feet into the stirrup, deftly swinging herself onto the horse's back. Her skirt hiked up to just below her knees, spreading out around her with little difficulty.

Emma moved forward in the saddle and put her hands on the horn, leaving the stirrups empty for him. Her heart threatened to beat out of her chest when he mounted behind her, reaching around her to take hold of the reins.

"Where to?" Scott asked, resisting the urge to pinch himself, just to be certain this wasn't a dream. He'd had fantasies like this, although he'd never begun to imagine how being this close to her might actually feel.

"Just go . . . toward the mountains. I know a place with a great view."

Emma became suddenly breathless as Scott heeled the stallion across the open meadow. She'd galloped this meadow countless times in her life, but never had it been so exhilarating. As he moved the horse into the foothills, she told him directions, which were the only words they exchanged.

Scott almost felt tempted to hold the horse back and make him go more slowly. He wanted this experience to last forever. Surrounded by mountain air and the fragrance of her clean hair so close to his face, he felt somehow closer to heaven. He liked the way his arms brushed hers as he maneuvered the reins, and he loved the feel of having her encircled in his care. It felt right and good and he wanted it to never end.

He became so caught up in absorbing her nearness that he was surprised when she said, "Okay, we're here." He halted the stallion and realized they were on a plateau ridge. He looked one direction to see the mountain rising behind them, and the other to see the valley below, where the station was completely visible, with the stables, the house, and boys' home all scattered among clusters of ancient trees.

"Extraordinary," Scott muttered as he dismounted and tethered the horse to a sturdy bush. He took another long look at the view before he turned to Emma and held out a hand to help her down.

"Uh . . ." she said, "I don't know that the terrain is suitable for bare feet."

Scott didn't hesitate a moment before he pulled her down from the horse and carried her to a large, somewhat flat—albeit lopsided—rock that just happened to be partially shaded this time of day.

Emma couldn't hold back a little laugh at the weightlessness she felt in Scott's arms. He set her on the shaded part of the rock before he sat beside her, propping his arms up on his knees.

Following a few minutes of silence, Scott felt the reality of the tension between them descend again. He reminded himself that she had apologized back at the stable, and with any luck, they were on the right track. Hoping to open the conversation back up, he said, "Is this not private enough for you, Sister Hamilton?"

"It's plenty private," she said, glancing toward him. "I'm just trying to remember what exactly you wanted to know."

"The reasons," he said. And when the silence continued he added, "The reasons you've been glaring at me."

Emma took a deep breath and reminded herself to stay calm and focused. He had good reason to be brusque and defensive; she'd been unkind and she knew it. She cleared her throat if only to give herself a few more seconds to think. "Well," she said, "first of all I must confess that my past experiences with men have not been necessarily positive. I had a lot of first dates, and a few second dates, and almost no third and fourth dates. On the rare occasions when I found a man worth going out with more than once, a change always occurred when something came up about my family's . . . circumstances."

"I'm sorry?" he said, not certain what she meant.

"My family's money, is what I mean."

"I see," he said.

"Once a guy realized I came from many generations of wealth, they either took the attitude that I was somehow destined to burn in hell, since they believed that a camel could go through the eye of a needle easier than any member of my family could get to heaven. They never opened their minds long enough to understand that it's the *love* of money that is the root of all evil, not the possession of it. The other attitude I dealt with was a sudden increase in attentiveness and adoration for me. A condition which I believe is based on the adage that it's just as easy to fall in love with a rich woman as it is a poor one. The bottom line is that many people are prejudiced about wealth, or they are willing to do anything to become a part of it. And the point of telling you all of that is to apologize for immediately slapping you into one of those categories. I was mortified to realize that you had practically read my mind, and when I heard you say my thoughts aloud—thoughts I had hardly recognized consciously—I realized how ridiculous and unfair they really were."

"Apology accepted," Scott said in a voice so tender that Emma had to turn and look at him. Their eyes met with an intensity that was almost becoming familiar—and even comfortable, now that she'd gotten past her own anger enough to see what she was really looking at. "That was one," he said, the edge in his voice not congruent with the warmth in his eyes.

"One what?"

"One reason. You said there were reasons. That's plural."

Emma sighed and looked straight ahead. She reminded herself that she had no reason to not be completely honest with this man. Her fears had come from within herself. And if he felt for her the way she suspected he did—the way she *hoped* he did—then complete honesty was the only possible way to build any kind of relationship that might have a ghost of a chance of lasting.

"This one's harder," she admitted.

"I'm listening," he said, this time more gently.

Emma swallowed carefully and closed her eyes, unable to face him as she admitted, "I'm scared."

Scott turned to look at her abruptly, startled by her words, as much as the trembling in her voice when she'd said them. Her eyes were shut tightly and her chin was quivering, as if she were trying very hard not to cry. Impulsively he touched that chin, making her eyes come open. He turned her to face him, looking into her eyes as he asked, "Scared of what? Me?"

Emma shook her head while his fingers continued to hold her chin, as if he feared she might turn and run otherwise.

"Then what?" he asked in little more than a whisper.

Emma knew she couldn't answer the question honestly without fully opening her heart. She could only hope and pray that he would handle her heart with care once she gave it to him.

Scott watched her closely and realized she was consciously gathering courage. He could see it in her eyes, in the way her face muscles tightened and she pulled her shoulders back.

"Tell me," he urged gently. "What is it that frightens you, Emma?"

Emma felt grateful for a distraction when she said, "That's the first time you've called me Emma." He showed a hint of a smile while his eyes never lost their expectancy in waiting to hear what she had to say. She swallowed hard and just forced the words to her tongue. "I'm not afraid of you. I'm afraid of . . . the way I feel about you."

Scott sucked in his breath and resisted the urge to let his mouth fall open. In his mind he had to replay the tape of what she'd just said three times before he was certain that he'd heard her correctly. Once he knew he had heard it right, his heart began to pound. Could it be possible? Were her feelings for him what he had always hoped and dreamed they would be? Drawing his own courage, he forced an even voice to say, "And how is that, Emma?"

Emma removed her chin from his grasp and looked away. "I'm not certain I'm ready to tell you. Why should I bare my soul when I have no reason to believe that you . . ." She stopped abruptly.

"That I what?" he demanded. "Are your feelings contingent upon mine?"

She shot bold eyes at him. "No, they are not. My feelings are what they are, but what I choose to do with them is up to me. And I know from experience that sometimes it's just . . . safer to keep your mouth shut."

"And I've learned from experience that sometimes keeping your mouth shut allows precious opportunities to slip by."

"Yes, I know," she said, looking down at her hands, clasped in her lap. "I'm here talking to you because I don't want that to happen, but that doesn't change the fact that . . . I'm just . . . scared; not only of my feelings, but what the future might bring."

"There's not a person alive who knows what the future might bring."

"I know some things," she said almost angrily. "I'm on dialysis, Scott. I need a kidney transplant. My life will never be completely normal."

His voice picked up that subtly husky quality as he said, "That's the first time you've called me Scott."

Emma met his eyes and felt that inner trembling overtake her as what she saw there penetrated her very heart and soul. She forced her eyes away and continued with her point. "I don't want to be a burden to any man."

His answer was quick and firm. "Any man who would consider you a burden, in any respect, would not be much of a man . . . in my opinion."

Emma didn't know where the sudden burst of tears came from, but with no warning she was crying like a baby, her face pressed into her hands. She felt both foolish and comforted when she found her face against Scott's shoulder, and his arms around her.

"Did I say something wrong?" he asked when she had finally calmed down.

"No. In fact, you say everything right; perhaps a little too right." She sat up straight and noted his confused expression. But she felt suddenly exhausted and a little bit sick. Knowing how far they were from home, she quickly added, "Would it be all right if we continue this conversation later? I'm suddenly not feeling well."

"Of course," he said, going immediately to his feet. Emma found his concern touching as he carefully picked her up and carried her to the horse. "Will you be all right?" he asked before he mounted. She nodded firmly, fearing she might cry again if she attempted to talk. He untethered the horse and mounted behind her and they rode home in silence.

When they arrived he helped her down near the door of the house. "Thank you," Emma said and moved toward the door.

"I'll see you later then?" he asked with an expectancy that quickened Emma's heart.

She offered him a genuine smile and said, "I'll be counting on it; after supper perhaps."

Scott nodded and watched her walk into the house. She seemed a little unsteady on her feet and he wondered if he should have gone in with her to make certain she was all right. But he knew there was at least one other woman in the house, and she would likely prefer their help over his. He walked across the lawn toward the stables, leading the horse by the reins. While he removed the saddle and thoroughly curried the animal, he recounted the conversation he'd just had with Emma. They'd made progress, and he felt a definite hope that had not been with him earlier today. He only prayed that the doors that had been opened—and closed again—would be reopened without too much grief. He longed for this chasm between them to be gone, and prayed that such a miracle might be possible.

When Scott returned to the house, he found Emily in the library. "Is Emma all right?" he asked.

"She's lying down. I think she might have overdone it, but she'll be fine."

He nodded and left the room, resisting the urge to go to her room where he could just sit beside her while she rested and hold her hand. Oh, how he longed to be the one who could hold her hand through whatever her forthcoming ordeals might entail.

Needing a distraction, Scott went to the boys' home and arrived just in time for library hour with the younger group. He sat in on story time, then helped some of the boys pick books to take back to their rooms. He went back to his office in the house and made a couple of phone calls, sent a fax, and checked his email, trying to ignore the ache inside of him that had become tangibly painful. He reminded himself that she had committed to talking with him after supper. He glanced at his watch and estimated the minutes left, praying that the sun would not set again with this rift between him and the woman he loved.

Scott forced himself to check over some records; something that needed to be done. He was relieved when supper time arrived, and disappointed when Emma didn't show. Having told her mother that she still wasn't feeling well, Emily had taken some supper to her room.

After supper Scott insisted on doing the dishes, fearing he'd go mad if he didn't have something to occupy himself, and he doubted he'd be very adept at bathing the children. When the kitchen could be no cleaner, he went out to the veranda and put his booted feet up on the rail, contemplating all that had happened since he'd sat there the previous evening. He almost cursed her for the time he'd spent with her, for the things she'd said that had given him hope—a hope that left him aching all the more when he had no idea where he really stood. He contemplated actually going to her room but decided against it.

The sun was going down before he looked up to see her standing beside him. She was wearing flowered pajamas and a long sweater, and fuzzy pink slippers on her feet. Her hair looked like she'd been in bed all day and she'd not bothered to take a brush to it. Even given that, she looked adorable.

"May I join you?" she asked.

"Of course." He put his feet down and sat up straight, motioning to the chair beside him.

"Thank you," she said and sat beside him.

"You had me worried," he said. "I thought maybe your not feeling well had something to do with me."

"And therefore you thought I wouldn't show myself this evening, even though I said I would."

"That's right."

"Well, in spite of certain . . . bad behavior on my part, I really am a woman of integrity—or at least I try to be."

Silence settled over them while Scott struggled to remember where they had left off earlier. He was relieved when she cleared her throat and spoke. "May I ask you a question?"

"Sure," he said, unable to take his eyes off of her.

His relief waned when she said, "I've told you why I was always glaring at you. Now why don't you tell me why you're always staring at me that way."

Scott looked away quickly, but not before Emma caught a distinct glimmer of guilt in his eyes. "Ah, so the tables turn," she said. "But are you willing to tell me the reasons?"

Scott attempted to find the right words. "I'm willing to tell you the reasons, but first I'd like to get back to the point where we started in the stable this morning."

"Which point was that?"

"When you said you'd like to start over." He stood in front of her and held out his hand, as if in greeting. "It's a pleasure to meet you. I'm Scott."

Emma smiled and shook his hand, not surprised when he held onto it. "Hello, Scott. I'm Emma, and the pleasure is mine."

"Is it?" he asked.

"Yes, it is."

"Would you consider taking a walk with me, if you think those slippers can handle the lawn?"

Emma stood with her hand still in his. "These slippers can handle just about anything."

Scott pressed her hand over his arm, placing his other hand over hers in a possessive gesture.

"The reasons," Emma said after they had ambled slowly for a few minutes.

"The reasons," he repeated. "Well, the reasons are difficult to put into words, Emma. It's complicated at best, and yet so . . . simple."

"Give me the simple version for now," she said. "I'm not sure my brain can handle anything too complicated right now."

Scott stole a quick glance at her in the early evening light and steeled himself to take the step that would change everything between them, irrevocably and forever. He could only hope that the change would occur in his favor. "The simple version would be that . . ." He took a deep breath. "I'm in love with you."

Emma stopped walking. Scott took another step then turned to face her. "Really?" she asked as if her very life depended on it.

"Really," he echoed with conviction.

Emma found it difficult to breathe as she stared at this man and tried to get her brain to accept what she had just heard him say. She had suspected his feelings for her, and at some level had believed she'd wanted to hear such words from him. But the reality struck her more deeply than she'd ever imagined possible. It was as if his words had magically opened the door into her own heart, allowing his confession to penetrate the feelings she'd had locked away there where she'd been unwilling—or perhaps afraid—to look at them.

Scott felt exposed and vulnerable as he waited for some further reaction. Then he realized that her eyes were clearly reflecting everything he felt. Knowing there was no point in backing down now, he lifted a hand to touch her face. She closed her eyes as if she relished his touch, and he felt his heart melt inside of him.

"Really," he repeated in a whisper. "Helplessly, hopelessly . . . in love with you."

He watched tears leak beneath her closed eyelids as she pressed her face closer to his hand. "Tell me the complicated version," she muttered, opening her eyes to look at him.

A wave of self-doubt rushed over Scott as moments of his life briefly paraded through his mind. She knew so little about him, his background, his past. Was he setting himself up for a fall by exposing his heart with so much left unsaid? Of course, he couldn't deny his feelings, and he couldn't regret sharing them. He feared if he'd kept them inside much longer they would have devoured him from the inside out.

Determined to forge ahead, he said, "Are you sure you want to hear it? Perhaps I'm not the kind of man you'd want to get involved with."

"Why not?"

"Well," he sighed loudly, "that would take some time to explain."

"You could include that explanation in the complicated version."

"Yes, I could. But for now, suffice it to say that I'm what some decent people would call a rogue."

He expected her to show some concern, or perhaps grill him with questions, but she only smiled and said, "My great-grandmother married a rogue. Her name was Emma."

Scott blew out a long, slow breath. "So there's hope for me, huh?"

"Yes," Emma said, "there's definitely hope."

Chapter Eleven

Emma watched Scott smile and felt its effect suffuse through every nerve in her body. She wasn't certain if he kissed her or she kissed him. She only knew that their lips came together, as if by some magnetic force. His kiss was meek and unassuming, and at the same time it betrayed an adoration that left her breathless. He kissed her again, pressing his hands down her arms and back up again as he did. She took hold of his arms, fearing she might topple otherwise, and was surprised by the strength she felt in them. He drew his lips slowly from hers, as if he was waking from a dream. And then he just held her close, absorbing her in silence, as if her nearness were like manna from heaven. Emma had never been held this way before. She'd never allowed herself to be close enough to a man to realize how intoxicating it could be. But then, she'd never met a man who had inspired her to want to be so close. Now, she felt her every sense come alive, as if they had only been working at minimum level her entire life, and now they had suddenly been stimulated to their full capacity, each one only wanting to experience the wonders of life and love to their greatest potential.

Emma closed her eyes and just breathed in the scent of him, a combination of leather and horses and mountain air, all the smells she connected to her father—and security. And blending them together was the vaguest hint of some masculine aroma he'd likely put on his face after shaving this morning. Opening her eyes she found a perfect view of the dark growth on his face that had appeared in the hours since he'd shaved. Impulsively she reached out to touch his stubbled face, again reminded of her father. But this was different—so completely different. The sense of security she felt in Scott's masculine presence was where the similarity ended. What she felt for Scott was unlike anything she'd ever encountered before in her life. He tipped his chin to look into her eyes and she felt as if she could see forever. Her purpose for being on this earth, for being a woman, suddenly made perfect sense, while she'd only had glimpses of that purpose before now. It was easy for her to say, "That's the other reason."

"What is?" he asked, looking baffled.

"When I told you I was scared . . . of my feelings. That's what I really wanted to say . . . needed to say . . . I was scared because I've never felt this way before and . . . given the present complications of my life, I was just . . . scared. Forgive me."

"It's in the past." He kissed her fingers that were still against his face. "We're starting over, remember?"

"Oh of course," she said and laughed softly. "Hello, my name is Emma, and I'm helplessly in love with you."

Scott laughed with relief to hear her actually say it. "I wanted to say something similar when I delivered pastries to your door on Valentine's Day."

"You did?" She laughed again. "Well, it's good you didn't, but . . ."

"Yes, it's good I didn't. But what?"

Her voice sobered. "I was feeling the same way."

"You were? Really?"

"Really."

"So, I have to ask . . . Why did you act the way you did when you came home and found me here?"

"Well, I've wondered that myself. I don't think I bothered to analyze it until after our little conversation on the veranda. But I believe now I was just assaulted with too much to deal with at once, and . . . well, I think it was not exactly how I'd imagined seeing you again. Look at me now." She glanced down at herself. "I'm a mess, and you're standing there telling me that you love me."

"I *do* love you," he said. "And I love the way you can just be you."

"Well," she chuckled, "I don't have to wonder if you would be turned off by seeing the real me, 'cause here I am."

"Yes, here you are." He touched her face again. "And you were saying . . ."

"Well, when I came home and found you here, I just felt . . . unprepared and thrown off balance, I suppose. And I was already off balance with having my mission cut short, and having to face that this disease is not going to be simply an inconvenience."

Scott pressed a lingering kiss to her forehead and said, "I can't even imagine how difficult that must be for you. I think a great deal of my frustration over the distance between us was simply that I knew you were struggling and I wanted to be able to do something." He looked into her eyes. "I want to do something now, Emma. Tell me what I can do to make this easier for you."

"There's not much anyone can do," she said sadly. "Just . . . be patient with me."

He smiled and Emma's stomach quivered. She could hardly believe this was happening to her. If she had come to accept that he was everything he seemed to be, then she had to admit that she had found the man of her dreams—and he loved her.

If only to ease the silence, she said, "You were going to tell me the complicated version."

"So I was," he said. "Do you think you're up to it?"

"I think that I want this night to never end. I've slept most of the day. The question is whether or not you're up to it."

"We can give it a try," he said, "but you'd better make yourself comfortable. While I'm at it you might as well know what a rogue I am, then we can just get all of that out of the way and you can decide if you still want to hang around with me."

Emma sat down on the grass right where she was. "Is this comfortable enough for you?" she asked, wiggling her feet to emphasize her fuzzy slippers. She eased her arms out of her sweater, feeling a bit too warm.

"It works for me." He chuckled and sat to face her. He leaned back on his hands and stretched out his legs, crossing his ankles. "Ah, the complicated version would probably have to start with the fact that I was raised as an orphan." Her eyes showed more compassion than concern, which made it easier for him to forge ahead. "As I understand it, my mother died of an illness when I was an infant, and my father was killed a few years later. I have a couple of vague memories of him, and they are not pleasant. I was passed around foster homes, never fitting in, always causing problems, until I was finally put into a boys' ranch at the age of eleven, where I stayed until I was old enough to be on my own. It was a tough upbringing; not conducive to producing really high-caliber people. By being with other troubled boys, I was exposed to far too much that could have been very detrimental. And do you know what my saving grace was?"

"No, tell me."

"Horses," he said and she laughed pleasantly. "It was as if this deep, innate love of horses had been planted into my heart, and that's what made me tick. I drew pictures of horses. The only books I read were about horses. And my desire to ride and help care for the horses at the ranch kept me on track. I learned that I could get what I wanted through good behavior, and that knowledge helped me through college and graduate school, and working my way up the corporate ladder, so to speak. Those horses, in a roundabout way, taught me that to attain success and acquire the things that I wanted, I just had to be good and be eager to go the extra mile. I cannot even tell you how those principles have saved me over and over."

"Amazing," she said expectantly.

"So, I left the ranch and got two jobs and worked my way through college. I quickly learned that to get the attention of people who could open the right doors for me I had to look good, and I had to be good to keep their attention. I found ways to dress well on very little money, and I worked hard to stay physically fit so that I could be in better control of my life."

Emma absorbed his appearance in a way she never had before, and she had to admit that he was right. There was no doubt that he was physically fit; she knew that from the way his arms had felt through the fabric of his shirt, and from sharing the same saddle with him earlier. And now that she'd gotten past her anger, she could see that he had a certain knack with the way he dressed. He dressed well without being showy, with a certain good taste that had nothing to do with money.

"And what exactly do you do for a living?" she asked quite seriously and he laughed. "What's so funny?" she demanded.

"You're serious," he said. "You don't know what I do?"

"Well, I know you spend a lot of time in that office of yours that used to be a sitting room, but . . ."

"Emma," he chuckled, "I am a full-time employee of Byrnehouse-Davies and Hamilton. Your brother put me in charge of the entire horse operation."

Emma realized now that she'd heard right after she'd come home that he was working some for Jess, but she hadn't fully digested it. Or perhaps she'd brushed the idea aside. "Okay," she said, somewhat embarrassed. "But what did you do before that? What brought you to Australia?"

"Well, I worked for a very large company that produced health products and distributed them worldwide."

"Ah, so you were a big corporate executive."

"Basically, yes," he said.

"Okay. I was just wondering. You can go back to telling me what a rogue you were."

"Ah, yes," he said. "The complicated version. Well, my weaknesses included smoking and drinking habits that I'd picked up from some of the boys I grew up with. I was too stupid to connect those problems with potential health hazards, but thankfully I never became dependent on either of them. For that I am truly grateful."

Scott's mind naturally went to the next part of his story and he felt knots gather in his stomach. Emma's expression had remained interested and accepting while she'd heard of his childhood and his bad habits. But the next one was a really whammy, and if she couldn't accept this part of his past, he wondered how he would go on. Still, it was something she had to know. Better to get it over with. As if to clarify his thinking, he came right out and asked, "You're still with me?"

"I am," she said.

"I haven't shocked you too badly?"

"Nope. I grew up with a home for troubled boys on one side, and a pack of stable hands on the other. And among them I have known many good people. I don't think there's much that could shock me."

"Well, I'm not finished yet. I was hoping perhaps that your family might have told you all about me, which would have saved me from doing it. But if you didn't know I worked here, then I'm guessing you don't know anything else."

"Sorry," she said, "they haven't told me much. I'm ashamed to say I didn't ask. But I'm asking now."

"Okay, well . . . this part is hard for me."

"I'm listening," she said gently and reached for his hand. Scott squeezed her fingers, wishing he could tell her how deeply such a gesture touched him.

"Okay," he said, "I'll try to get this over with. My habit was to work hard through the week and spend Friday and Saturday nights in the bars, then sleep it off Sunday and go back to work. It was in a bar that I met Callie." He paused to check Emma's expression, barely visible in the dusky light. Her eyes didn't even flicker. He pressed on. "Her habits were similar, and we quickly became close. Our lifestyles and values were very similar, and we hit it off rather well. And somewhere during that period of time, I met your brother while he was serving his mission. I had a good job and what I considered a good life, and his implication that I needed to change angered me. You know how that part eventually turned out, but what you don't know is that I was married."

Scott watched her closely, holding his breath. He was amazed when her only reaction was a slight widening of her eyes as she said with surprise, "Oh, I *didn't* know that."

"And now that you do know, are you still willing to sit here and hold my hand?"

"You're not *still* married, are you?"

"No." He chuckled.

"Then I don't see a problem. Go on."

Scott let out a sigh and continued. "I want to clarify something. In spite of my sinful past, Callie is the only woman I ever slept with, but I was sleeping with her long before I married her."

"It was before you joined the Church?"

"That's right. And when I *did* join the Church, my marriage gradually fizzled. It finally reached a point where she left me. But I know it was for the best. I couldn't live with her while she lived that kind of life. I could never be happy, never grow spiritually, living in such surroundings. The divorce was difficult. I respected those vows, but I wanted to live a righteous life. And eventually I came to terms with it."

"What finally helped you do that?" she asked, her tone showing curiosity more than anything.

"Well, it was a scripture I came across in the New Testament. It was one of those experiences where I knew I'd been led to it, and its meaning pierced me deeply. I knew I had found my answer."

"Tell me," she urged.

"I remember it well," he said. "Matthew, chapter 10. Verses 37 through 39, I believe. 'He that loveth father or mother more than me is not worthy of me: and he that loveth son or daughter more than me is not worthy of me. And he that taketh not his cross, and followeth after me, is not worthy of me. He that findeth his life shall lose it: and he that loseth his life for my sake shall find it.'"

Emma felt his gentle recitation of the scripture pour into her heart. No explanation was needed for her to perceive what those words meant to him, and how they had shaped his life. She felt compelled to say, "So you chose to take up your cross and follow the Lord, and you found peace in putting behind you the woman you loved."

Scott glanced at her then looked down, a little alarmed to be talking with the woman he loved about the love in his life gone by. "That's right," he said.

"And did you find your life?"

Scott met her eyes and felt her question strike him deeply. "Yes, I did," he said firmly.

"Then you have no regrets?"

"No, I don't. It couldn't have turned out any other way. I was the one who had changed, and she resented it. The divorce was quick and easy."

"But difficult, nevertheless, I would imagine."

"Yes," he looked down, "it was extremely difficult."

"You loved her," Emma stated, wondering if she wanted to ask the follow-up question that came to mind. *Did he love her still?* Were there feelings in his heart for this woman who had once shared every aspect of his life? Was she glamorous and gorgeous, the kind of woman that wouldn't easily leave a man's heart?

Scott answered immediately, "I thought I did. But given other events in my life, it didn't take me long to realize that what I felt for Callie was trivial and relatively shallow. I missed her for a while, simply because I was lonely. Once I found a place where I was no longer lonely, she just became a wisp of a memory."

"What other events in your life?" she asked.

"Meeting you," he said, surprising her. "I felt more for you in our first two brief encounters than I had felt for Callie through the duration of our marriage. She was more like a drinking buddy and a roommate, and when I quit drinking, we had little in common."

"Still, it's a part of your life—your history."

"Yes, it is. And that's why I needed to tell you. And that, in essence, brings me to the complicated version of why I was always staring at you. I was hopelessly in love with you, but a little afraid to open my heart again, especially seeing how . . ."

"Stubborn and obnoxious I was?" she suggested when he hesitated.

Scott chuckled. "I was searching for words that were a little more . . . diplomatic."

"Well, you're very kind," she said, "but I want you to promise me that no matter what, you will always be completely honest with me. I have to know that no matter what happens, you will never patronize me or say what you think I want to hear. If you're not willing to agree to that without question, then I'm going to stand up and walk away right now."

Scott was a little taken aback by her vehemence, but he easily said, "Of course. I wouldn't expect it to be any other way. Did you believe I would be otherwise?"

"Not necessarily, but we are not dealing with normal circumstances here. My health issues are real and they're not going to go away."

"And they make no difference to how I feel about you."

Emma's smile was barely visible as dark settled around them, but he felt her hand on his face and turned to press a kiss to her palm. The joy he felt was in direct proportion to the frustration and anguish he'd been struggling with not so many hours ago. He silently thanked God for blessing his life so abundantly, and especially for putting this incredible woman into his path.

He was just contemplating how badly he wanted to kiss her when he heard Jess holler Emma's name, and a moment later the beam of a flashlight came around the corner of the house.

"I'm here," she called, easing her hand away from Scott's grasp.

The light caught them sitting together on the grass just as Jess said, "Oh, there you are. We were just worried, wondering where you'd gone."

"Sorry," she said. "We're just talking."

"I'll see that she gets safely to bed," Scott said.

"Very good," Jess said and turned around. "I'll see you both in the morning."

"Goodnight," Scott and Emma both called at once.

The darkness of night descended fully as they continued to talk, bouncing back and forth from his past to hers, analyzing their struggles, their growth, and the impact the gospel had made on their lives. As the night air settled around them, Emma slipped back into her sweater, then gradually ended up wrapped in Scott's arms, leaning against his chest as they talked on and on. When they ran out of words to say but neither felt inclined to be separated, they lay back on the lawn and contemplated the stars aloud, holding hands. Scott finally insisted that they both needed to get some sleep and he helped Emma to her feet. They ambled slowly back to the side door of the house and went inside.

At the foot of the stairs, Emma said, "Oh, I think the tired just hit me. Give me a minute." She leaned heavily against him and he just held her a long moment before he pulled her up into his arms and carried her up the stairs. Emma laughed softly at the same weightlessness she'd felt earlier when he'd carried her to the rock on the mountain.

"My father used to carry me up the stairs and tuck me into bed," she said dreamily with her head against his shoulder. "I don't know if I've ever felt this secure since I grew too big for such things."

Guided by a light left on in the main upstairs hall, Scott carried Emma into her room.

"What are you doing?" she asked.

"I'm going to tuck you into bed."

"Okay," she laughed softly, "but I need a minute in the bathroom first."

He set her carefully on her feet and watched her toss her sweater into a chair and disappear into the bathroom before he turned down the covers on the bed. When she came back out he immediately picked her up again, making her laugh. "Shhh," she said, "you'll wake Mother."

Scott chuckled softly. "I'm not the one making all the noise," he said and she laughed again, more softly. He placed her on the bed, removed her fuzzy slippers and tucked the covers up over her. He pressed a kiss to her forehead and pushed her hair back off of her face.

"I love you, Emma Hamilton," he said quietly.

"And I love you," she said in a sleepy voice. He left the room and closed the door, but the dreamlike sensation of being with her hovered around him as he returned to his own room and climbed into bed. He slept quickly but woke before dawn and couldn't go back to sleep. His body refused to rest while his mind attempted to catch up with the happenings of the previous day. He felt deliriously happy, and at the same time a sense of urgency, as if there was something he needed to be doing that couldn't wait. He turned his mind to prayer and kept it there until it was time to get up and shower.

He wasn't surprised to find Emma absent at breakfast. Once they got past the usual greetings, his mind wandered while the others discussed their plans for the day. He was brought back to the conversation when Emma's dialysis appointment was mentioned.

"I'll take her," Scott said without even taking a moment to think about it. In response to several astonished expressions he added, "I have some business in town anyway. It's not a problem."

"Oh, that would be wonderful," Emily said. "That suddenly makes my day doable instead of stressful."

"Glad to help," Scott said.

After breakfast he went to the computer to check his email and see what business had to be attended to. He went to the stables and went over some things with Murphy. He managed to get done what was mandatory, but his mind kept wandering to Emma and this sense of urgency that hovered around his thoughts of her. Keeping a prayer in his heart, he hoped that he could find the answers. He felt as if the Spirit were guiding him to something important, but he couldn't quite figure it out.

Back in his office, Scott was startled by a knock at the door and absently called, "Come in." Then his heart leapt when he turned to see Emma.

"Hello," she said, leaning against the door to close it.

"Hello," he replied while their meaningful glances acknowledged all that had changed between them.

She glanced down coyly and gave a nervous laugh. "I . . . uh, slept late and . . . I was just going to get something to eat before I go to my appointment, so . . . I just wanted to see you before I leave, and—"

"Actually, I volunteered to take you. I hope that's all right. It seems that your mother has a busy day."

"Oh," she looked pleased, "that will be nice."

Scott came to his feet and moved toward her. "How are you today?" he asked, taking both her hands into his.

"Physically, I will be much better this evening."

"And otherwise?"

"Otherwise . . ." she looked into his eyes, "I feel as if I'm dreaming." Her voice lowered to a whisper. "Pinch me, Scott, so I'll know I'm not dreaming."

"My hands are busy," he said, gently squeezing her fingers.

"Kiss me, then," she said as if she might die if he didn't.

"With pleasure," he muttered and pressed his lips to hers. "If you're dreaming," he said, his lips still close to hers, "then we're both having the same dream."

"May we never wake up," she said, kissing him again.

Scott smiled and pressed a kiss to her brow. "You'd best get something to eat, or we'll be late, I think."

"I'll hurry," she said.

"I'll finish up here and meet you downstairs in half an hour."

She smiled and slipped from the room, but a warm glow remained in her absence. Scott had to tear himself away from her lingering presence in order to finish up what he'd been doing. Half an hour later he found Emma waiting for him in the kitchen.

"Shall we?" he asked as she stood, and he followed her outside to his car. He opened the door for her, then got in himself and drove toward town.

The first ten minutes passed in complete silence, until Emma said, "Do you suppose we're just tired, or we talked so much last night that we've run out of things to say?"

Scott smiled at her and admitted, "I'm afraid my mind is churning with so many thoughts that I'm not sure I can think and talk at the same time."

"Yeah, I know what you mean," she said, turning to look out the window.

Emma finally said, "So, you know my faults, what are yours?"

Scott chuckled. "Do I know your faults?"

"I'm stubborn and willful," she said, "or so my family tells me. I'm sure they're right."

"Well, being stubborn can be a strength if it's put to the right purpose."

"Like what?" she asked, leaning her head back on the seat and turning to look at him through the sunglasses she wore.

"Like . . . your stubbornly loving me for the rest of my life, for instance."

"Oh, that kind of stubborn," she said and laughed. "So, tell me, Scott, what are your faults? There must be something wrong with you."

He chuckled. "I'm sure there's plenty wrong with me, and it may take time for you to figure it out. But one of my biggest faults is that I actually struggle with some OCD behaviors."

"Really?" she said, more intrigued than concerned.

"You actually know what that means," he said, surprised.

"College psychology. My parents suggested that it would help me deal with people in every aspect of my life, but most especially as a mother."

"Good advice," Scott said.

"So . . . what exactly are you obsessive-compulsive about? Is it the way you wash your hands? Do you divide your M&M's into color categories before you eat them? Or is it the way you line up your shoes? Do tell."

Scott laughed. "No, no . . . and maybe. I actually talked to a counselor about it when I was going to school. I think it stems from the foster-home thing. I always felt so out of control of my surroundings and circumstances, that when I was finally on my own and could control my environment, I *really* wanted to control my environment. The counselor suggested that as long as I didn't allow the compulsions to disrupt my life, it wasn't anything to worry about. At the time I think it was disrupting my life, but I've worked on it."

"So, what is it?" she asked.

He chuckled. "I'm obsessively tidy."

"Ooh," she said as if a red flag of warning had gone up, "I'm rarely tidy at all. I keep things clean, but not necessarily in good order."

"It's really okay, Emma. I've learned to not let what other people do with their belongings bother me. As long as I keep my own belongings in order, I'm fine. I learned a long time ago that I can only control me, and that's the way it should be."

"So, how did your wife deal with this? Was she tidy too?"

"No, she was a slob. But she just let me pick up after her and we got along fine."

Emma laughed and he added, "Is that funny?"

"Yes, actually," she said. "I don't know why; it's just funny."

"Well, you might not think it's funny when I have to make the bed and leave my clothes folded before I can go anywhere."

"Does it make you late for wherever you're going?"

"Nope," he said proudly. "Like I said, I've learned to manage it so that it doesn't disrupt my life." He chuckled. "I just set the alarm early enough that I can have everything under control before I go wherever I need to go."

Emma laughed again and he laughed with her. A few minutes later he asked, "So is this our first date?"

She gave a scoffing chuckle. "I don't think four hours of having my blood filtered qualifies as much of a date."

"Okay, but . . . we could go out to dinner after, couldn't we? You usually feel pretty good right afterward, don't you?"

"Usually."

"So?"

"So, what?" she asked and he turned to her, looking confused. "If you want to take me on a date, you're going to have to ask properly."

Scott smiled and said, "Would you go out to dinner with me? I promise to be a perfect gentleman."

"I don't ever recall seeing you any other way."

"Oh, I have my moments."

"Well," she said lightly, "there was the other night on the veranda." She lowered her voice to mimic him. "Or perhaps my delivery of German pastries lacked some degree of finesse."

"You're mocking me," he said with laughter.

"No," she said quite seriously, "just feeling rather grateful that you had the courage to set me straight."

Scott reached for her hand. "It was either that or completely lose what was left of my mind."

She smiled and a minute later she said, "Yes."

"Yes what?"

"Yes, I would love to go out to dinner with you."

Scott grinned. "I'll look forward to it."

Silence reigned through most of the drive, while Emma absently played with the ring he wore on the little finger of his right hand, and Scott's mind began to perceive an idea that he believed might be the answer to the urgency he'd been feeling.

"If you'd like," he said, "I could get a chain and you could wear my class ring around your neck and then all the other guys would know we're going together."

Emma laughed and took notice of the ring. "Is that what it is? A class ring?"

"University of Utah," he said and she tugged it off of his finger.

"It's very nice," she said, examining it closely, then she found one of her own fingers that it fit onto perfectly. She held up her hand. "I don't need a chain. I'll just wear it like this."

Scott chuckled. "It's a little . . . overbearing for that pretty little hand."

"A bit too . . . masculine for my taste, I think." She put it back on him. "But thank you anyway."

When they arrived at the clinic he went in with her, then asked, "Would you prefer that I leave you alone?"

"You're welcome to stay, but it's not a pretty sight."

"Well, I have some errands, but not four hours' worth. If it's all right with you, I'll stick around for a while."

"I won't complain," she said, still holding to his hand.

"It smells like popcorn," he said and she laughed.

"That's because everybody in here likes to eat it."

"I thought you couldn't eat popcorn—too salty."

"I can while I'm hooked to that machine."

"Really?" he said and she kept hold of his hand when she was called back. She let go only long enough to step on a scale while a nurse wrote down her weight and joked about how much she was going to lose today. He felt a little startled when Emma unfastened the top two buttons of her blouse. He glanced away until she chuckled and said, "It's okay, Scott. I'm stopping there."

He looked again to see the tubes that had been surgically implanted in her upper chest, and within minutes they were connected to a machine and he was watching blood move through them. His thoughts wandered as he watched the process, and Emma's voice startled him, "Maybe you should reconsider."

"Reconsider what?"

"Whatever it is you seemed to be considering the last time you told me you loved me."

"Maybe you should get it through your stubborn little head that my feelings have nothing to do with your kidneys."

She smiled and glanced toward the blood pumping through the tubes, saying in a simpering voice, "My heart bleeds for you."

Scott laughed then excused himself to do his errands. "The humor is getting a little sick in here. I'll see you in a couple of hours."

Scott left the clinic and spent half an hour just sitting in his car, praying very hard and pondering what he was feeling. He finally pressed himself to do his errands, knowing in his heart that he was on the path God intended for him to take. Whatever the outcome, he would go forward with faith. He returned to the clinic in time to spend another forty-five minutes reading to Emma from a magazine. As they returned to the car, he commented, "I do believe you've lost weight, my love."

"You think?" she said with light sarcasm.

When they got into the car she said, "I should call home and let them know we'll be later than expected, so they won't worry."

Scott pushed a speed dial to the house on his mobile phone and handed it to her.

"Hello, Mother," she said when Emily answered.

"Hello, dear. How are you feeling?"

"Much better, thank you. Listen, Scott's taking me out to dinner; I'm not sure when we'll be home, but I didn't want you to worry." She smiled toward him as she added, "He promises to take very good care of me."

"I'm sure he will," Emily said. "Have a good time."

Emma got off the phone and handed it back to him. "Thank you," she said and he drove to the restaurant where he'd made reservations amidst his errands.

"Oh, this is nice," she said once they were seated. "It's been a long time since I've been out for a really nice dinner."

"Well, it's about time, then."

Between ordering and eating their meal, Scott initiated conversation that would help them get to know each other better. While they were waiting for the dessert they had ordered, Scott said, "You know, it's extraordinary. In a way I feel like we're practically strangers. I've spent so little time with you, and know almost nothing about you in many respects. And yet, I feel like I know you deeply and personally, as if being here with you this way is something we've done a thousand times."

"Funny," she said softly, "that pretty much describes how I feel about you."

Scott smiled and took her hand across the table. He measured his feelings and thoughts once more, carefully balancing what he felt in his heart and knew in his head. Finding no stupor of thought anywhere inside of him, he forged ahead.

"There's something I'd like to tell you," he said.

"I'm listening."

"When I made the decision to join the Church, I did so because there was a feeling inside of me that it was simply something I had to do. That same feeling has compelled me to live the gospel as fully as I am capable of in spite of certain sacrifices in my life. But I've never looked back, and I have no regrets."

Emma felt his conviction and tingled from the inside out. For as long as she could remember, spiritual conviction had been at the top of her list of requirements in the kind of man she wanted.

"You know that kind of feeling?" he asked.

"Yes, I do," she said firmly. "I felt that way about serving a mission, for one thing. I know that feeling well. It's not necessarily strong, but very powerful."

"Well said." He tapped his fingers on the table and she realized he was nervous. "I'm glad you understand what I'm talking about. Otherwise, it would be difficult to explain why I want certain things in my future."

The server brought the single serving of dessert they'd ordered, and two forks. Emma took a bite and made a delightful noise.

"Did you enjoy your meal?" he asked.

"Oh, very much," she said. "I'm glad I can take some of it home so that I had room for dessert."

"So, I did okay for a first date?" he asked.

"You did marvelously," she said.

"I'm glad," he said. "I was hoping it would be memorable."

"Why is that?" she asked with a smile and took another bite of cheesecake.

"Because . . . one day I want you to tell our children that our first date was incredible, especially the part where I proposed to you."

Emma held her breath and stopped chewing, wondering if she'd heard him correctly. Her heart quickened as the words echoed in her mind with a clarity that told her he'd really said what she thought he had said. The words he'd spoken leading up to this moment suddenly made sense. His talk of the feelings that compelled him to join the Church and live the gospel, his reference to certain things he wanted in the future. She was still trying to absorb the full breadth of the implication when he reached into his jacket pocket and set a little black box on the table in front of her. She set her fork down as if it suddenly weighed ten pounds. Looking at the box as if it might bite her, she asked, "What are you saying, Scott? I think you'd better make yourself perfectly clear."

He leaned back in his chair while his eyes locked with hers intently. "I'm asking you to marry me, Emma. I'm pledging all that I have and all that I am to your happiness and security. I'm not asking because I feel sorry for you and I think you need me to help you get through whatever lies ahead with your health. I could do that without marrying you. I'm not asking you because your family has money. I have plenty of my own, and I have a good job that has nothing to do with you. I'm not asking you because your family has become my family, and they've given me the home I never had. Obviously, I can be a part of the family without any connection to you. I'm not asking for any reason of convenience or opportunity. I'm asking because I love you, because I felt something deeply significant toward you the moment I saw you. I'm asking because I know we share the same values, the same convictions; combined with the way we feel about each other, I believe we could make a good marriage, raise a good family, have a good life." He leaned forward and his voice lowered. "I'm asking because I want to be with you forever, Emma."

Scott took a deep breath and absorbed her countenance. When she only gazed at him and said nothing, he added gently, "My heart and my head are in complete agreement on this, Emma, and I have searched them carefully. You must do the same, because I don't want you to marry *me* for any reason of convenience or opportunity. I know it seems fast, but when I think of how long I've felt this way, and how my feelings have only grown, it doesn't feel fast at all. Nevertheless, I will respect your wishes, whatever they may be."

Still she said nothing. He let the silence reign for a few minutes, certain she had much to take in. But he finally had to say something or go insane. "Speak to me, Emma," he pleaded in a whisper.

"Okay," she said with a tremor in her voice, "but . . . I just don't know what to say."

"Just . . . share your thoughts with me."

Emma sighed, hating the way her most prominent thoughts were always the health problems that plagued her life. But she had to be honest with him. It was her greatest concern, her deepest reservation. If there was any chance for the two of them to share a future, she just had to tell him how she felt.

Chapter Twelve

"Okay," Emma finally said, "I can't help wondering if you have any idea what life would be like with me, given this condition I have."

"It really doesn't matter, Emma."

"It *does* matter," she said with quiet vehemence. "Tell me what you know. Tell me!"

"I know your kidneys are not functioning and you need a transplant in order to survive without dialysis every two or three days. I know that your quality of life has been greatly decreased, and your limitations are many. I also know that your spirit is strong and your heart is good, and that is all that matters to me."

"That may be easy for you to say now, Scott, but living with the reality might not be so easy. I appreciate your noble approach to this; truly I do. But I don't want you to wake up one day and wonder what you got yourself into. If the kidney my brother gives me doesn't take, it could be years, if ever, before a suitable match is found. My health could continue to deteriorate, until my limitations leave me stranded in bed, and my quality of life is nonexistent. And whether I end up with a healthy kidney or not, I don't know if I will ever be able to have children. I'd like to say that I'm going to approach what little may be left of my life with a positive attitude, that I will make the most of what I have, that I will be strong and cheerful no matter what cards I am dealt. But this has been difficult for me to accept, and I can't promise that I will always be pleasant and perky. And I fear that you are looking at this unrealistically, because at this point I am still capable of functioning almost normally. It does matter, Scott. It does!"

Scott realized he was actually feeling angry. He swallowed carefully and counted to ten. "It doesn't matter, Emma," he growled quietly. "Listen to me with your heart when I tell you that if your body were completely crippled and I had to carry you and feed you and take you to the bathroom it *would not* matter. And do you know why? It is my spirit that is drawn to your spirit, Emma. The love I feel for you transcends any earthly restriction or form of opposition. What I'm asking for here is eternity, and whatever challenges we may meet as we move toward that goal are simply to better prepare us for that."

Scott leaned forward and the intensity in his eyes deepened. "When I embraced the gospel, I was awakened to the existence of a spiritual universe that exists all around us. What the Holy Ghost taught me made the instincts I'd felt all my life suddenly make sense. For years I had tried to drown out those instincts, believing I was somehow crazy for trying to explain feelings and desires that had no logical explanation. And then the doors were opened to me, and I could not deny what I felt, nor what I knew in my heart to be true. But do you know what the most difficult thing for me has been in being a member of the Church?" She shook her head and he went on. "I am continually amazed at the Latter-day Saints who go to church every week and go through the motions of living the gospel and they seem to be completely unaware of the spiritual existence they are living that is far more important, far more real and valid, than the garbage we must endure in this world."

Scott leaned further across the table and reached an arm toward her. "That is one of the biggest reasons I know we could be happy together, Emma. You understand those spiritual matters; you live by them. And it is because—and only because—of those spiritual stirrings within me that I am asking you to be my wife. So, you are going to have to get past your own fears or prejudice or whatever it is in regard to your illness that holds you back. Tell me yes or tell me no, but give me an answer that has nothing to do with any earthly restriction that is now—or may become—a part of our lives."

Emma shook her head and squeezed her eyes closed. He watched as tears trickled down her cheeks and his heart beat painfully as he feared she would close herself off from him and refuse his proposal. When she said nothing he felt compelled to share one more thought that wouldn't leave his mind.

"May I ask you a question?"

"Of course," she said and opened her eyes, wiping at her face with her napkin.

"Hypothetically speaking, let's say that we got married, and in only a few months I was thrown by a horse and broke my neck. I'm in a wheelchair, on a ventilator, completely immobile. Would you regret marrying me? Would you love me any less?"

"Of course not," she said with fervor.

"Why?"

Emma knew she didn't have to answer. The reasons were plainly evident, and she knew the point he was trying to make. As if he'd read her mind, he said, "I know it's obvious, Emma, but I want you to say it."

"Because I love who and what you are inside. True love has nothing to do with the restrictions of your earthly body."

Emma waited for him to ask her why his feelings for her were any different, and she had to admit that his analogy had made her think. But he cut her to the quick when he said, "So, are you saying then that I am a man of so little depth and character that I would base my love and commitment on your physical capabilities? Are you saying I'm the kind of man who would renege on my vows because it suddenly became more difficult than I'd anticipated?" She sensed that he was fighting to keep his anger in check. His voice tightened as he added, "Tell me you think I'm that kind of man, Emma, and I will walk away and leave you in peace."

She countered bitingly, "And would you walk away from my family, as well?"

"Absolutely not. My relationships with them have nothing to do with you, Emma. They are the family I never had, and they have blessed my life immeasurably. I do my best to contribute in a positive way and remain grateful for such a miracle in my life. And I will not turn my back on that out of some pathetic measure of pride or hurt feelings because you and I don't end up together."

Emma looked at him long and hard, once again marveling at the depth of his integrity, his character, his strength. She prayed for the words to express all she felt, and all that he had just taught her over dessert about life and love.

"Are you finished?" she asked and Scott felt certain she was going to tell him where to get off.

"Yes," he said quietly and looked down.

"Good, because I would like to tell you what kind of man I think you are."

His mind responded with a sarcastic, *I can't wait. Just cut me off at the knees and get it over with.*

"You are absolutely the most . . . incredible, honorable, spiritual man I have ever met. And I love you."

Scott looked up at her, holding his breath while he absorbed the fresh emotion in her softened eyes. She took hold of his hand across the table and added with conviction, "I would be a fool not to marry you."

Scott's heart responded with what she had said by threatening to jump out of his throat, but his head needed clarification. "Yes, I know you'd be a fool," he said. "The question is . . . *Will* you?"

Tears again spilled over as she said with fervor, "Yes, Scott, I will marry you."

Scott squeezed his eyes shut, deep relief filling his heart. A one-syllable noise erupted from his mouth, something between a laugh and a sob. Fearing he'd break down and cry like a baby, he attempted some humor to counteract it. "You haven't looked at the ring yet. Maybe you'll feel differently. I don't really know you well enough to know your taste."

"And I can exchange it if I hate it, right? I mean, as long as you paid for it, wearing it means we're going together, right?"

Scott smiled. "Right." Somewhat seriously he added, "Are you sure you don't want to think about it? Eternity's a long time."

"I don't have to think about it," she said. "When I get past all my concerns about my illness, I cannot deny that my heart and my head *do* agree. I know beyond any doubt that this is the best thing I could possibly do with my life."

Scott laughed as he rose to his feet and tossed his napkin to the table. He took Emma by the hand urging her to stand and face him. And then he kissed her, oblivious to what anyone else might think. He laughed again and reached for the little box on the table. Holding it close to her face, he opened it, watching her expression closely. She gasped pleasantly when the ring came into view. "Oh, it's beautiful," she said and gave a disbelieving laugh. "It's the most beautiful ring I've ever seen."

"No exchanges?" he asked.

"No exchanges."

Scott took it out and set the box aside before he slid it onto the third finger of her left hand. "And it fits," she said. "How did you know?"

"You were trying on my ring earlier, which gave me some idea of the size. There was some guessing involved—and praying," he added with a chuckle.

"But I was bloated earlier," she said.

"I took that into account," he said and laughed again before he kissed her once more, silently thanking God for yet another miracle in his life.

Following another kiss, Emma forced herself away from him so they could finish their dessert. She loved the way he kept laughing for no apparent reason as he fed her bites of cheesecake.

Once in the car, he asked, "So what kind of wedding do you want?"

"A temple one," she said firmly.

"Of course," he laughed. "But I mean . . . the other stuff. I want it to be exactly the way you want it."

"Well, I'm the youngest in a large family. We've had many weddings, and so there seems to be an established mold. To be quite honest, I don't really care about all of that stuff. But as my mother would say, friends and family should be privileged to celebrate with us on such occasions. I think I'll just let my mother plan the wedding. She likes that kind of thing."

"So, tell me about these . . . traditions."

"Well, the most recent was Jess and Tamra. I was the only one who hadn't gone to the temple yet, so I watched about three hundred kids at a hotel in Sydney during the wedding."

"Three hundred, eh?" he laughed.

"No, but it seemed like it. All of my nieces and nephews. It was probably fifteen or twenty—seemed like three hundred. Anyway, everybody met at a hotel in Sydney and we had this big family gathering the night before the wedding, since my sisters flew in from all over the place. After the wedding we had a big luncheon back at the same hotel, then Jess and Tamra left and drove home, having sort of a honeymoon on the way. We had a reception at the house a week after the wedding with lots of food, too many people—even dancing. That's Jess's favorite part."

"Sounds delightful," he said.

"What about you?" she asked.

"Anything is fine with me," he said. "It's only the temple part I need."

"But . . . what about your first wedding? What was that like?"

She saw his countenance darken slightly. "It was tacky," he said. "We went to Vegas, actually. We'd been living together for months and one day I just told her that I wanted to make it right, so we got in the car and drove to Vegas. We got married in one of the classier places, but that's not saying much. When it was over I remember thinking, 'Is that it?' The whole thing just seemed so . . . unimportant. Not long after I went to the temple myself, I was invited to the wedding of a business colleague. It was simple and just . . . beautiful. It was perfect. The contrast was incredible."

"I've never been to a temple wedding," she said. "I guess mine will be the first."

Scott laughed and said, "I can't believe it. We're getting married."

"Yes, we are," she said, laughing with him.

"I guess we should set a date," he said.

"It could be a long time before I'm up and about after my surgery and feeling up to a wedding." Scott tossed her a confused glance and she asked, "What?"

"You look plenty up to a wedding right now."

"What are you saying?" she asked breathlessly.

"I'm saying I want to marry you as soon as possible—I don't want to wait."

"But . . . but . . ." She couldn't put words to a sudden storm of thoughts.

"But what?"

"There's so much . . . uncertainty."

"Exactly," he said. "For now, you're doing well. The surgery will hopefully bring long-term good results, but it will take you months to feel completely up to par. And what if it doesn't take? What if something goes wrong?"

Emma started breathing heavily with a hand pressed over her heart. Scott pulled the car to the side of the road and stopped it. "What?" he asked gently, turning toward her and taking her hand.

"What *if* it doesn't take? What *if* something goes wrong?" She gasped for breath and started to cry.

"It's all right," he said, urging her head to his shoulder. "Come on. Breathe deeply. Calm down. Take a deep breath or you'll hyperventilate; come on."

Emma forced her breathing to slow down while she clutched onto his upper arms and kept her face pressed into the folds of his shirt.

"Now talk to me," he said once she'd calmed down.

"I don't want to lose you; I don't want to lose what we have." She sobbed and held to him more tightly. "I want to live. I want to spend fifty years with you in *this* world before we go on to the next one."

Scott took her face into his hands and looked directly into her eyes. He ignored her whimpering as he said with conviction, "That's what I want too, Emma, and we are both going to do everything in our power to make that happen. We have to remember that this is in God's hands. And we must trust in Him. We will live each and every day to its fullest, my love, and we will live like any other couple starting out together—as if we *will* have fifty years together. We're going to talk about the future and work toward it, and we're going to do it together. That's why I want to marry you *now!* I want to be your husband through all of this, not some distant bystander that isn't allowed to get too close because I'm not a member of the family. Let me help you through this, Emma, whatever the outcome may be."

Emma marveled at the hope and peace he could give her, and she had to wonder how she had ever managed without him, when only two days ago she had been angry with him at best. She nodded firmly, unable to speak and he urged her closer, holding her tightly, pressing his lips into her hair.

"Everything will be all right, Emma. We're going to get through this . . . together."

When she had calmed down he drove on toward home. They were nearly there when she said, "You call the temple and I'll pack a bag and maybe we can be back before my next appointment."

Scott laughed. "We might need a little more preparation than that, but I like the theory."

"Seriously," she said, "I don't need the fancy wedding; all the things that take time and preparation. All I really want is enough time to get my family gathered in the temple."

"Sounds good to me."

"You know, of course, that we can't have much of a honeymoon if I need dialysis every couple of days."

"I'm sure there are places all over the country where we can get that done. We can call around and make some arrangements. You'll have to get it done at least once in Sydney if we're getting married there."

"That's true," she said.

He pulled the car up beside the house just as the sun was setting over the west horizon.

Emma looked out over the yard and chuckled. "What were you doing twenty-four hours ago?"

Scott took her hand and kissed it. "I was praying you would still talk to me after I spilled my heart to you."

"It worked," she said and he kissed her quickly.

"I think," he said, glancing toward the house, "that we need to have a little chat with your family."

"Yes," she sighed loudly, "it would seem we do. But you mean *our* family."

"Yes," he smiled, "*our* family."

"And since they're probably in the middle of putting children to bed, that would give us time for a little walk before we go inside."

Following a leisurely stroll, Scott and Emma went into the house, first putting their dinner leftovers into the fridge. They wandered up the long hall and Scott whispered, "We're in luck," when they peered quietly into the lounge room to see Jess, Tamra, and Emily each reading different books.

"Hello there," Scott said as they entered the room, and all eyes were drawn to the fact that he was holding Emma's hand. Emma was glad he held her left hand, which left the ring concealed by his fingers.

"Hello," they all said haphazardly, then Emily added, "do we detect something romantic here, or would you just be taking my daughter out to dinner and holding her hand as . . . friends?"

Scott laughed and sat down, urging Emma beside him on one of the couches. "Don't beat around the bush, Emily. Just come straight out and ask."

Jess and Tamra both chuckled. Emily smiled at him expectantly until he added, "Yes. So you don't all have to lose sleep over it, I would definitely say you could detect something romantic here." He turned to Emma with mock concern. "At least, I think so. Is there something romantic here, or are you just humoring me?"

"It's definitely romantic," Emma said as if it were a serious business matter.

Scott turned back to Emily and said firmly, "Yes, it's romantic." He comically added, "I hope that's all right with everyone. Should we take a vote?" he asked Emma.

"No, I don't think so. My vote is the only one that counts."

"Okay," Scott said, "how about a poll?" He looked around the room again. "Is that all right with everyone?"

"Not to worry," Jess said. "You passed the worthy-of-my-baby-sister test a long time ago."

"I second the motion," Tamra added.

"And what about the worthy-of-your-best-friend test?" Emma asked her brother. "You know me better than anyone. Maybe you should be taking him out behind the stable and giving him fair warning."

They all laughed and Jess added, "She has her days."

"Yes, I've seen some of those days," Scott said. "I think I must have nine lives since I've gotten several of those looks that could kill."

Emily laughed heartily then asked, "So, I take it dinner was nice?"

"Very nice," Emma said, smirking at Scott, "thank you."

Nothing was said for a couple of minutes until Scott cleared his throat and broke the silence. "I was really wishing Michael were here."

"My father?" Jess asked.

"That's right," Scott said.

"Why is that?" Emily asked, seeming intrigued.

"There's a question I'd like to ask him. But seeing that he's not here, I guess his wife and son would be an appropriate substitute."

"Okay," Jess said, his tone serious.

Scott gave Emma a long, cautious gaze before he turned to face the others. "Jess, Emily, I want you to know that I've asked Emma to marry me, and she has accepted."

"Really?" Tamra squealed. Emma lifted her hand to show off the ring and the women both gasped.

"Oh, that *is* romantic," Emily said.

Jess and Tamra both let out a joyful laugh before Scott went on soberly, "I want you to know that I will always do everything I can to contribute to her health and happiness. If Michael were here I would ask for his blessing. As it is, I hope that you will be willing to give it."

"Of course," Jess said easily.

"I think it's wonderful," Emily added.

"Thank you," Scott said and reached for Emma's hand.

"Well, we have plans to make," Emily said. "When your surgery is over you can—"

"Actually," Scott interrupted, "I want to marry Emma *before* the surgery."

Scott held Emily's eyes as he waited for her to perceive what he'd just said. It was her support that mattered most in this. He knew well that Emily Hamilton was not easily ruffled or flustered, but she was now. He watched her take a deep breath and sensed her measuring her words carefully. "But why, Scott? It's so complicated. If you wait you can have a real honeymoon without having to worry about dialysis and—"

"Forgive me, Emily, but complicated is relative here. I'll tell you what I see as complicated. I realize that nobody wants to think it, let alone say it out loud, but the hard truth is that any number of things could go wrong, and I have to accept the possibility that Emma may not ever be healthy enough to have a real honeymoon. And the bottom line for me is that I will *not* spend days—maybe weeks—on the outside of those doors of the intensive care unit, staring at the sign that says, 'only immediate family admitted.' Since I have convinced her to be my wife, I intend to make the most of every minute of every day that we have together."

Scott heard the fervor in his voice and paused to take note of the astonished expressions in the room—all except for Emma. She was staring at him with something close to adoration glowing in her eyes. He pressed her hand to his lips and turned back to face her family. He couldn't miss the fact that Emily was crying. Jess and Tamra looked as if they were about to. "Forgive me for being so brash," he said.

"If I may be brash for a moment," Emma added, "I would like to say something that no one has been willing to say since I came home. We all want to hope for the best, but the reality is that my condition is serious, and Scott is right when he says that things could go wrong. This may not work out the way we hope it will. Like it or not, I have to be prepared for the possibility that my life could be cut significantly short."

Emily put a hand over her mouth as if to hold back some kind of protest. The silence grew heavy until Jess said to Scott, "And what if she does die young? Are you willing to face being a widower at your age?"

"You'd better believe it," Scott said with fervor, "so long as I can have forever. In my heart I believe she'll be all right. I'm going to count on that and expect it, but that doesn't mean we shouldn't be prepared for every possibility. Whatever happens, I want to be holding her hand through every possible minute of it. And I want the covenants and ordinances in place that will make it possible for us to be together again—no matter what happens."

Scott watched Emily as she visibly seemed to be collecting herself and considering what she'd just heard. He glanced at Jess and Tamra and noticed them watching Emily as well, as if they all sensed that she wasn't necessarily happy about this. While Scott was trying to come up with words that might help her understand his conviction, she cleared her throat gently and said, "Forgive me, Scott . . . Emma. I don't want to embarrass either of you, but I have a concern that I feel has to be addressed. We're all adults here, and if the two of you are going to be married, it's something that must be discussed."

"Okay," Scott said, noting that Emma looked much more nervous than he felt.

"The thing is," Emily said, "I must admit that one of my greatest concerns is the possibility of Emma getting pregnant." He heard Emma sigh as she put a hand over her eyes to cover her embarrassment, but Emily pressed on. "A single woman with strong moral values does not run the risk of having her illness complicated by pregnancy. But once she's married . . ." Emily shook her head. "We cannot even begin to imagine what complications could occur if she were to get pregnant with her body in such condition. I honestly don't know, because it wasn't an issue when we spoke with the doctors about her condition. It might be too risky for her to *ever* have children. We don't know. But I cannot in good conscience support something that would add risk to Emma's life."

Scott leaned his forearms on his thighs, looking directly at Emily. "I understand what you're saying, Emily, and I want you to know that it's something I have considered carefully."

"You have?" Emma gasped.

Scott glanced at her then back to Emily. "I understand this is moving quickly, and Emma and I have not had a chance to discuss every aspect of the situation, but I promise you, Emily, that we will take every possible precaution to keep her from conceiving so long as it is not completely prudent according to her doctor's advice. I agree with your feelings emphatically, and I swear to you, I will do everything in my power to protect her health. And as far as whether or not she can have children in the future, well . . . we will do whatever we have to in order to raise a family. There are plenty of unwanted children out there who need loving parents and a good home. I'm living proof of that. They do not have to be our biological offspring to be our foreordained children. I believe that with all of my heart."

Scott glanced from Emily's thoughtful expression to see that Emma had warm tears in her eyes. He leaned back and took hold of her hand while they waited for Emily to respond. Following a long, tense moment, Emily rose and moved toward Scott. He stood to meet her and they shared a tight embrace before she looked into his eyes, saying with conviction and emotion, "Nothing could make me happier than this. You have my every blessing."

Scott let out a long sigh, followed by a breathy chuckle, then he hugged her again. Emily then hugged Emma and Jess stood to give Scott a brotherly embrace. "It's a miracle, you know," Jess said.

"Yes," Scott said, glancing at Emma, "I believe it is."

Tamra stood and hugged them both.

They all talked for a few minutes before going their separate ways to bed. Scott was walking Emma toward the stairs when she said, "I don't want this day to end. Let's sit outside for a few minutes."

"I'd love to," he said, not feeling sleepy at all.

Once they were seated on the veranda, Emma said, "Scott, there's something I need to say."

"I'm listening," he said cautiously, sensing the concern in her tone.

"Everything you said in there . . . Did you really mean it?"

"Every word of it."

Emma sighed loudly. "Forgive me; I'm not doubting your integrity. I'm more . . . concerned about . . ."

"What?" he asked when she didn't go on.

"I just . . . well . . ." She looked directly at him. "What if I die, Scott?"

"What if you do?" he countered. "Who knows when any of us will die, for that matter?"

"Answer the question. What if I die as a result of this?"

"Then I have eternity to look forward to. In essence, I already said that."

"I know," she said, glancing down. "I guess I just . . . need some time to let all of this settle in. It's been a very eventful day."

"Yes, it has," he said. "Perhaps you should get some sleep."

"Perhaps," Emma said, but she only put her head against his shoulder and relaxed.

When Scott realized Emma was almost asleep, he lifted her into his arms and carried her up the stairs, tucking her into bed.

"You're tucking me in again," she said sleepily.

"Yes, I am, my love." He pressed a kiss to her brow. "I'll see you in the morning."

Emma listened as he left the room, then she habitually tuned her mind to prayer as she drifted to sleep. She woke up in the darkest part of the night and couldn't go back to sleep. All of her deepest fears related to her health and the pursuit of this relationship came tumbling through her mind. She prayed to feel the peace and conviction she'd felt earlier, and to be free of the darkness of doubt and anxiety. After several minutes of prayer, Emma felt compelled to get up and read in her missionary journal. It was something she'd gotten in the habit of doing on her mission. At times of discouragement, she could go back and read evidence of her growth and the good experiences she'd had. For more than an hour Emma sporadically thumbed through the journals, reading different segments, before she came upon words that left her in awe. She had begun recording her mission experiences the night she had been set apart as a missionary, and Jess had given her a blessing. She had written down the ideas expressed in that blessing, and now they struck her more deeply than they ever could have at the time. As she read the words over and over, an undeniable warmth consumed her, letting her know beyond any doubt that what she was feeling now was right and true.

Emma didn't even glance at the clock before she threw on her bathrobe and went to Scott's room. Without knocking she opened the door and eased to the edge of the bed, guided by the light from the hall.

"Scott," she said, nudging his shoulder. "Wake up. I need to show you something."

"What are you doing here?" he asked, looking startled then confused.

"I have to show you this," she said. "It can't wait."

"Okay," he said, squinting as she flipped on the lamp on the bedside table. She put the journal in front of him but he said, "You're going to have to wait until my eyes adjust, or you'll have to read it to me."

"Fine," she said with a little laugh, sitting on the edge of the bed. "I couldn't sleep and I was reading in my missionary journals. This is what I wrote the night I was set apart, after Jess had given me a blessing."

"Go on," he said.

"'In the blessing I was told that the location of my mission had not been happenstance, that the Lord was mindful of me and my afflictions, and I would be led to great blessings and opportunities as a direct result of where I would be serving. I was also told that in the same respect, my family would reap great blessings as well.' Don't you see?" she said excitedly. "The only possible tangible blessing that came out of where I served my mission was the fact that I met you, and my meeting you brought you here to my family, and to me and . . ." She threw her arms around his neck. "Oh, Scott. I love you so much. We were meant to be; I know that now, beyond any doubt. And I will never question it again."

Scott laughed and hugged her tightly, and Emma knew that, somehow, everything was going to be all right.

* * *

The following morning Scott walked into the kitchen to find only Emily there, sitting at the table with her usual cup of cocoa.

"Good morning," he said and she just gave him a smile so wide that it looked as if it might spread right off of her face. "What?" he asked with a chuckle.

"I think you have made me the happiest woman alive."

Scott chuckled and poured himself a cup of hot water for his herbal tea. "I don't know," he said. "The last time I saw Emma, she couldn't stop laughing."

Emily laughed. "Now *that* is a miracle. Until last night I don't think I've seen her laugh since she came home."

"Well, she's making up for it now," he said, sitting at the table. "I'm just glad she finally figured out that she didn't hate me."

"We're all glad for that," Emily said. "And apparently she figured it out rather quickly. A couple of days ago I was under the impression that she wouldn't give you the time of day."

"I was under that impression as well," Scott chuckled.

"So, what happened? If you don't mind my asking."

"I don't mind," he said. "I confronted her, basically telling her that I had a right to know why she was so angry with me. And I think she couldn't come up with an answer."

"We had a long talk after that," Emily said. "I sensed she was getting the picture, but I had no idea what she might end up doing."

"Well . . . she apologized and asked if we could start over. Eventually I was able to admit that I'd fallen for her the first time I saw her." Emily smiled but he felt he had to say, "You knew."

"I suspected."

"I never said anything because . . . Well, I don't know why completely, but I think a part of me feared that you might think my coming here had only been a ploy to worm my way into Emma's life because I was attracted to her."

Emily smiled again. "No, I never would have thought that. I could feel your reasons for being here, right from the start. And this is just . . . icing on the cake." She reached her hand across the table to set it over Scott's and he lifted his eyes to meet hers. "I just want you to know," she said, "that you would forever be a part of our family, regardless of any connection by marriage. But to have this happen is just doubly wonderful. She could not have found a better man." She leaned back and sighed. "And you must understand that this works out much better for all of us."

"How's that?" Scott asked, leaning back as well.

"We've talked many times of how nice it would be if Emma could settle down here; the way her and Jess have always been so close, and . . . well, it's such a big house. It was something we always wanted, but we were realistic enough to realize that with all the time she spent in the States, going to school and such, that she was much more likely to marry an American and settle down there, just as two of her sisters did."

"Well, you got the American part right," he said, "but I think this one is pretty deeply rooted right here."

Emily smiled again. "For which I am deeply grateful." She then let out a spontaneous laugh, and Scott laughed with her.

He sipped his tea for a minute while his mind wandered, then he felt compelled to share his thoughts even before Emily said, "You look . . . concerned. Is something bothering you?"

"Perhaps," he said. "It's just that . . . there are moments when I look at my life and feel so completely blessed that I have to wonder why. Why me? I'm not so special. Look at the way I grew up—the bad choices I made, my rebellion. Why would God give me so much?"

Emily sighed and smiled. "Well, first of all, I know many people who have at least as much as you have, maybe more, who don't consider themselves necessarily blessed. I think you have a gift in being able to appreciate the good things of life, and to acknowledge God's hand in those blessings. And secondly, I don't have to wonder why you're so blessed. You made some bad choices; we all do. But you didn't have the guidance of the gospel at the time. I don't look at you and see a rebel. I see a man who made choices—difficult choices—to put that rebellious part of you aside. I see a man who has been blessed because he works very hard at living the gospel and staying close to the Spirit, in spite of some tough circumstances in your past. I know you've read our ancestors' journals, but I wonder if you remember what Alexa Byrnehouse-Davies wrote about her son-in-law, Michael."

"Remind me," he said eagerly.

"She said that he was such an incredible man because he'd risen above the worst of circumstances to become great, as opposed to men in this world who rose above nothing to become the same. I would say the same applies to you."

Scott reveled in her wisdom, her love, her acceptance, and he could only feel all the more blessed. Perhaps one day he would stop feeling unworthy of all he'd been given. Or perhaps that very attitude would keep him aspiring to do better.

Before Scott went out to begin his work, he helped Emily fix breakfast. Once they had eaten he took a tray up to Emma's room and surprised her with breakfast in bed.

"So, it wasn't a dream," she said as he set the tray over her lap, then leaned over to kiss her in greeting.

"Depends on what you think you dreamt, I suppose," he said, sitting on the edge of the bed.

"I dreamt that you promised to love me forever."

Scott smiled and took her hand. "No, it wasn't a dream." He kissed her hand then held it in front of her face, comically drawing attention to the ring she wore. "And here's tangible proof, just in case you ever wonder."

Emma let out a joyous laugh.

"You've been doing a lot of that," he said.

"What?"

"Laughing."

"Oh, and it feels so good to be happy again. I don't think I've ever felt completely happy since my father got sick. Now, I just have so much to live for."

Scott grinned. "You just keep up that attitude, my love, and just keep living."

"I'll do my best," she said and he kissed her again before he forced himself away to get to work.

As soon as Emma was finished with her breakfast, she got on the phone to share the good news with her sisters. She had a long talk with each of them, and didn't end up getting a shower until after lunch. Following a long talk with her mother, she went in search of her fiancé. She found him in the office attached to the main stable, leaning back in a chair, talking on the phone about an agreement to provide several well-trained horses for an elite riding school. He smiled when he saw her and motioned her to an empty chair. He held up a finger to indicate he would just be a minute. Emma sat and watched him for a few minutes while they exchanged knowing smiles, then she impulsively moved to his lap, kissing him quietly while he was listening to the voice on the other end of the phone. When he finally hung up, he made a comical growling noise and hugged her tightly. "You are terribly distracting, my love," he said and kissed her again.

"Is that a problem?" she asked as if she didn't care in the least.

"Oh, no," he said, "you just keep distracting me for the rest of my life, and I will be a happy man."

"Speaking of the rest of your life, we need to set a date. We've got wedding plans to be making and not very many weeks until the surgery is scheduled."

"I have nothing to work around," he said. "Murphy will cover for me here whenever we do it, so . . . just plan away. Let me know what I need to do."

"Oh, don't worry. I'll keep you plenty busy," she said and laughed as he bent her backward and briefly tickled her. He held her that way for a minute and she said, "Is there a reason you're holding me upside down?"

"Yeah. It'll keep the blood in your head and you won't pass out."

Emma laughed and he tipped her upright, hugging her tightly as he did.

"I haven't got time for this," she said, slipping off his lap.

"Where are you going?" he asked, his disappointment evident as she moved toward the door.

"I'm going to make an appointment at the temple," she said and they exchanged a deep, long gaze.

With perfect sincerity Scott said, "I love you, Emma Hamilton."

"I love you too, Scott Ivie," she said before she turned and left the office.

Scott watched through the windows as she walked away, in awe of the life he'd been blessed to live, here in paradise with the woman of his dreams. It was truly a miracle.

Chapter Thirteen

Emma was grateful for her mother's expertise in planning weddings as they plunged into putting one together in a hurry. Once the date was set with the temple, and all of the family had been notified so that they could arrange to be there, Emily took Emma into town where they ordered announcements from a place that could have them ready in a couple of days. Before the announcements were picked up, Emily had made phone calls to arrange all they needed for the reception. Once she found a catering company with that date open, the rest was easy. Normally Emily would have done a good deal of the decorating and food herself, but given the time element and circumstances, she chose to just put it all in someone else's hands.

Since Emily had all the addresses in the computer, and they had been updated when Jess was married, labels were quickly printed out and the family worked together to get the announcements ready and mailed. When that was done, Emily declared that everything was under control except for outfitting the wedding party. It didn't take Emma long to find a wedding gown that she liked, given that she'd never been terribly fussy about clothes anyway. The dress made her feel beautiful, and it was white. She concluded that those were the only two mandatory requirements. Jess took care of helping Scott get what he needed, and since they'd made the decision to have no formal receiving line, what anyone else wore really didn't matter. Emily had suggested that since Michael was gone and Scott didn't have any family beyond the one he was marrying into, it would be more comfortable and appropriate for the bride and groom to receive guests formally, and everyone else could just mingle and visit.

Through every step of the preparations, Emma kept a close eye on this man she had committed herself to, marveling at how he had come into her life and turned it upside down, leaving her on top of the world. She quickly learned that he kept his camera close by and he was often snapping candid pictures of his surroundings—most especially her. After a while she almost got used to it, and she loved the way he would laugh or wink at her after he snapped the picture. As for Emma, she found herself taking mental photographs, attempting to absorb his presence, his character, his personality, fully into herself. He would often catch her staring at him and ask, "What are you looking at?"

Emma came up with a number of responses, most of which made him laugh. But one particular evening, she said, "I'm just wondering how I could have been so stupid. I should have just hurled myself into your arms the minute you walked in the kitchen and found me there."

"Yes, you should have," he said. "But that does give us something in common."

"What?"

"I too was wondering how you could have been so stupid," he said, then he laughed and she threw a pillow at him.

* * *

Emma knocked at the door of Scott's bedroom, hoping he wasn't still in the shower.

"Come in," he called and she did. She found him sitting on the edge of the bed, pulling on his boots and adjusting his jeans over the top of them. "Well, good morning," he said when he looked up. She handed him the cup she was holding and he asked, "What is this?"

"Herbal tea, of course," she said and he smiled.

"Thank you," he said dramatically and rose to kiss her. He set the cup on the bedside table then pulled her into his arms to kiss her again. "Good morning," he said close to her face.

"Good morning," she replied, smiling widely. "Guess what?"

"What?" he asked without letting her go.

"We're getting married tomorrow."

"Yes, we are," he said and laughed. "A fact for which I am inexpressibly grateful."

"And if we don't hurry, we will never get to Sydney before that dialysis appointment."

"I'm ready," he said, "as soon as I drink my tea."

"I'm ready, too," she said. "But I don't know if everybody else is ready. With all that stuff Tamra is packing for the babies, I don't know how we're all going to fit in one plane."

"We're not," Scott said, apparently knowing something she didn't. "In fact, we don't have to wait for the others. We can leave as soon as you're ready, so we can make that appointment."

"Oh, is Murphy flying us to Sydney?"

"No," Scott drawled, "Murphy is covering for me while I'm gone." Emma gave him a confused scowl and he said, "I wonder how long it will be before we stop being surprised at what we don't know about each other."

"What don't I know?" Emma demanded.

"I am flying the plane to Sydney, my love. And your mother is going with us. Jess is taking Tamra and Rhea and the kids."

"Really?" Emma laughed. "I didn't know you—"

"Obviously," he said. "Once Jess took me up in one of those planes, I was hooked. I got my license in record time."

"Wow," Emma said and kissed him quickly, "a man of many talents."

A moment later Emma giggled.

"What's funny?" he asked.

"I was just thinking about poor Rhea. Last time I got stuck at the hotel tending all the kids during the ceremony. Now she gets to do that."

"And she seems pleased as punch to do it," Scott said.

"Yes, well . . . a lot of those kids are a few years older, and they can help with the younger ones. But then there are Jess's three little boys to add to the mix." Emma giggled again. "Let's just say I'm glad I'm the bride and not the babysitter."

"We are both glad about that," Scott said.

An hour later they were flying south and Scott turned to see Emma staring at him. "What are you looking at?" he asked, as he often did.

"I was just thinking what a miracle you are."

Scott chuckled uncomfortably. "Me? No, I think you mean what a miracle I've been blessed with."

"No, that's not what I meant," Emma said. "Stop being humble for a minute and listen to me. Just for a minute, mind you. Your humility is one of many things I love about you. But I love the way you're such a miracle."

"It's about time you figured it out," Emily said from the rear seat.

Emma glanced over her shoulder to see her mother's nose buried in a book. "I thought you were reading."

"I am, but I'm not deaf. Don't mind me."

Emma turned back to Scott, feeling compelled to finish her thought, "I mean it, Scott. I've heard Jess and my mother both say how you filled a void in this family that's been here ever since the loss of James, and Jess's friend Byron; a void that was made deeper when we lost my father. And I've come to see that's true. But it just occurred to me that you filled the same void in my life. There's an emptiness that's been inside of me, especially since Dad died. And while I will always miss him, and no one could ever replace him, you have definitely filled that hole inside of me, and I want you to know that I'm grateful."

Scott gave Emma a humble smile and said, "It is I who am grateful, Emma. Sometimes I feel like Job in the respect that he lost everything, even though I think sometimes that I really didn't have that much to lose; I never had much to begin with. But now all that I never had, and all that I lost, has been given to me tenfold. There is no doubt in my mind, Emma, that God is mindful of us, guiding our lives for good as we live for those blessings. And that is truly the miracle."

"It is indeed," Emma said, and a silent moment later they heard Emily sniffling.

Emma glanced over her shoulder and asked, "What are you crying for?"

"I'm just . . . reading," Emily said and blew her nose. "Don't mind me."

"You know," Scott said to her in a lighter tone, "tomorrow you're going to legally be my mother. Do you think you're up to that?"

"Since I've been your mother emotionally for several months now, I'm pretty certain I can handle it." She chuckled and added, "Just fly the plane and let me read."

"Yes, Mother," he said and she chuckled again.

A few minutes later Emma said, "You know, Scott, that's another thing I love about you."

"What?" he asked. "You've lost me."

"Well . . . it's the way you always find blessings and miracles in everything. I love that; I just wanted you to know."

"It's a gift he has," Emily said.

"Oh, will you just read?" Scott asked with mock anger. "Any more of this ridiculous praise and I'm going to make you fly the plane, and I'll read."

"If you know what's good for you," Emily said with mock severity, "you'll just be humble and gracious and fly the plane."

"Yes, Mother," he said again and Emma laughed, as if the happiness inside of her simply had nowhere else to go.

* * *

In spite of having some difficulty finding the clinic where Emma was scheduled for a dialysis treatment, they arrived less than five minutes late. Scott and Emily left her there once she was settled and went to the hotel to unload their luggage and get settled in. Emily checked with the hotel staff to make certain everything was ready for the family gathering they would have that evening, and the wedding luncheon the following day, then they went back to sit with Emma through the last half hour of her treatment. They arrived back at the hotel just in time for Emma to get cleaned up before her family was due to arrive. Emily went to the meeting room they'd reserved downstairs to be there as they began to arrive, but Emma decided to rest for a short while and go down after they were all assembled. Scott chose to sit in a chair near the bed where Emma was lying. He started out looking at a magazine, and ended up just watching her sleep. He contemplated the love he felt for her, and the incredible reality that he was marrying into the greatest family in the world. He'd lived with them long enough to know their weaknesses, and they certainly knew his. He'd seen disagreements and minor difficulties come up, some even involving him, and he'd seen how they were effectively solved through appropriate communication and a mutual willingness to admit mistakes and be forgiving. He hadn't yet met the rest of the family, but he knew they were from the same blood,

the same upbringing, as the people he'd been living with. And whatever
their shortcomings might be, he didn't have to live under the same roof
with them. Still, he knew enough about Emma's sisters and their families
to know they were good people. Glancing at the clock, he actually felt a
little tense with the reality that he *was* meeting the rest of the family very
soon. He'd not had the normal experience of dating a woman and *then*
meeting her family. It had been the other way around—until now. And
he was decidedly nervous.

He had promised Emma that he wouldn't let her sleep past a certain
time, so he nudged her awake then gave her a few minutes to freshen up
before they went downstairs. Before they left the room, Scott tugged at
his jacket and asked, "Do I look okay?"

Emma looked him up and down. "Perfect in my opinion." Then she
took notice of his fidgety hands and chuckled. "You're nervous."

"Yes, I am," he declared firmly.

"About marrying me?" she questioned as if the idea troubled her.

"Oh no," he chuckled and kissed her, "I'm not nervous about that. I
just hope the rest of your family likes me."

"They will love you," she said.

"You didn't," he said quite seriously.

"Well, I'm a much bigger fool than the rest of them. Come on, let's
get it over with."

Downstairs they hesitated at the door of the room. Emma took in
the noises of bustling and chattering and laughter that were all so
familiar. She noted Scott taking a deep breath and couldn't help chuck-
ling. "It's okay," she said. "They'll love you."

"Okay," he said and pushed open the door.

Scott momentarily forgot about his nerves as Emily approached
him, pressing a kiss to his cheek and taking hold of his arm. A moment
later he was approached by Emma's oldest sister, Allison, who hugged
him as if they knew each other well. She looked into his eyes and said
with firm emotion, "I can't tell you how good it is to finally meet you. I
think you're the best thing to happen to this family since sliced bread."
She introduced him to her husband, Ammon, and a handful of kids
with names that he forgot as soon as he heard them.

Scott then met Amee and Alexa and their husbands and children.
And he was finally able to meet the famed Sean O'Hara and his family,

the young man who had been taken in by the Hamiltons when he'd been disowned by his own family. Scott couldn't wait to get to know him better; he felt sure they'd have much to talk about.

Once the formalities were over he completely lost his nervousness. Five minutes with these people and he already felt the family connection. He told himself he should have known that would be the case. They spent the evening eating and talking and laughing, and he decided that this tradition of the pre-wedding gathering was a good one. It had been Emily's idea several weddings ago, since the wedding day itself was so busy and full. This way the bride and groom could relax and visit with family members and catch up.

Eventually the children were all taken up to their different hotel rooms and put to bed, with older children being left in charge of younger ones. The adults continued to visit until very late, while he considered a new layer of blessings from this marriage. He knew that such family gatherings were rare, given that they were spread out over two continents, but he still felt a secret thrill at the idea of having extended family. As of tomorrow he would be gaining four sets of sisters and brothers-in-law. And he liked them all.

He was surprised to hear Jess start bragging about him, but in a light, teasing kind of way that didn't embarrass him. "He's done so many amazing things with the family business," Jess said to the group, "that I'm thinking it should be Byrnehouse-Davies, Hamilton, & Ivie."

Everyone laughed while Ammon said, "I think that's a great idea."

"I think it sounds like a law firm," Emma said, and they all laughed harder. Scott concluded that it probably wasn't really that funny, but given the late hour, they'd all become delirious.

Emma found it easy to finally say goodnight to her family, given her sudden exhaustion. But she found it difficult to say goodnight to Scott when he left her at the door to her room with a long, savoring kiss.

"Until tomorrow, Miss Hamilton," he said close to her face.

"Not for long," she said.

He grinned. "Precisely."

Once they finally parted, Emma feared she would have trouble sleeping, but she slept quickly and deeply. And the morning became a delightful frenzy that finally climaxed with the perfect serenity of seeing her entire family gathered in a sealing room of the Sydney Temple.

While they were waiting for the sealer to arrive, Emma looked around the room, holding Scott's hand in hers. She realized that this was the first time her entire family had been together in the temple. When she had gone through for the first time, prior to her mission, two of her sisters had been unable to join her. She couldn't help feeling that her father was there, as well. Of course he would be there, she reasoned. He wouldn't have missed this event, no matter the restrictions of the veil.

Scott squeezed Emma's hand tightly as the sealer entered the room and closed the door. He greeted them warmly and with laughter before he embarked on sharing some words of wisdom. When his little talk was apparently finished, he paused and said matter-of-factly, as if it were the most natural thing in the world, "I feel strongly impressed to tell you, Sister Hamilton, that your father is present, as well as other members of the family, and he shares the family's joy at this event."

Emma felt tears press into her eyes, as if to verify the truth of what she'd just heard. And when they cleared enough for her to see, a quick glance around the room made it clear that there wasn't a dry eye. Even Scott had tears in his eyes. He put his arm around her and pressed a kiss to her brow just before the sealer said, "Now, Brother Ivie, if you would escort your bride to this side of the altar, and then kneel across from her."

Scott laughed softly as he stood and took Emma by the hand. When they were facing each other over the altar, Emma's mind was far from the disease plaguing her body. It didn't even cross her mind that her illness might be a burden to him, or that her life might be cut short. Through those precious moments of her marriage and sealing, Emma could only see forever reflected in the eyes of this incredible man that God had sent into her life. She realized then that while she had felt cheated out of being able to complete her mission, the true purpose of her mission had been to bring Scott Ivie into the family. She had needed to serve her mission in order to meet her eternal companion. The year she had served following their meeting had been a bonus, a gift from her Heavenly Father. She'd not been cheated at all, but immensely blessed. And the full reality of those blessings rushed over her as they shared a sealing kiss over the altar. She knew then, beyond any doubt, that whatever life might bring, however long or short her life turned out to be, every day would be a gift and a blessing so long as she had Scott by her side.

When the ceremony was complete and the rings exchanged, Emma and Scott stood at the door and received reverent congratulations from their loved ones. Then they went together to the celestial room, holding hands as they absorbed the perfect peace of their surroundings.

"Whatever happens," Scott said, looking into her eyes, "I want you to remember this moment, and hold onto this feeling. No matter how much time we are given together in this world, Emma, this is what we are working toward as our final goal. Always remember."

"I will," she said fervently and he kissed her with the same reverence that had sealed their marriage over the altar only minutes ago.

The remainder of the day felt like a dream for Emma—a beautiful, ethereal dream. Following countless pictures taken on the temple grounds they all returned to the hotel for a big luncheon that involved the entire family and a few close friends of the family. Every adult in the room took a turn at standing and giving the newlyweds some words of wisdom, and tender wishes for a happy future. There was much laughter and even a few tears, while Scott possessively held Emma's hand, often kissing it or fingering the rings she wore that bound her to him. Occasionally he just reached over and kissed her lips, as if he simply couldn't contain himself. And the happiness she saw in his countenance mirrored her own feelings perfectly. Watching him closely she tried to comprehend that a few weeks ago she was angry with him and trying to convince herself that he was nothing but a thorn in her side. Oh, what a fool she had been!

When the luncheon finally wound down, Scott and Emma gave their loved ones a dramatic farewell and went together to the room they would share at this hotel for the next few days. They had decided that honeymooning here in the city was the best solution with Emma needing dialysis every other day. Scott had reserved tickets to an opera and a musical on two different evenings, and they felt sure there was plenty in the city to keep them occupied. Although, Emma felt certain as Scott carried her over the threshold, with her wedding gown rustling in his arms, that a honeymoon anywhere would have been perfect, as long as she could be alone with Scott.

"Welcome home, Mrs. Ivie," he said and set her on her feet, kissing her in a way he never had before. And Emma concluded that she'd never felt so happy.

* * *

Emma held tightly to her husband's hand as he flew the little plane over the breathtaking landscape of her homeland. She thought of how eagerly he had embraced this land as his own home, and she considered his love for Australia an added blessing in her life. Given the likelihood of her chronic health problems, living in the same family home with her mother and her brother's family would certainly tend to make life's challenges easier.

"Almost there," he said as if his eagerness to be home was the same as hers. She heard him laugh as the station came into view, and then again when he circled low over the house and stables to alert the family of their arrival. By the time he brought the plane down for a smooth landing, Jess was leaning against the parked Cruiser next to the hangar. He greeted them with tight hugs and much laughter, as if they'd been gone six weeks, rather than six days.

When they returned to the house, the welcoming committee was the same that had bid them farewell from the wedding luncheon. The entire family had been staying at the house in order to be present for the reception, using the wedding as an excuse for a vacation. Emma became suspicious when several people followed them to the bedroom that she would share with Scott. She didn't mention to Scott that her brother would have good cause to get even with her. She just reveled in his laughter when he opened the bedroom door to find the room filled with balloons and confetti.

"Well," Jess said sheepishly, "it wouldn't have been any fun to decorate your car in Sydney, since it was rented and we wouldn't see you leave in it. So . . . I just followed my sister's example."

"Oh, so this is your fault," Scott said to Emma before he scooped her into his arms and carried her over the threshold.

"Don't worry about it," Emma said to Jess. "Scott will have the room perfectly tidy in less than an hour."

"Really?" Jess said, hovering in the doorway while Emma grabbed the helium balloons and began handing one to each of her nieces and nephews that had followed them upstairs. "So, how is it living with a man who is compulsively tidy?"

"Oh, it's heavenly," Emma said with drama. "He waits on me hand and foot; treats me like a queen."

"That has nothing to do with my tidiness," Scott argued lightly.

"Okay, well . . . he picks up after me, too." She winked at Scott. "It's heavenly."

"Well, I'm glad you're back," Jess said. "Maybe you brought some heaven with you. I really missed you guys."

"How could you miss us when the house is overflowing with siblings and in-laws and children of every size with—"

"I'm well aware of what the house is overflowing with," Jess said. "I still missed you."

"Well, it's good to be home," Scott said, "but if you'll excuse me, I'm going to find the vacuum, or we will be finding this confetti on our fiftieth wedding anniversary."

Emma laughed and just kept passing out balloons to what seemed an endless stream of children. "How many grandchildren do you have?" Emma asked her mother who had hovered nearby, watching the revelries with a grin on her face.

"Not enough," she said with a little laugh. "Although, having them all here at once is . . ."

"Insane?" Jess provided and they all laughed.

Later that evening, when the adults were all gathered in the lounge room, talking and laughing, Emily plopped a wrapped package onto Emma's lap. "You should open this now," Emily said. "Although, I wouldn't expect it to be much of a surprise."

Emma looked briefly confused, then her eyes filled with an excited enlightenment. "Oh, my gosh," she said. "I've waited my whole life for this."

"What is it?" Scott asked, his attention perking as he eased closer to Emma. He lifted the little tag dangling from the bow to read, *For Scott and Emma. The legacy goes on.*

"We all got the same when we were married," Allison said.

"Even me," Jess added like a bragging child.

"Then it must be good," Scott said as Emma peeled away the silver wrapping paper.

She lifted the lid on the box at the same time Emily said, "We call it the legacy gift."

Scott felt chills rush over his back as Emma folded back the silver tissue paper that lined the box. "Oh, they're even more beautiful than I remembered," Emma said, reverently pressing her hand over the white linens folded neatly there.

"You'd better explain it to Scott," Jess said to Emily. "He looks confused."

"I'd be happy to," Emily said and Scott turned his attention to her at the same time Emma pulled out a lovely white tablecloth with intricate lace crocheted around the edges. "You see," Emily explained, "in her later years, Alexa became rather adept at crocheting lace, and she taught her skill to the other women in the family. There were many pieces that have been carefully preserved and distributed as wedding gifts among the family."

Scott said, "By Alexa, you mean . . ."

"My great-great-grandmother," Emma said and Scott took a sharp breath.

"Wow," he said then chuckled, pressing a reverent hand over the pillow slips Emma had spread over her lap.

"Michael's mother made this particular set of pillow slips. His grandmother, Emma, made this tablecloth, and his great aunt, Lacey, made the other tablecloth. Alexa made the dresser cloth."

"Alexa?" Scott asked. "Really? As in . . . the woman who wrote the words that are on the wall in the gabled attic? The woman who helped found the boys' home?"

"Yes, Scott," Emma said with a little laugh.

Scott touched Alexa's handiwork and muttered, "It's incredible. I think that's the most amazing gift I've ever been given."

"I'd have to agree," Emma said. Her mother helped her refold the pieces and put them back into the silver lining of the box while Scott still felt a little dazed. He could never say how grateful he was for this remarkable token of the great legacy he'd inherited by marrying into this incredible family.

The following morning Scott took Emma into town for the usual treatment, then they returned home in time for Emma to get some rest before the reception that evening. The entire celebration went so smoothly that it was difficult to believe how quickly it had been pulled together. Scott had told Emma he didn't need this aspect of the wedding, but he couldn't deny that he appreciated the opportunity to meet many friends and colleagues of the family that he'd not met before. And he was thrilled with the ward members that came, along with the stable hands, the staff of the boys' home, and even the boys, all dressed in their best and behaving like little gentlemen—for the most part. The evening was exhausting but perfectly enjoyable, and by the time it was over Scott felt that he was finally beginning to accept the reality of being a literal member of the Hamilton family.

A few days later the last of the family finally left and the house returned to its usual condition. Jess commented frequently on the peace and serenity of the house, which was usually followed by comments about the three toddler boys that were anything but peaceful and serene.

Scott quickly settled into a life that had become completely comfortable for him, except that now he shared that life with the woman who had stolen his heart the moment he'd laid eyes on her. To have her by his side in every aspect of life was more joyous to him than he could ever express. Barring the tedium of their regular visits to the "blood-filtering monster" as Emma had come to call the dialysis machine, life was close to perfect. There was only one thing that marred his happiness at all, and it crept up much faster than any of them had expected. Scott felt completely unprepared for Emma to undergo the surgery to get her new kidney, but as the date loomed quickly closer, he knew the entire family shared his lack of enthusiasm for what had to be done. They discussed their feelings openly, and many tears were shed. But if nothing else, they were all in it together. A part of him wanted to put it off indefinitely, mostly because the dialysis had become comfort-able and tolerable, and the surgery was taking them into unknown territory. But as Emma began to struggle with growing side effects that had not troubled her much before, they all knew that the surgery simply couldn't be put off. She was blessed enough to have a suitable donor, and they needed to get it over with.

The day before Jess and Emma would both report to the hospital, the entire family, on both continents, participated in a unified fast. The local ward joined the fast, as well, and Jess and Emma's names were both called in to two dozen temples. Jess and Emma were each given priesthood blessings, as well. They all knew they couldn't be any better prepared, emotionally as well as spiritually, but Scott still felt terribly unprepared.

On the designated morning, Scott and Emma, Jess and Tamra, and Emily, all drove into town before the sun came up. Beulah, a friend of the family who worked at the boys' home, would be staying at the house with Rhea to help with the children, while the family all planned to keep a constant vigil at the hospital until the outcome was certain.

Scott took his camera along and appreciated the way it gave him something to do, and a certain sense of security. He told the others he intended to keep a photo journal of this experience that they would all share with their grandchildren someday. When he was snapping pictures of Jess and Emma both wearing hospital gowns while they waited to be prepped and taken away, Jess commented, "It's a good thing they won't let you into surgery with that thing, or you'd take pictures of us both cut open."

"Oh, my gosh, don't say that," Emma said.

Jess squeezed her hand. "Sorry," he said then kissed her hand.

The waiting seemed endless, while Scott wasn't sure what exactly they were waiting for. Then suddenly a team of nurses were hurriedly doing final preparations and wheeling Jess and Emma toward the surgical area. Scott walked beside Emma with his hand in hers, well aware that they were both trembling.

"I'm scared, Scott," she said softly. "I'm trying not to be, but I am."

"I know," he said. "I am too. But it's going to be all right."

"Okay," one of the nurses said as they came to a huge set of swinging double doors, "this is where you kiss and say, 'see you later.'"

Emily took a minute with each of her children, and Tamra was having as difficult a time letting go of Jess's hand, as Scott was letting go of Emma's. When they finally stepped back, the doors were opened and the patients were rolled away. One of the nurses said to the three who were left waiting, "Someone will come out and give you reports at regular intervals. We were able to book one of the larger surgical rooms, so they will be right there together, probably holding hands until they go under," she added with a sensitive smile. Scott felt Tamra take hold of his hand as the nurse said the last, and they watched her walk away. Emily took hold of his other hand and the three of them stood in the hallway for several minutes before they found the motivation to seek out some comfortable chairs in the nearby waiting area.

In spite of the regular reports of the progress of the surgeries, indicating that all was going well, the hours dragged incessantly. Being in the company of these two women he cared for so deeply, Scott truly wanted to be strong and positive, but the fear and concern he saw on their faces clearly expressed how he felt. He did his best to keep his mind focused on prayer, begging his Father in Heaven to help him replace his fears with faith, and to help get Jess and Emma through this without any trauma. He refused to entertain the thought of what they would do if the kidney didn't take, or if complications arose that added any further threat to Emma's life—or Jess's.

Scott was long past feeling that he was going to scream when the team of surgeons finally appeared, talking quietly between them as they approached. Scott, Tamra, and Emily all stood in unison to meet them.

"It couldn't have gone any better," Jess's surgeon said.

Emma's surgeon added, "They are both stable and doing well, and Emma's new kidney is functioning."

Scott laughed and hugged both Emily and Tamra at the same time. The doctors spoke briefly about what to expect, and answered some questions before they left. Scott, Tamra, and Emily all exchanged long, firm embraces, with laughter and a few tears. Then they waited again until Jess and Emma were both settled into rooms in the ICU for observance. As a nurse led them to the room they were sharing, Scott couldn't help noticing the sign they passed that said, "Immediate Family Only." How grateful he was to be included in that elite group. As they entered the room where Jess and Emma were both hooked to many monitors, and barely coming to, Scott was also grateful that they were allowed to be in the same room. There were curtains that could be drawn for matters of privacy, but having them together allowed Emily to be with both her children at the same time, and for Scott and Tamra to offer each other support and encouragement. They each took their places, holding their spouse's hand as they emerged slowly into consciousness.

The next couple of days proved to be difficult and exhausting as Jess and Emma were both in a great deal of pain and the others suffered from acute fatigue. Even having places available for them to sleep didn't give them the peace of mind to get much rest. Then Jess and Emma both reached a point where they had gotten past the worst and they were moved to regular hospital rooms, two doors from each other. Jess was up and about, albeit moving slowly, but Emma's surgery had been more complicated and her incision much larger. Still, she showed steady improvement and the more time that passed, the more thrilled they all were to know that her new kidney was doing its job, and doing it well. Still, Scott felt uneasy without understanding why. Certain he was just being paranoid, he continually reminded himself to put the matter in the Lord's hands and have faith that all would be well. He just knew he'd feel better when Emma was home from the hospital and getting back to normal.

Tamra finally decided she was going home for the night to spend some time with her children. Jess was doing well and she was exhausted. Scott encouraged Emily to go with her so that they could both get a good night's sleep.

"Maybe you should do that too," Emily said.

"No," Scott said, "I'm fine. I can sleep just about anywhere. I feel like I need to be with her."

Emily reluctantly left her daughter, but Emma assured her that everything would be fine.

Scott actually slept fairly well in the recliner in Emma's room, but he was glad to be there in the predawn hours when Emma woke him, saying that she didn't feel well. It turned out that she actually had a fever, and it was declared that she had developed some kind of infection. When Scott heard the word *infection* he had trouble keeping his expression steady and his knees from buckling. Once the nurse was finished giving him a report, he hurried from the room and found an empty men's room before he allowed his fear into the open. He locked the door and pressed himself against it. He prayed and cried for several minutes before he finally got hold of himself and returned to Emma's room. Jess was at the door, actually looking rather well, except for the concern on his face. He was dressed in his own clothes, albeit having bare feet, and Scott recalled that he was supposed to go home today.

"What's wrong?" he demanded of Scott. "They won't let me in."

"She's got some kind of infection," Scott said in an even voice that gave no hint to his internal fears. "They're doing some blood work and they're going to change the antibiotic they're giving her. That's all I know."

Jess's countenance clearly expressed Scott's feelings, but he appreciated Jess's calm voice as he said, "I'm sure it's nothing to worry about. They'll get it under control." Scott nodded, wanting to believe him.

"Have you called Mother?"

"No," Scott glanced at his watch, "they're probably barely up, or sleeping in a bit, which they could both use."

"Yes, but . . . we promised we'd call if anything changed. Are you going to do it, or do you want me to—"

"I'll do it," Scott said.

He insisted that Jess sit down since he was looking pale, then he left to find a pay phone, since the use of cell phones wasn't allowed in the hospital.

"What's wrong?" Emily asked as soon as she heard Scott's voice.

"She's got an infection," Scott said and went on to tell her all that he knew.

He could tell she felt panicked, but she told him that she and Tamra needed a little time with the children. "They're starved for their mother and grandmother," she said. "We'll be there as soon as we can this afternoon, and I'll stay with you while Tamra takes Jess home."

"Thank you," Scott said and went back to find that Jess had now been allowed into the room, and they both took up a silent vigil at Emma's bedside. She admitted that she didn't feel well at all, and Scott's heart wanted to break when she told him that she felt scared.

"I don't want to leave you, Scott," she said, holding weakly to his hand.

Scott prayed her words weren't some spiritual sense she had of what might happen. "You mustn't leave me," he said, pressing a kiss to her brow. "I need you."

"Surely it's not as serious as all that," Jess said and a few minutes later Emma drifted to sleep.

Chapter Fourteen

Over the next few hours Scott and Jess literally held onto each other as they watched their fears turn into a full-fledged nightmare. Scott realized he'd never been so afraid in his life. He found himself fighting a fear so tangible that the pain in his chest threatened to devour him from the inside out. Emma's blood pressure dropped dramatically. Her oxygen saturation became critical, and her fever soared. Then the monitors in her room sounded an alarm and he realized she had stopped breathing. But his attempt to get to her side was thwarted by two male nurses who rushed him into the hall, past a medical team running into the room, shouting quiet commands to each other above the orderly chaos.

Scott felt as if a tremendous weight had been thrown over him and he wouldn't be able to breathe unless he could get it off. His chest tightened and his breathing became sharp. He became oblivious to anything but his need to get back into her room, as if he could save her by his will alone.

"Now stay put," Jess ordered, holding him against the wall. "Calm down. Breathe. Are you hearing me?" Scott nodded and squeezed his eyes shut. "You can't go in there, Scott. They can help her. You can't." Scott groaned and pushed against Jess who held his arms tightly. "I haven't got the strength to hold you here. You've got to calm down."

Scott's labored breathing turned to heaving sobs as he slid down the wall and ended up sitting on the floor, oblivious to whether or not he was making a scene. Jess knelt beside him and Scott was barely aware of him glancing down the hall, then he muttered something under his breath and Scott looked the same direction to see Emily and Tamra frozen there, as if they'd just turned the corner in time to see Scott crumble. He attempted to get control of himself for their sakes, but he couldn't find the strength to move. Emily seemed jolted out of a stupor and she rushed toward Jess, demanding quietly, "What's happened?" Tamra followed slowly after her, as if her legs had turned to lead.

Scott felt his own emotion return again as he heard Jess's voice falter in his attempt to explain. He stammered incoherently until Scott interrupted with a shaky voice, "She stopped breathing."

"What?" Emily choked. "But how could—"

Scott found the will to get to his feet when the door opened and a doctor appeared, his eyes going straight to their four anxious faces. He reported with compassion, "I fear she's gone into septic shock. They're putting her on a ventilator."

"What exactly does that mean?" Tamra asked. She was apparently the only one who could find a voice.

Scott listened to the doctor's lengthy explanation with growing horror. Some kind of infection from an unknown source had completely taken over her body. The ventilator would keep her breathing. They would do blood cultures to try and pinpoint the bacteria and fight it aggressively with antibiotics. Beyond that, all they could do was hope for the best.

"What are you saying, Doctor?" Scott demanded as anger rose to overtake his every other emotion.

The doctor's voice remained compassionate as he said, "It's serious, Mr. Ivie. I can't make any promises. We'll do everything we can."

Scott pressed his back to the wall as if it could save him. He watched the doctor walk away, vaguely aware of the shock and horror in his loved one's faces. He slid down the wall again as his strength drained completely away. He groaned and pressed his hands brutally into his hair. Then he felt hands on his shoulders and looked up to see Emily's face close to his. With more anger and vehemence than he had ever seen in her, her voice rumbled as she said, "We will not lose her! Do you understand me? We won't!" Hot tears rose in her eyes as she added, "I will not outlive any more of my family members! Do you hear me?"

Scott nodded as tears burned into his own eyes, then Emily crumbled into his arms and they cried together. Jess and Tamra cried together as well, but at least they made it to some nearby chairs.

The medical team finally emerged from Emma's room, declaring that she was stable and they could go in. The jolt of seeing Emma on the ventilator nearly sent Scott over the edge all over again. But a blanket of shock enveloped him as he moved to a chair close to her side and sat there, taking her hand into his. He absently fingered her wedding rings, hearing Emily's voice sound distant as she talked about the sound of the ventilator taking her back to when Jess had been in a coma following his accident. Then the sound of the ventilator and monitors beeping became the only sound at all for what seemed hours as they all sat and watched Emma, lost in unconsciousness. Tamra slipped from the room to make some phone calls. She was apparently the only one who could pull herself together enough to do it. She came back to report that she'd informed the family and had spoken with the bishop and the Relief Society president. Later in the day the bishopric made a visit and gave Emma a blessing, which Scott and Jess both appreciated, since they were both so upset that it was difficult to focus.

In the evening Tamra insisted that she take Jess home. "They won't keep you as a patient," she said, "because you've been released. But you need some rest. They'll call you if anything changes," she said firmly and nudged Scott's shoulder. "Won't you?"

"Of course," Scott said. Then to Jess, "You need to rest." To Tamra he added, "Drug him with pain pills or something."

"I just might do that," Tamra said, urging Jess to his feet.

Jess snarled as he left the room, "Just as well—I can't sit here and watch her die."

Scott glanced over his shoulder to watch Jess and Tamra leave the room, then he turned back to look at Emma. Was that what he was doing? Sitting here watching her die? As if Emily had read his mind, she scooted her chair closer and took hold of his other hand, saying gently, "She'll be okay."

Scott wanted to believe her, but a part of him wondered if her positive attitude was mostly denial because she was unable to face the possibility of losing another family member.

Through the next few days, nothing changed. Scott and Emily shared their constant vigil, taking turns sleeping in the recliner in the room, and forcing themselves to eat if only to avoid the nagging growls of hunger. Frequent phone calls with Tamra let them know that Jess had almost become despondent, sleeping a great deal with the help of the pain pills he'd been given, and having practically nothing to say when he was awake. She was concerned for him but didn't know what to do beyond love him and see that he had what he needed. She'd offered to take him back to the hospital to offer support and at least see Emma, but he'd adamantly refused.

Scott was inexpressibly grateful for Emily's company and wondered what he would ever do without her. And then Emily started to feel like she was coming down with something. Not wanting to spread it to Emma or anyone else, she called Tamra to get a ride home, and Scott found himself alone with the ongoing sounds of life support, and the beating of his own heart.

The next day Tamra let him know that Emily apparently had some kind of flu, and wasn't feeling well at all. She tearfully expressed her frustration and concern as both Emily and Jess clung to their beds, behaving as if the world had ended.

"It's as if they believe she's already dead," Tamra said, "but I'm not willing to give up that easy."

"I can't give up," Scott said, his voice cracking. "I just can't."

"You are in my prayers, as well," she said gently. "I'll keep you informed; you do the same."

"Of course," Scott said and got off the phone.

Hours crept into days for Scott while he lost all sense of time, of night and day. His mind wandered sporadically through bits and pieces of his life, as if the darkness surrounding him lured every difficult episode from the past directly into the forefront of his mind. In spite of his preoccupation with Emma's survival, he felt compelled to sift through the recesses of his mind, to sweep out the corners of latent pain, and dust off the outdated perceptions of an abandoned child who feared being left alone again. Consumed with the prospect before him, he felt he had nothing left to lose. Scott found himself digging deeper into his heart and soul than he'd ever done before. He begged God for strength and understanding while he cried for the discarded child who had grown into a man whose deepest fear was being left alone in this world, abandoned by the only woman he had ever truly loved. With time and pondering Scott came to more fully understand the source of his fear, and he struggled with all his heart and soul to turn that fear over to the Lord, knowing that Emma's life was in His hands, and His hands alone. But a part of him just couldn't let go of a deep-seated belief that he simply had to accept it; he was destined to be alone. Whether his being alone was the result of desertion, divorce, or death, he was still left alone.

Scott tried to count his blessings, to remind himself of the miracles in his life. But with Emma's lifeless hand in his, everything else he'd been given seemed empty and hollow. And when he thought of Tamra's report concerning Jess and Emily's state of mind, an unfathomable despair threatened to overtake him completely. How could it have come to this? How could he—and these people he loved—ever endure such a horrific loss?

For the hundredth time since this infection had set in, Scott attempted with everything inside of him to completely turn this over to the Lord, and to make it clear that he would accept the Lord's will and allow Him to take Emma from this world. But he just couldn't do it. He felt consumed with grief and a stupor of thought that threatened to make his head burst. And the result was a growing belief that he simply didn't have the faith or the strength or the courage to truly accept God's will.

Scott dozed in the chair, as he often did, and came awake to the realization that nothing had changed, and his fears and anguish had been laced into his dreams. He took Emma's hand and pressed it to his lips, and it occurred to him that he had figuratively reached his Sweetwater. He just couldn't go any further. He couldn't face life without Emma. He couldn't give Jess and Emily the love and support they needed and so richly deserved. He just couldn't go another step. He felt completely weary and spiritually sapped. He closed his eyes and attempted to pray, but even that felt dried up and depleted. He heard someone in the room and waited for one of the nurses he'd become familiar with to talk to him. Then he felt a hand on his shoulder and looked up to see Jess standing beside him. Nothing was said as Jess scooted a chair close enough that he could put that hand back on Scott's shoulder as he sat down. "How long has it been since you've eaten anything?"

"I . . . don't know," Scott said. "I . . . can't eat. I just . . ." Tears poured out of him and he found his head against Jess's shoulder.

"Talk to me, brother," Jess said.

"I can't lose her; I just can't. I thought I could be brave. I thought I could be happy with whatever time God gave us together here, that eternity would be enough. But it's not! I can't lose her! I just can't!" He sobbed like a frightened child while Jess rubbed a soothing hand on his shoulder and muttered comforting words. When his emotions were finally spent, he said in a croaky voice, "I thought I had faith enough to accept God's will in this, but everything inside of me is screaming that this is all wrong. I just can't accept this. I can't let her go."

"Maybe," Jess said gently, "you feel that way because it *is* wrong." Scott drew back to look at him, checking his eyes for sincerity. He'd been imagining Jess at home, curled up in bed, despondent and depressed. But something had changed. There was a light in his eyes, a distinct peace and serenity in his expression. "Maybe you feel that way because it really isn't her time to go. And if it *is* her time to go, the Spirit will eventually let you know and you *will* be able to let her go; you will be able to accept it."

"I've prayed so hard to know if it's her time to go, and if that's truly what I will be left to face, and I just can't accept it. But I don't know if the Spirit is really telling me that, or if I'm just so scared that I can't feel the Spirit at all."

"Well, if it's any consolation, I'm feeling the same way."

"You are?"

"I am. When my dad had cancer and I was finally kicked out of denial with the cold, hard fact that it was indeed terminal, I just couldn't believe it. It felt so wrong. But after a fair amount of prayer, I got an answer."

"What was it?"

"I knew beyond any doubt that he was appointed to die, and nothing I could do would save him. It was hard, but I knew in my heart that it would happen and I had no choice but to accept it. I did my best to accept it with faith and dignity, but that doesn't mean it was easy. Still, if nothing else, that experience has helped me recognize something now."

"What's that?"

"Well, I admit that I've been having a pretty rough time with this. Tamra gave me some time to be depressed, then she reminded me of something I learned the hard way after that suicide attempt."

"What was that?" Scott asked, already feeling a little better, simply from the companionship and understanding of his brother, his friend.

"I learned that I'm the only one who can fix it. I can't do it alone. I need the Lord, but I'm the one who has to reach out and ask for that help, trust in it, and apply in my life the principles that I know to be true. So, I stopped feeling sorry for myself and I started praying. I've prayed very long and hard, Scott, and I've pondered the way I felt when my father died, and the way I feel now. I've puzzled and studied and wrestled, and I can honestly say that I don't feel the same feelings now. Maybe there's something I don't quite understand, but in the deepest part of my heart, I really believe she's going to pull through. And maybe, just maybe, that's why you feel the way you do. I know you do your best to live close to the Spirit, and I believe that if anyone would be entitled to have the Spirit prepare him to lose his wife, it would be you. So, I suggest that we just take this on as if we know she'll make it."

Scott drew in Jess's words and found that he actually felt better. Through the following hours as he watched her sleeping, he found the stupor of thought leaving his mind. He felt free from confusion and grief, and he truly did believe she would come through. And if she didn't, he would deal with that when it happened. For now, he chose to believe the best and count on it.

"Hey," Jess said, coming to his feet, "I don't think she's going anywhere while we go get a decent meal in your stomach. Look how pathetic you are when I'm not around to take care of you. You look terrible."

Scott came to his feet and actually teetered a little. "Yes, I must admit it, without you I'm pathetic." He impulsively embraced Jess, holding to him tightly. "Thank you," he said. He pulled back and looked at him directly. "I do believe you've just carried me across the Sweetwater."

"Excuse me?" Jess said.

"Come on, brother. I'll tell you about it over lunch."

"Uh . . . lunch was a long time ago. It's about supper time now."

"Okay, supper," Scott said. He turned to take Emma's hand long enough to press a kiss there, then they left the room together.

After sharing a good meal and some good conversation, Scott felt strengthened emotionally and physically. He was pleased that Jess had brought him some clean clothes, and he was able to get cleaned up in the little bathroom that was part of Emma's room. Returning to his bedside vigil he had to admit that he felt better in every respect. And now, with a change of perspective, he focused his thoughts on simply believing that Emma would come through this, and he did his best to trust in the Lord to make that happen. Analyzing the difference in his feelings as he steered his thoughts in that direction, he had to admit that he felt a definite peace. He believed that Jess had been right. In comparing stupor of thought, or confusion, to peaceful feelings, Scott realized that it was easier to accept the Lord's will when the Spirit guided you to what His will would be. The more Scott pondered and prayed with that concept in mind, the more confident he felt that Emma would come through this, and she would be all right.

Three days after Jess had carried him across his personal Sweetwater River, Emily came to Emma's room, looking a bit pale but declaring she'd gotten past the virus completely and she felt much better. As they sat side by side, watching Emma with relaxed expectancy, Emily said, "I owe you an apology."

"Whatever for?" he asked quickly.

"Through the course of all this—even long before the surgeries— I had trouble dealing with what was happening."

"Which is certainly understandable," Scott said. "I see no reason for you to be apologizing."

"Well, my faith has been tested through this, Scott, and I fear that my losing faith may have contributed to other members of my family doing the same. For that I am sorry. I know in my heart that Emma's life is in God's hands, and my protests and fears will not change that. But they can make the experience more difficult."

"Perhaps we all had to face our own personal difficulties through this."

"Perhaps we did," Emily said. "I heard once that when a person can find the gift within the trial, then the trial will have served its purpose. It's when we flounder through the same type of trial over and over and never learn anything, never find the gift, that we keep going through the same, seemingly fruitless struggles. It's a theory, anyway."

"It makes sense, I think."

"Yes, I believe it does. And I can see now that we have each grown through the course of Emma's illness, especially since the surgery. At least I know I have."

"Well, I certainly have," Scott admitted, briefly contemplating the internal searching and personal evolution he'd struggled through.

"And now that I've waded through my fears and grief," she said, "I believe she's going to be all right."

Scott inhaled deeply, cherishing what seemed to add one more witness to what he and Jess had both felt.

They sat together in silence for several minutes before Emily reached into her purse and pulled out an envelope. "I think you should read this," she said, handing it to him.

"What is it?" he asked.

"It's Emma's patriarchal blessing," Emily said. "It was funny . . . this morning as I realized I had finally come to terms with this, and that I truly felt the peace I'd been seeking, I felt compelled to find this. And I wonder how long it's been since Emma has read it. Has she ever shared it with you?"

"No, she hasn't," he said, turning the envelope over in his hands.

"Well, you're her husband. You should read it. Now would be good, I think."

Scott pulled out the page of heavy paper filled with single-spaced type on both sides. He read silently to himself, amazed at this written evidence of what an incredible woman he was married to. But his heart unconsciously quickened as a certain feeling came through in the subtle tone and wording. He paused for a minute to analyze what that tone was, and he realized that it simply seemed to take for granted that she would live a long life. He read on and turned the page to read on the back. He caught his breath when he read the sentence, "You shall be taken to the holy temple and there be sealed for time and all eternity to a man who will be a stalwart to you and to those you love." He read that line three times, trying to comprehend that it was talking about him. He marveled at the miracle of personal revelation that came through patriarchal blessings as he read on. Then with no warning his quickened heart raced wildly, and his breathing became sharp. He blinked away the mist that rose into his eyes in order to make certain that he'd read it correctly. Then he realized that it wasn't so much what he'd read as the way it made him feel. He was still attempting to absorb the feeling when Emily said, "Yes, I felt that way too when I read it."

Scott glanced at her then back to the page, focusing carefully on the words enough to read them once more. "You will face many challenges, but you will be blessed with miracles to counteract those challenges. As you care properly for your body and spirit, you will be blessed with an abundance of years on this earth, and you will be surrounded by a vast posterity that will honor you in the maturity of your life before you eventually pass through the veil to be met by loved ones gone before. You will share a great reunion as you are reunited with them after many long years of separation." Scott read the promises once again, oblivious to the tears coursing down his cheeks, but well aware of the warmth consuming him.

"It's a miracle," he muttered.

"Yes, it is," Emily said and he embraced her tightly. They held to each other and wept while Scott absorbed the reality into himself. He knew beyond any doubt that his sweet Emma would be all right, and the life ahead of them would be long and good.

Late that evening Emma was taken off the ventilator, but she remained unconscious and Scott couldn't say that she looked any better. He reminded himself to appreciate each small step that indicated improvement.

The very next morning Scott woke from a nap in the recliner to find Emma looking at him with vibrant eyes that shone brilliantly with a zest for life that completely contradicted her physical condition. He rushed to her side and held her close, crying into her hair and relishing the feel of her hand moving over his shoulder and touching his face.

"I love you, Scott," she whispered and pressed her lips meekly to his.

Scott laughed and kissed her again. "I love you too," he muttered. "Oh, I love you too!"

When their greetings seemed complete, Emma looked around the room. "Where is everybody?"

"Jess went to get something to eat. Your mother is home, but she'll be here in a few hours."

He picked up the phone and quickly dialed the house number before he held it so that both he and Emma could hear. Emily's voice said, "Hello."

"Hi, Mom," Emma said and they could hear Emily laugh and cry so hard that she couldn't speak at all for a few minutes. When she finally found her voice, she simply said, "Oh, my sweet Emma. What a joy you are to me! But I must get off the phone so I can be on my way. We'll be there soon."

Scott hung up the phone then eased close to Emma on the bed, putting his arm around her shoulders, silently thanking God for giving him back his sweet Emma. Never had he known such perfect joy!

A nurse came in to check Emma and be certain all was well. She gave a good report and left the room only seconds before Jess came in and froze with his hand on the door. He responded much as Emily had before he sat on the edge of the bed, opposite of where Scott was sitting. And that's how Emily and Tamra found the three of them when they arrived less than an hour after Emma had talked to her mother on the phone. The greetings they shared were filled with tears and laughter. Scott kept Emma's hand in his, observing the love shared among his family, certain that no man on earth was as happy as he.

* * *

With Emma conscious and steadily improving, Scott brought his camera out again to record these events on film. He loved seeing her interact with Jess and Emily, and the laughter they shared. He especially enjoyed the way Jess teased her about his fine characteristics that she would find herself adapting now that she had his kidney inside of her.

The day Emma returned from the hospital was filled with celebration. Her happiness was evident each time Scott looked at her, in spite of her fatigue. But he knew in his heart that she couldn't possibly be any happier than he.

As the weeks passed, Emma's health showed a steady and firm incline, while Scott settled more thoroughly into his work. He continually felt his roots deepening as his place with the family became firm in his heart. Months after Emma's surgery it was difficult to comprehend how bad off she had been and how far she had come. They were all educated enough to know that many transplant patients struggled with a number of complications and side effects from the medication that Emma would need to take for the rest of her life. But Emma's challenges were few, and they were all extremely grateful.

As Christmas approached, Scott often looked at his incredible wife and marveled at the changes that had occurred in their lives. Two years earlier he had been struggling to come to terms with his divorce, living alone in Salt Lake City, and she had been serving a mission. A year ago the complications in their lives had seemed insurmountable and perhaps life threatening. And now Emma was busily engaged in Christmas activities as the house was prepared for "the Christmas invasion," as Jess had dubbed it. The entire family would be coming for Christmas, with many extra activities planned to take advantage of them all being together. One of the first things on the agenda was a formal family portrait. Pictures had been taken of the family together at Scott and Emma's wedding, but this would be different. Emily had made the family aware of her plans several weeks in advance so that everyone could acquire some degree of matching attire.

Jess had hired a professional photographer to come to the house so the picture could be shot on the lawn with the house in the background. Scott enjoyed snapping pictures as the photographer attempted to get everyone positioned just right. Emily sat on the lawn in the middle of what seemed a hundred grandchildren, frequently laughing at their antics, and at the same time admiring the patience of the photographer. When the children were finally in place, Scott put down his camera and took his place with Emma. Between shots Scott said, "Wow, I'm going to be in a family portrait. It's like a dream."

One of the younger children started to cry and Jess said, "Or a nightmare." Everyone laughed and the photographer snapped another picture. He did versions of only the children, and only the adults, and Emily with her children. When they were finally finished Emily insisted that the photographer stay for dinner. He stayed into the evening while they all crowded into the lounge room to sing Christmas carols. When he commented on what a wonderful family they were, and the warm spirit in their home, Emily made sure he didn't leave until he had a plateful of Christmas goodies for his family, and a copy of the Book of Mormon.

Christmas itself was filled with noise and chaos and perfect joy. And Scott reveled in being right at the center. He and Emma found pleasure in helping keep the younger children occupied and looked after, and they talked often of how they looked forward to having children of their own. Whether those children came to them biologically or through other means was something they were putting into the Lord's hands, and they were keeping an open mind.

Through the duration of the family's visit, Scott enjoyed best the late-evening conversations among the adults after the children had all been put down for the night. He loved to hear them reminiscing of years gone by, of their struggles and heartaches, of their joys and triumphs. As they shared a great deal of laughter, and even a few tears, Scott felt like he was one step closer to knowing and understanding the profound history of this family he'd been privileged to become a part of. And one of the greatest highlights of having the entire family together was the way they would all kneel together and share family prayer. They often did it once before the children went up to bed, and again before the adults parted for the night. The experience added one more level of meaning to the concept that families can be together forever. He was so grateful to be a part of such a great family—something he could never take for granted.

Before the family all departed for home, the copies of the portraits that had been ordered arrived. They had turned out beautifully, especially the very large one that Emily would have framed to hang in the front hall. The women and girls were all wearing white dresses, and the boys and men wore white shirts and dark pants. The effect was marvelous against the lush, green lawn, with the house in the background. Scott's favorite picture was the one with the adults. The women were all seated on the lawn, with Emily in the middle. Their legs were tucked up beneath them, and their white skirts flowed into each other and onto the lawn. The men knelt behind their wives so that their dark pants were hidden, and only their white shirts could be seen. The remarkable thing was that Emily ended up with three couples on one side of her and two on the other, but the angle of the picture left it looking slightly off balance, in an artistic kind of way. It was Jess who commented, "I think this is where James and Krista were when the picture was taken."

Everyone gathered to see what he meant, and there was a great deal of gasping and pleasant agreement as they speculated over the possibility. While they were discussing it, Scott noticed the gap between him and Jess, and just behind Emily. "And that's where Michael was kneeling," he said, pointing it out. A sudden hush fell over the room, and most everyone got a little teary, but it quickly became evident that the reason for their emotion had more to do with a mutual feeling that Michael was close by, as opposed to any excessive sorrow in missing him. Seeing the image of the family all together in white, it wasn't difficult to imagine the day when they would all be united for a similar gathering on the other side of the veil. Pondering the possibility, Scott took hold of Emma's hand and squeezed it. She smiled and kissed him as if she understood perfectly how he was feeling. He laughed and kissed her again, amazed at how he could just continue being so happy, day after day. Still, this was only the beginning.

* * *

The day after the last of the family left for their homes, Scott found himself drawn to the gabled attic in the boys' home. He thought of the wonderful events he'd seen take place in this room. He had grown up a world away from here, but in a way, it seemed as though he'd always been there, that this wonderful place that nurtured troubled boys was important to him.

Scott slowly read the plaque that hung there, as he had at least a dozen times. But the words never stopped amazing him. He hovered over the sentence, *My deepest prayer is that every boy who has the opportunity to stand at these gabled windows and watch the sun rise, will leave here changed for the better and more capable of finding a life of happiness and peace.* He *had* watched the sun rise through these gabled windows, but more importantly, a figurative brightness had come into his life through his opportunity to be in this place, and among these people. He knew well the traditions this family had of taking in lost souls, and he felt privileged to be among the lost that had been taken in, and among the elite few who were actually blessed enough to literally become a part of the family. He thought of the family journals he'd read of generations past, and the amazing people who had descended from those who had first homesteaded this land and created this gilded world. The purpose of this room and all it represented had most certainly accomplished what had been hoped for. Scott had most definitely become a better and stronger person; and he certainly had found a life of happiness and peace.

Scott thought of Jess and Alexa Byrnehouse-Davies, and he wondered what they might be thinking to look down upon their posterity now, and all the good that they were doing, and to see the ongoing dream of the boys' home pressing forward.

Scott was startled from his thoughts to hear Jess say, "Oh, it's you."

"Hello," Scott said.

"I was just . . . on my way to the house and saw the door open." He sauntered into the room. "Mind if I join you?"

"Not at all," Scott said. "I was just attempting to comprehend how amazing this room is, and all that it represents. I'm certainly one of the lost souls taken in that has benefitted greatly."

Jess chuckled. "Well, some of us lost souls are just born here." Scott chuckled as well and Jess added, "However, I have to say that the healing in my life had a lot to do with being able to know my ancestors through their journals, and perhaps even to feel them with me on occasion. I have no doubt that the love present in our family today has a great deal to do with the legacy of love that's been passed down for many generations. And I'm grateful for that."

"Indeed," Scott said, leaning in one of the gabled windows to look out into the early evening light.

Jess leaned a shoulder on the opposite side of the same window and stuffed his hands into the pockets of his jeans. "The really wonderful thing, however," he went on, "is the way the gospel is now a part of that legacy. Sometimes it's difficult to believe that my father had reached the age I am now before he joined the Church, and it was most definitely my mother's influence that brought him to it. Now the work has been done for all of those great ancestors, and the promise of an eternal family is a big part of who and what we are. And you know, when I look back at my own personal struggles, and see where I've come, I'm amazed at how evident God's hand is in our lives. There is no doubt in my mind that when we trust in Him, our lives are orchestrated in ways that we never could have worked out on our own."

"Amen to that," Scott said. "It's truly a miracle."

"It truly is, my brother," Jess said with a little laugh, putting a hand to Scott's shoulder. "Come along; I think it's about supper time."

They walked together from the room after Scott hesitated just a moment to put his fingers on that plaque, and the words written by Jess and Emma's great-great-grandmother. "Extraordinary," he muttered under his breath and they went together to the house, talking and laughing comfortably.

Scott and Jess entered the kitchen to find the women chattering and laughing as they worked together to prepare supper. It was a common scene, but Scott found deep comfort in it. He considered it a great privilege to share this home with extended family. The blessings of such an opportunity far outweighed the occasional challenges. When the women realized they were there, Emma hurled herself comically into Scott's arms, and Tamra wrapped her arms around Jess's neck. Once their wives had given them their typical greeting, Emily gave each of her sons a tight hug, then Scott helped Jess get the twins situated at the table while the meal was set out.

About halfway through the meal, Jess handed Scott a large envelope. "What is this?" Scott asked.

"It's a gift, from the family; we all pitched in. Quite honestly, we were supposed to give it to you for Christmas and it was so crazy, we forgot."

"Does that give any indication of how crazy this family gets when they're all together?" Emily asked.

"Oh, you loved every minute of it," Scott teased.

"Yes, I did," she said. "But the peace and quiet is nice, too."

At that very moment one of the twins starting hitting his bowl on the table and the other wailed over having dropped his food on the floor. The adults all laughed and dealt with the problems before Jess said to Scott, "Come on, open it."

"It's for both of you," Tamra said.

"You open it," Scott said, handing it to Emma.

"What if it bites me?" Emma asked, laughing. She gingerly took the envelope and opened it, then she gasped. "Oh, my gosh!" she said, then Scott couldn't tell if she was laughing or crying.

"What is it?" he asked, but she only waved the envelope excitedly and said nothing.

Scott grabbed it from her hand and looked inside to realize they'd been given an all-expense-paid trip to Hawaii. "Oh my gosh!" he repeated, making everyone laugh. "I can't believe it."

"Well," Jess said, "we all thought it was about time the two of you had a real honeymoon, without dialysis every other day."

"Oh, it's incredible," Emma finally managed to say.

"It certainly is," Scott agreed. "Of course, I have to say it's all the better for me, knowing that when the honeymoon is over, we get to come home."

"I like that part, too," Emily said.

Tamra sighed loudly and said, "You know what they say, 'Home is where the heart is.'"

"They do say that, don't they," Scott said, somewhat facetiously.

"You know what else they say," Jess said, then added in a ridiculously dramatic voice, "There's no place like home."

"Oh, my gosh," Emma said, "that is quite enough. This is beginning to sound like some ridiculous romance novel."

About the Author

Anita Stansfield has been writing for more than twenty years, and her best-selling novels have captivated and moved hundreds of thousands of readers with their deeply romantic stories and focus on important contemporary issues. Her interest in creating romantic fiction began in high school, and her work has appeared in national publications. *Gables of Legacy: The Miracle* is her twenty-fourth novel to be published by Covenant.

Anita and her husband Vince are the parents of five children. They and their two cats live in Alpine, Utah.

ABOVE SUSPICION

BY BETSY BRANNON GREEN

As the sun rose over the white sand beaches behind the Bethany Arms Hotel, Mary Grace O'Malley dropped a pile of sheets onto the floor of the laundry room. She loaded both washers and added the recommended amount of industrial-strength detergent. The wash cycles started, and she leaned against the window to watch the waves, painted pink by the sun, pound against the shore.

Her appointment with Justin's lawyer was only minutes away, and she didn't have a second to spare, but the incoming tide was irresistible. So she stood and stared for a moment, wondering how it would feel to be that powerful. Finally, with a sigh, Mary Grace pulled her thoughts back to practical issues.

Leaving the laundry room, she walked toward her office. She needed to go over her figures again before Heath arrived. After their meeting, she would help Lucy clean up the mess created by the continental breakfast they provided for their guests, then prepare the additional rooms reserved for the weekend.

When she reached the small office, Mary Grace sat behind Justin's big, imposing desk. Opening her file of financial statements, she tried to concentrate, but her eyes strayed back to the window and the beach. Heath was going to say the same thing this morning that he had every time they'd met since Justin died. A part of her wanted to follow his advice, but the other part . . .

She transferred her attention from the window to the framed snapshot of Justin taken several years earlier. He was standing in front of his sailboat, smiling at the camera.

"He loved that old boat," Heath Pointer said from the doorway, and Mary Grace looked up, startled. Heath was an attractive man in his early forties who always dressed like a model from *Gentlemen's Quarterly.*

"Good morning, Heath."

He pointed out the window. "If you'd listen to me, you could be lying out on that beach instead of cooped up here with a stuffy old lawyer." He gave her a charming smile, then waited for her to assure him that his self-description was erroneous.

Instead, Mary Grace responded, "I never was all that crazy about lying on the beach."

Heath cleared his throat. "Aztec made another offer yesterday." He moved into the office and dragged the chair from in front of the desk around to the side before sitting down. "If you sell the Arms, you'll have almost a million dollars after taxes and legal fees."

"I'm happy running the Arms, and money doesn't interest me," she said.

"Money interests everyone," Heath assured her. "And you're just breaking even with the Arms. There are several repairs that need to be made, and advertising, while essential to success, is something you can't really afford."

She was pleased that he had introduced this subject for her. "You're exactly right," she agreed wholeheartedly. "I do need to make repairs and advertise. That's why I asked you to come over today. I want you to help me get a business loan."

Heath frowned. "How much?"

Mary Grace pushed her proposal across the desk, and he picked it up.

Heath read for a few seconds, then his eyes widened. "Pretty comprehensive."

"There's no point in doing it at all if I'm not going to do it right."

"If you borrow this kind of money and sink it into the Arms, you'll be committed. Are you sure you want to run a small-time hotel for the next thirty years?"

"I love the Arms," she said softly.

"That doesn't mean you have to sacrifice your life for it." Heath's tone was gentle. "The Arms was Justin's dream, not yours. And he never meant for you to work so hard. You have to get up before dawn to wash sheets and towels for the guests. Then you have to spend time in the kitchen to compensate for the fact that your cook is blind . . ."

Mary Grace couldn't control a laugh. "Lucy is not *completely* blind."

"Close enough," Heath muttered.

"She's worked at the Arms for years, and I can't fire her just because she's getting old." Mary Grace tucked a wisp of dark hair behind her ear. "Besides, she's talking about retiring."

Heath leaned back and crossed his legs so that one tasseled, Italian leather shoe swung very close to her. "I hope she retires soon, for your sake. And in the meantime, why don't you consider dropping dinner from your list of services? That would save you time and money."

"Dinner at the Arms is legendary," she reminded him.

"It's expensive," he reiterated. "But delicious," he relented with a smile. "What's on the menu for tonight?"

Mary Grace recognized the hint. "Lasagna, and you're welcome to join us."

"I might just take you up on that. And don't dismiss Aztec's offer without giving it some thought. I've studied it carefully, and it's a good one."

"I appreciate your concern and your advice, but I'm not ready to sell the Arms. So you can tell the people from Aztec to stop making offers."

Heath smiled. "For such a pretty girl, you sure are a tough negotiator."

"I'm not trying to get a better offer out of Aztec," Mary Grace insisted. "I really don't plan to sell."

Heath glanced at his watch. "Okay, then. I'll call around and see if I can find any takers on a small business loan." He stood and moved toward the door. Mary Grace accompanied him, and just before he stepped into the hallway, he turned to face her. "Hey, I've got an idea. As good as dinners at the Arms are, you must get sick of them. Why don't you let me take you out to a restaurant for dinner?"

For a second Mary Grace was too surprised to respond. She had always thought of Heath as Justin's friend, Justin's lawyer. The idea of a personal relationship with him was unnerving. Pasting a polite smile on her face, she shook her head. "Thank you for the invitation, but there can't be dinner at the Arms without a hostess. My presence is required."

Heath frowned. "Don't you ever take a night off?"

She walked into the hall, hoping to rush his departure. "No. Never."

"Well, maybe we could go to lunch sometime," he suggested as she led the way through the lobby.

"You know I'm chained to this place, Heath," she discouraged him gently. "Breakfast, lunch, and dinner." She opened the front door. "But thanks anyway."

Accepting defeat, Heath continued outside. Mary Grace followed him as far as the cobblestone drive that encircled the courtyard in front of the Arms. She watched Heath climb into his gold-tone Volvo, then waved as he drove away. Surveying the courtyard, she realized that the grass was going to have to be cut before her teenage yardman returned from vacation the following Saturday. It had been awhile since she'd pushed a lawn mower, but maybe it was like riding a bike—something you never forgot.

Mary Grace returned to the lobby of the Arms and straightened magazines on an antique occasional table. She pulled dead leaves off a plant and stirred the sea breeze potpourri on the registration desk. Then, accepting that she could delay it no longer, she went to the kitchen and called for Lucy.

"I'm here, Mary Grace," a voice responded from the storage room.

Mary Grace stuck her head in to see the elderly black woman with cotton-white hair stretched out on a cot, watching *The Today Show* on a small television. "Is something wrong?" she asked.

Lucy nodded. "I got to feeling a little dizzy and knew you'd want me to lie down before I fell."

Mary Grace controlled a sigh. "I certainly wouldn't want you to fall. I'll clean up the dining room."

"Don't worry about dinner. I'm sure I'll be better by then."

Mary Grace didn't comment but instead pulled a metal cart from the kitchen into the dining room and started collecting dishes and silverware. The buffet table only took a minute, but the long banquet table where her guests had eaten was a mess. The snowy white linen tablecloth was littered with crumbs, and two crystal jelly jars were turned on their sides, the contents seeping into the expensive fabric.

As Mary Grace pried a spoon covered with cheese grits from a butter plate, she rejoiced that the Lovejoys and their demon children would be leaving the next morning. Glancing down, Mary Grace saw a strawberry and two squashed grapes under the table. She crouched to retrieve them and was in this undignified position when she heard footsteps echoing on the hardwood floor of the lobby. Before she had time to stand, the form of a tall man filled the doorway.

The chandelier in the lobby was at his back, causing a shadow to hide his features. But there was something familiar about the way he stood with his feet wide apart and his head thrust forward. Mary Grace felt her scalp start to tingle . . .

The man was holding several bulky pieces of luggage, which he dropped abruptly, then stepped into the dining room, and her eyes focused on his face. The dark, wavy hair was cut a little shorter than it used to be. The brown eyes were older, wiser. Only his lazy grin was just as she remembered. "Hey, Gracie," he said.

Mary Grace had thought about John Wright many times during the past five years, but never had she imagined that when and if she ever saw him again she'd be crawling on the floor holding squashed fruit. She stood and clasped her sticky hands behind her. "Nobody has called me that for a long time," she told him.

He took a step closer and looked around the dining room. "So you *own* this place?" he asked.

"I do," she confirmed. "What brings you to Bethany Beach?"

"Business." He smiled. "I called last week to make a reservation, but the girl who answered the phone said it wasn't necessary since you always have plenty of vacancies."

Mary Grace wished fervently that her desk clerk had prepared her for John's impending arrival. "We have rooms available, but I'll warn you in advance that the Arms is not luxurious."

"I've been on the road for three weeks, so luxury is a distant memory. I just need a quiet place to work for a few days. And this looks perfect."

She wiped her hands on the already-soiled tablecloth, then walked past John Wright and into the lobby. "Would you like a room that faces the beach or the courtyard?"

"It doesn't matter," he said as he followed behind her. "I'll be too busy working on my article to look out the window."

"Article?" she asked as she opened the hotel register.

"I'm an investigative reporter for the *Savannah Sun Times,* and I'm here to write a story."

She paused in her efforts to find the correct page in the register. "You always said you were going to be a journalist. Did you get to play for the NBA too?" she asked, then regretted the question, realizing she had shown him that her memories of him were quite detailed.

He shook his head with a smile. "No, I lost my edge during my mission and had to give up on a pro basketball career." He ran his hand along the polished mahogany surface of the registration desk. "This place is pretty nice."

Mary Grace was instantly conscious of all the needed repairs and wished that he had waited to come until after the improvements had been made. "It's a wonderful old house," she told him with pride. "But we're a little off the beaten path, and I don't advertise much anymore, so I'm surprised you found us."

John gave her another smile. "I met Stan Guthrie at the Atlanta airport last summer, and I asked him about you. I'll admit it was a shock to learn you were here. I figured you'd be in a desert with dirt under your fingernails instead of running a classy little hotel. What happened to your dreams of being an archaeologist?"

"Circumstances changed my dreams," she responded vaguely.

"That happens sometimes." He studied her for a few seconds, then continued. "Anyway, when I got the assignment to come to Bethany Beach, I decided to stay here so I could see how your life has turned out."

She laughed. "I don't think my life has 'turned out' yet. I'm just kind of in a holding pattern."

His eyes surveyed her quickly. "You cut your hair."

Mary Grace absently put a hand to her head. For years she'd worn her hair long, but recently Jennifer had convinced her to try a more sophisticated look, and now the bottom layer barely brushed her collar. "Yes."

"I like it. Even though it makes you look so . . . mature and serious."

"I am very serious," she assured him. "And mature."

"But you're not computerized?" he asked as she wrote his name in the register.

"We don't have many guests at a time, so this system still works for us," she told him as she mentally added a computer to her list of things she would buy with her renovation money. Then, reaching behind her, she took a set of keys off a hook. "You'll be in the Robert E. Lee Room, courtside. It's the most convenient to the parking lot and should be quiet."

"Thanks." He took the key, and she couldn't help but notice that he wasn't wearing a wedding ring.

After pausing to let him retrieve his luggage, she led the way outside. "Follow me, please."

"Don't you want my credit card number?" he asked.

"My desk clerk will be in soon, and she'll handle the payment arrangements with you." Mary Grace glanced at him. "I'll trust you until then."

"I guess I have an honest face," he said, and she smiled.

She opened the door with her passkey, then stood back and admired the room with pride. The furniture was mostly antique, and a large, limited-edition print of General Lee himself hung above the huge, four-poster bed.

"Wow," John said as he stepped inside. He put his suitcases down and walked around, looking at the Civil War memorabilia. "Is this stuff authentic?"

"Mostly. Some are reproductions."

"Are all your rooms named after Civil War generals?"

"Confederate generals," she corrected.

He returned from his tour of the room to stand beside her. "That was clever."

"I can't take credit for the idea," she told him.

"And you said your rooms weren't luxurious," John said with satisfaction. "You should have seen the Annie Oakley Motor Inn that I just checked out of."

Mary Grace smiled at this. "Well, I've got to get back to work. Call the desk if you need anything, and stop by after ten o'clock to give the clerk your credit card number."

Before John could reply, Mary Grace left the Robert E. Lee Room and took two calming breaths as she returned to the lobby. John Wright was staying in her hotel. She couldn't wait to call Jennifer and give her the news. When she walked through the front door, she saw that her teenage desk clerk had arrived.

"Oh, my gosh!" the girl cried with her hand to her heart. "I saw our new guest!"

"Mr. Wright?" Mary Grace clarified.

"Didn't you recognize him? He's John F. Kennedy, Jr.!" Windy exclaimed.

Mary Grace exhaled slowly. Windy worked for almost nothing and was eager to please, but she was not the brightest person. "John F. Kennedy, Jr. is dead. He and his wife and sister-in-law were killed in a plane crash several years ago."

Windy grasped Mary Grace by the arm. "Don't you see? He must have faked his death, and now he's hiding out! He probably stays in small towns like Bethany Beach to keep from being discovered by the press." Windy held to her original theory.

Mary Grace couldn't control a laugh. "Windy, John Wright *is* the press. He works for the *Savannah Sun Times.*"

"John Wright must be a fake identity," Windy insisted. "And he probably uses his *real* first name to keep from getting confused!" She lifted her eyebrows meaningfully.

"I can promise you that John Wright is not a famous dead person," Mary Grace reiterated. "We knew each other when we were in college."

"Oh, I get it," Windy replied with a conspiratorial nod. "He asked you to cover for him. I can understand that you want to help him, but it seems like you could tell me, since I work here and everything . . ."

Mary Grace shook her head and moved away from the desk. "He'll be back in a little while to pay for his room." She stopped and glanced at the teenager. "And he said he called last week and you told him he didn't need to make a reservation."

Windy looked down at her faded blue jeans. "If I'd have known I was going to meet someone important today, I'd have dressed better."

"Dressing professionally is something you should do every day, regardless of who you expect to meet, and record keeping is very important. I've asked you to make reservations when people call."

The girl was instantly contrite. "I'm sorry! But when he called, those Lovejoy people were checking in. Their kids were jumping on the couch, and it made me so nervous I forgot."

Mary Grace sighed. "It's okay. Just try to remember next time," she said, then walked back to her office. The answering machine was blinking, and she checked her messages. There were two calls—one from her mother and one from Bobby Chandler. She didn't have time for a lengthy conversation with her mother, but it seemed wrong to return one call and not the other. She had just about decided not to call either of them when the phone rang. It was Bobby.

"I called a few minutes ago, but no one answered," he said.

"Sorry. I was taking an unexpected guest to his room."

"Oh, an unexpected guest," Bobby sounded impressed. "That's a good thing."

An image of John Wright's face floated before her, and Mary Grace suppressed a sigh. "Maybe."

"How did your meeting with Heath Pointer go this morning?" Bobby asked.

"About like you'd expect. He tried to talk me into selling the Arms."

"But you resisted?"

"Firmly," she assured him.

"I hate to agree with your snooty lawyer on anything, but you ought to unload that place," Bobby advised. "Justin will forgive you."

"I've already discussed this enough for one day."

"Am I invited for dinner?" Bobby changed the subject.

"Of course. You have a standing invitation. But I have to warn you that Heath may also be there."

Bobby groaned, and Mary Grace had to laugh.

"Lucy and I made lasagna," she told him. "Maybe that will compensate for the company."

"I'll be there," Bobby promised, concluding the conversation.

After they hung up, Mary Grace reviewed her list of reservations for the weekend. The Lovejoys were leaving the next day at noon, but the ladies from Haggerty were due in just a few hours. That would fill four of her remaining rooms. A couple from Texas who had spent their honeymoon at the Arms in 1978 would arrive by six o'clock and had requested the Robert Hatton Room. Her perusal was interrupted by a sharp knock. Mary Grace looked up to see John Wright standing in the doorway. He held an American Express card in his hand.

"The girl at the front desk says she doesn't remember how to do credit cards," he explained.

Figuring it would be useless to get mad at Windy, Mary Grace stood. "I'll take care of it for you."

He stepped aside to allow her through the doorway, then followed her into the lobby. When they arrived at the registration desk, Windy gave Mary Grace a sheepish look. "Sorry."

"It's okay," Mary Grace said. "Just watch me so you can do it next time." She pulled out the old manual imprint machine while John leaned on the aged wood. He extended the card toward her.

"I didn't know anyone used those things anymore," he commented as she made an impression of his card onto the carbon paper.

"We like to keep things simple." Mary Grace tried not to sound like she was making excuses for the Arms. "How many days are you planning to stay?"

"At least through Friday. I have to be at my next assignment on Monday, so I'll finish up before then."

Mary Grace made a notation on the slip, then handed it, along with the credit card, to Windy. "Can you handle it from here?" she asked the girl.

Windy nodded. "I'll call this in and be right back," she told John with a giggle.

Hoping to distract John from Windy's peculiar behavior, Mary Grace asked, "What are you working on? Or are you allowed to say?"

He leaned closer and whispered, "I think I can trust you. I'm investigating an unsolved mystery that began twenty-five years ago. A girl named Victoria Harte was killed in a motel here. Have you ever heard of her?"

Mary Grace frowned. "No, but our mayor is Richard Harte."

John nodded. "Victoria was his sister."

Windy returned at this moment. "His credit card is good," she announced. John raised an eyebrow, and Mary Grace regretted the girl's lack of tact.

"That's a relief, I can tell you," John teased.

"I had no doubt that it would be," Mary Grace said with as much dignity as she could muster. "It's just standard procedure," she added with an embarrassed look in John's direction.

"No problem," he assured her.

Windy gave the card and the charge slip back to their new guest. "Thank you, Mr. *Wright*." She emphasized his last name, then winked at Mary Grace.

Mary Grace was glad that John didn't even seem to notice the girl. "I hope you enjoy your stay," she told him, then turned and walked to her office. She didn't realize that John had followed her until he spoke from the doorway.

"You look natural in here," he said.

"I should, I certainly spend enough time at this desk."

"I guess running a place like this takes a lot of dedication." He looked around. "It must be about a hundred years old."

"Almost," she affirmed. "It was built in 1910 by a railroad baron named Peter Bethany. It was *one* of his family's summer homes."

John whistled in appreciation. "The architecture is kind of unusual. It's shaped almost like a V."

"Peter Bethany could afford the best, so he brought in craftsmen from the northeast who were skilled in building homes that could withstand high winds. The shape of the house protects the courtyard from gusts blowing up from the ocean. They built it up here near the bluff to avoid flooding, even during hurricanes. Because of that, it's one of the few surviving structures from its era."

John seemed impressed by this information. "So when was it turned into a hotel?"

"In the 1940s. But then it changed ownership several times, and by the time Justin bought it, the Arms had fallen into disrepair. He restored it and made a good living."

"No easy task, I'm sure. This Justin—is he your husband?"

She shook her head. "Just a friend."

Now it was John's turn to look embarrassed. "I'm sorry."

She smiled. "That's okay. Lots of people make that assumption."

"Did you buy this place from him?"

"No," she told him. "Justin left it to me when he died."

John looked even more uncomfortable. "I'm sorry again. Did he die recently?"

"He's been gone for almost four years." She forced a smile.

There was an awkward silence, then John said, "Can I ask a favor?"

She nodded. "Of course."

"I need to fax some information to my office in Savannah." He held up a handful of papers, and his eyes strayed to the economy fax machine on the credenza behind her desk. "If it wouldn't be too much trouble," he added.

"It's no trouble." She extended her hand, and he relinquished the pages.

"I hate to bother you, but I'm already in the doghouse with my editor, and if this arrives after my deadline, I'm toast." He gave her the fax number, and she put the papers into the tray. There was a few seconds of awkward silence. Neither of them spoke while they watched the first page slip slowly into the machine.

Finally Mary Grace felt obligated to make conversation, "What could possibly be interesting enough about a twenty-five-year-old murder for the *Savannah Sun Times* to send a reporter all the way to Bethany Beach?"

John leaned his hands against the edge of her desk. His shirtsleeves were rolled up, and as Mary Grace saw the muscles in his forearms flex, she wondered if he still played basketball to keep in shape. "Summers are always a little slow news-wise," he told her. "So somebody came up with the idea of doing a series of articles on old unsolved murders. They've given me a less-than-generous expense account and sent me to little towns across the southeast."

Mary Grace raised an eyebrow. "Maybe your limited expense account was the *real* reason you wanted to stay here—since my rates are cheap."

He looked over her shoulder out the window at the beach. "I'll admit I was pleased to get a bargain."

She removed the papers from the fax machine and handed them back to him. "All done."

He took the pages. "Thanks. Now I'll get to work." With a wave, he turned and left the room.

Mary Grace stared at the empty doorway for several minutes after John left. Then the phone rang and she picked it up absently. "Bethany Arms."

"Gracie?" It was John's voice. "The phone in my room doesn't work."

She cleared her throat. "It sounds like it's working fine to me."

"I'm calling on my cell phone. The one in the Ulysses S. Grant Room is dead as a doornail."

"Robert E. Lee," Mary Grace corrected. "The jack is probably loose. I'll be right there."

She hung up the phone and walked out of her office. When she passed the front desk, she saw Windy painting her fingernails. "Windy," she whispered, "please don't paint your nails at the front desk."

Windy looked up with a blank expression. "Why not?"

Rather than try to explain professionalism to Windy, she said, "It's a waste of money for me to buy that expensive potpourri when the only thing our guests can smell is nail polish."

Windy considered this for a few seconds, then nodded as she put the little bottle of polish away.

"We've got several guests arriving today," Mary Grace told the girl. "Please check the register, then turn on the air conditioners in the appropriate rooms."

"Who'll answer the phone while I'm gone?" Windy asked as she blew on her damp nails.

"I will," Mary Grace replied.

With a shrug, Windy sauntered slowly toward the back door. Once the girl had disappeared, Mary Grace took a deep breath, then walked outside and down the sidewalk to the Robert E. Lee Room. John was unpacking his clothes when she knocked on the open door.

John smiled. "Well, that was quick service." He pulled dress shirts from a suitcase and hung them on the wooden rack provided for that purpose.

"Service is something we're very serious about here at the Arms," Mary Grace assured him as she walked across the room. She leaned over the desk and pushed the loose phone cord firmly into the jack, then stood and picked up the receiver. The dial tone hummed steadily in her ear. "All fixed." She turned back toward the door, but his voice stopped her.

"I might be getting a fax back from my office."

She nodded. "If you get anything, I'll have Windy call you."

"Your desk clerk?"

"Yes."

He walked over and stood a little closer than absolutely necessary. "Her name is Wendy?"

"No, Windy," Mary Grace emphasized the vowel sound.

John frowned. "Windy isn't a name, it's an atmospheric condition."

She smiled. "I can't be held responsible. I didn't name her."

John acknowledged this with a little nod. "It says on my welcome note that you provide a continental breakfast for all your guests."

His close proximity was unnerving, so she took a step back. "Yes, from seven to nine during the week, eight to ten on weekends."

"It also says that a buffet dinner is served every night at seven o'clock."

"That is correct. It's included in the price of your room."

He gave her a speculative look. "So, do you join your guests for meals?"

Mary Grace nodded, then turned her stare to the picture of General Lee. "Yes, it's a long-standing tradition."

"Well then, I'll look forward to seeing you tonight."

Mary Grace nodded, then walked back to the lobby. She sat down at the desk and dialed a number from memory. Jennifer Sanders Guthrie answered on the third ring. "Hello!"

Mary Grace could hear the twins in the background. "Jen, it's me, Mary Grace."

"Calling me in the middle of the day? Did someone die?" Jennifer demanded.

Mary Grace laughed. "Not that I know of. What are you doing?"

"Wiping noses, cleaning toilets, thawing hamburger . . ."

"You're watching Judge Judy, aren't you?"

"It's very educational," Jennifer admitted without a trace of guilt. "It really should be on PBS. So what's up?"

"Do you think Stan would keep the boys for you tonight so you could come for a visit? I'll make you a root beer float."

"I'm due for a night out, but what's the occasion?"

"I just have some interesting news and wanted to share it with you. Be here at nine o'clock. I'll be finished with dinner by then."

There was a brief pause, then Jennifer said, "I know you don't expect me to wait until tonight to find out your news. The suspense will kill me."

"Not if the twins haven't," Mary Grace responded with confidence. "See you at nine."

Rather than try to explain professionalism to Windy, she said, "It's a waste of money for me to buy that expensive potpourri when the only thing our guests can smell is nail polish."

Windy considered this for a few seconds, then nodded as she put the little bottle of polish away.

"We've got several guests arriving today," Mary Grace told the girl. "Please check the register, then turn on the air conditioners in the appropriate rooms."

"Who'll answer the phone while I'm gone?" Windy asked as she blew on her damp nails.

"I will," Mary Grace replied.

With a shrug, Windy sauntered slowly toward the back door. Once the girl had disappeared, Mary Grace took a deep breath, then walked outside and down the sidewalk to the Robert E. Lee Room. John was unpacking his clothes when she knocked on the open door.

John smiled. "Well, that was quick service." He pulled dress shirts from a suitcase and hung them on the wooden rack provided for that purpose.

"Service is something we're very serious about here at the Arms," Mary Grace assured him as she walked across the room. She leaned over the desk and pushed the loose phone cord firmly into the jack, then stood and picked up the receiver. The dial tone hummed steadily in her ear. "All fixed." She turned back toward the door, but his voice stopped her.

"I might be getting a fax back from my office."

She nodded. "If you get anything, I'll have Windy call you."

"Your desk clerk?"

"Yes."

He walked over and stood a little closer than absolutely necessary. "Her name is Wendy?"

"No, Windy," Mary Grace emphasized the vowel sound.

John frowned. "Windy isn't a name, it's an atmospheric condition."

She smiled. "I can't be held responsible. I didn't name her."

John acknowledged this with a little nod. "It says on my welcome note that you provide a continental breakfast for all your guests."

His close proximity was unnerving, so she took a step back. "Yes, from seven to nine during the week, eight to ten on weekends."

"It also says that a buffet dinner is served every night at seven o'clock."

"That is correct. It's included in the price of your room."

He gave her a speculative look. "So, do you join your guests for meals?"

Mary Grace nodded, then turned her stare to the picture of General Lee. "Yes, it's a long-standing tradition."

"Well then, I'll look forward to seeing you tonight."

Mary Grace nodded, then walked back to the lobby. She sat down at the desk and dialed a number from memory. Jennifer Sanders Guthrie answered on the third ring. "Hello!"

Mary Grace could hear the twins in the background. "Jen, it's me, Mary Grace."

"Calling me in the middle of the day? Did someone die?" Jennifer demanded.

Mary Grace laughed. "Not that I know of. What are you doing?"

"Wiping noses, cleaning toilets, thawing hamburger . . ."

"You're watching Judge Judy, aren't you?"

"It's very educational," Jennifer admitted without a trace of guilt. "It really should be on PBS. So what's up?"

"Do you think Stan would keep the boys for you tonight so you could come for a visit? I'll make you a root beer float."

"I'm due for a night out, but what's the occasion?"

"I just have some interesting news and wanted to share it with you. Be here at nine o'clock. I'll be finished with dinner by then."

There was a brief pause, then Jennifer said, "I know you don't expect me to wait until tonight to find out your news. The suspense will kill me."

"Not if the twins haven't," Mary Grace responded with confidence. "See you at nine."